Death by Deadline

Death by Deadline

Can Out of Control Local News Kill People?

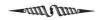

Larry Kane

This book is dedicated to Donna, Michael, Alexandra, Jen, Doug, Aiden and Benjamin.

Special thanks to Janet Benton, one of the finest book editors in the business, and Joe Kelter of Bad Cat Design for the unique cover art.

Note: Although this book includes some real-life newsroom circumstances, policies, challenges, and accomplishments, none of the characters are based on real individuals, and none of the TV stations reflect actual Television operations. This is a work of fiction, with a definite point of view. Fiction? Yes. Reality? Maybe on some dark day in the future, if, indeed it is not too late.

CHAPTER ONE: **WHACK IT AND TRACK IT**

*H*ow the hell did I get here? After forty-seven years of covering the news, thirty-seven as an anchor, now I'm in the middle of it. I'm on my back on the asphalt, and my head doesn't feel too good. I feel blood dripping from my nose and forehead and seeping through my shirt. I was just thrown from my car onto the Route 422 Bypass near Oaks, Pennsylvania, a gridlocked suburb of McMansions and strip malls. My car is burning a few feet away. I hope it doesn't explode. All four lanes are blocked by the twisted carnage of melted metal. I have no idea what is going on, but I see thick black smoke in the air, and I smell death. Nothing smells like death more than burning human flesh. I've smelled it at accident scenes, during violent protests, and in war zones. But this is different. I'm one of the victims.

Up above, the clouds are spinning fast, like small jets moving in circles, or little ghosts. I must be having vertigo. The dizzy nausea brings an involuntary spasm to my chest. Liquid pours out. The smell of burning tires isn't making me feel any better. Neither are the bodies.

A dead woman, thrown from her car like I was, lies a few feet from me. She wears a beautiful daisy-print dress, but it's covered with blood. I keep looking, trying not to think about the pain shooting from my face down to my chest and legs. My legs feel like they're on fire. I take a breath. Judging from how I feel, I will probably be dead soon, too.

My lungs are burning, scorched by smoke. I gasp for air. But there is no clear air to breathe. My neck does not turn, but in my peripheral vision I see what looks like a head protruding from a car directly to my left. It is. The rest of the body must be on the other side of the dashboard.

I try to get up. I position my elbows on the ground. But I can't do it. I try to pick up my head, but I start vomiting blood. The blood is choking me up. I can't breathe. I must divert my mind from the gagging. I think about Rebecca, the kids, the cop, the son, the boss, the blood-soaked map, the missing parts, Bernie, the newsrooms, and the voice I heard while I was driving—the newsman on Newsradio 1070, who said, "This is a nightmare scenario." What scenario? The one I'm in, or is there something bigger? Then the station went silent and I ended up in this mess. What the hell did he mean?

Up above I see smoke from the east and west converging, turning day to night. All of a sudden, a video plays in my mind. First I see people whose faces look like what they were when they were, then old places, children laughing and crying, explosions, ceremonies, births, ashes. It's all in black and white. My God! Am I going into shock? Suddenly the pictures vanish. I see nothing. Am I blind? Then suddenly I feel limp. The pain goes away. One long breath flows out of my mouth, a huge vapor. And as the air escapes, the lids of my eyes close, and I fade to black.

CHANNEL FIVE NEWSROOM
NOVEMBER 16, 2007

I should have known. I should have known from the Lakeview High School fiasco. I worry myself sick over the power of the newsroom, the power that can kill. I've been worrying for years, and frankly, I was getting too tired to complain. But I've had enough. I'm not going to throw away decades of hard work so that the bastards can win.

I love news. I love getting it. I consume it like food. I've been hungering for news since I started gathering information for class projects in seventh grade. I love calling people. I love breaking news. I devour newspapers and magazines, and I watch CNN at all hours of the day. I have a passion for people and the things they do. News has been a piece of my life for fifty years. Oh, the sound of it gets my adrenaline going. But like all the merry men and women in newsrooms everywhere, I whistle in the dark, if you know what I mean. "Stand by. We are dealing with a police emergency in progress."

The sound of the police dispatcher's voice is piercing, and it never stops giving me or my news buddies a sense of impending doom. "Stand by. All cars. Move in with care to the Cambria area, Second and Cambria. Be cautious." Her voice is trembling. "Sear—sear—search for suspect," she says. "Two men down. Police by radio."

Scanners are the soundtrack of newsrooms. Most days the sound fades into the background, becoming a disjointed sort of music to work by. But the newsperson's mind always jumps to attention at the words "police by radio." They mean that a cop is on the scene and may be in danger.

"All units in," she continues. "Citywide call for units. Move quickly. Highway Patrol . . . move in available units."

Highway Patrol? In Philadelphia, the Highway Patrol is not what you might think. It's not police who cruise the roadways. It's an elite group of super cops who are called in when there is deep trouble, or the threat of it. Believe me, you don't want to mess with Highway Patrol. In a town where eight police officers have been killed in the past few years, Highway Patrol moves first and asks questions later, which frankly is the way it should be when danger is facing you. Hesitate and it might be over. Personally, I give cops the benefit of the doubt if they are forced to shoot and kill an approaching madman.

On the Channel Five scanner at the round assignment desk in the center of the newsroom, the Philadelphia Police Department radio blasts out several more shrill beeps.

The dispatcher's agitated voice seems to rise as each minute passes. "Once again, Second and Cambria. Proceed with caution. Please be advised—Car One is headed to the scene."

Car One is not exactly Air Force One. But it's a large Ford LTD with enough radio controls and GPS systems to steer the space shuttle. Inside the car is the nervous, thug-hating police commissioner of Philadelphia, Douglas Underwood.

"Underwood's en route," I yell out from my office near the police radio to the others in the newsroom. "It must be big."

Around the assignment desk is an octagon of cubicles. The anchors, pampered as we are, have separate desks facing out to the street. Mine is in the corner nearest the assignment desk, just off the elevator entrance to the tenth floor. At the next blast of beeps, I look toward the assignment desk. Archer McDonald, the executive producer of the 11 o'clock show, rises from his seat. Senior Writer Quinn Michaels looks pale. His father is a cop. The harried radio dispatcher now begins to scream through the speaker.

"Repeat. I repeat! Nineteenth District. Shooting. Second and Cambria. All medical squads in. Again, all medical squads—rescue one, rescue two, all in. All in now. Approach--approach with extreme caution. Officer on scene."

I get up from my desk and walk over to the assignment desk. I lean on the counter, which is filled with empty coffee cups and a pile of suburban county phone books, and watch News Director Barbara Pierce. Barbara Pierce is someone who keeps failing up. I mean, this woman keeps getting promoted, even though she keeps screwing things up. I always wonder: Does she have pictures, photos of someone where they shouldn't be? How does a person like Barbara keep moving higher? She went to a big time journalism school, but I've always presumed they didn't teach ethics. I mean, Barb worked for Susan, the Philadelphia native who came down from network to save Channel 9. Channel 9 was resurrected, and I mean, you would think that Barb learned from Susan, and would bring some honesty to the place when she jumped ship to join the "mighty five," as she calls our place?

I guess people get rewarded in America all the time for failure. At the moment of the emergency call, Barb sits at her desk across the room from mine. The afternoon sun blazes through the window, a sweeping panorama of glass extending from the building's Market Street side to the view of City Hall and wrapping around to the side that faces the concrete canyon of West Market Street. We are seven blocks away from Ben Franklin's home. But journalism was much different in Big Ben's day.

Barb and I have the closest desks to the assignment desk. We flank the desk like two news birds waiting to attack. Barb is tensed in her chair, her eyes bulging, face contorted with anxiety. Barb chews on the remains of a cheese danish left over from a meeting with advertisers a few days before. This. Unfortunately, is a newsroom-wide habit. It looks tasty, but at several days old, it's not something I would eat. Her mouth is full as she screams in that sweet way of hers, "What the fuck is going on?" She runs to the assignment desk, half of the danish still in her hand, the rest in her mouth.

Bob Harris is the assignment manager. He's the guy who finds the news, gets it covered. If he misses a story, his life will be unbearable. Bob is indefatigable. He eats news, and getting it eats him alive. There is no assignment manager in local news in America who sleeps well. Bob will be fired; he knows it and waits for the day; but in the meantime, he salivates for news.

Bob is now seated on a stool at the assignment desk in the center of the newsroom, surrounded by scanners and a six-foot-tall map of Philadelphia, the suburbs, New Jersey and Delaware. His "office" is the spine, the nerve center of the newsroom, resembling the oval counter of the maitre de at a fancy restaurant. Leaning on the counter, Bob stands up and roars back to the nervous news director: "It's a shooting at Second and Cambria."

"Where?" Pierce asks.

"Second and—"

"Isn't that a rundown, shitty neighborhood?" she says, her hands gesturing in the air, a conductor without form.

"Yeah—but we've got two men critically wounded."

Pierce puts her hands on her hips and answers in her cigarette-scarred, gravelly voice, "Bag it. Nobody gives a fuck about that godforsaken, bombed-out neighborhood. Shootings there are a dime a dozen. It's not worth a reporter. Just get some video. Whack it and track it back here. I'm not biased, mind you. I just know what sells tickets to TV in this town."

"Whack it and track it" means bring back the footage, edit thirty seconds of video and treat it as news that means little to the viewer.

"Whack it, Bobby," Barbara says. "You can't make cream cheese out of shit. So whack it, and get that crew out of there. You get me, Bobby boy?"

He winces. He looks down, as if he's been ordered to the back of the class or the bus. The word "boy" does not sit well, either.

Barb goes inside the assignment desk area, squirming, her arms locked together over her chest. At this anguished stage in her career, I believe she could screw up a two-car funeral. I think she's capable of anything. She is sly and cynical, and there hasn't been one day in her life when she hasn't feared for her job. I watch from across the assignment desk and wait for her next move.

I blame this situation on Bernie. Bernie the owner. Bernie the greedy jerk. Bernie who screws with life. But I have to admit there is plenty of blame to go around. Let's face it, local news has gone to hell. In this town and around the country, ratings are down by 35 percent. So all of us, even the alleged ethical intellectuals like me, are fighting for a bigger piece of a smaller pie.

Decision time nears. Barb is about to hold the three o'clock meeting. Every newsroom in America holds a three o'clock meeting. That's when they decide what blood and guts, sex and gossip, and unsubstantiated health advisories will go on tonight. That's when the real good newsrooms look for stories that impact directly on people. Frankly, To Barb, murders of minorities are not news, and in that sick, decadent way of hers, she is convinced that if the victims are black, it doesn't count. Is she bigoted? She says not. But if that's not bigotry, what is?

Barb is feeling even more pressure than usual, because this has not been a good November. The overnights—the ratings— are not good. They suck. So Barb is looking for anything to lure the folks in, except that she's blind to the day's biggest story. Barb is a deer in the headlights.

CRIME SCENE—SECOND AND CAMBRIA

When Garcia Perez sees the men sprawled on the pavement, his right hand shakes so violently that he can barely hold the two-way radio microphone.

"Oh my God!" he calls.

Cops are tough, but cops are people. They put on a great show of pride, an appearance of invulnerability. But inside, they cry just like the rest of us. When they see death, they get depressed.

Cops hold this society together. They get paid peanuts for dodging bullets, breaking up domestic dustups, and taking care of all of us. I respect cops in a way that few people do because I have watched them on the job, not through the glamour of TV but in the real-life messes they have to clean up after.

Once they deal with that, the gore, the idiocy of crime, the process of looking for the reasons begins. Cops are paid to be suspicious. The weapons between their ears can be more powerful than the automatic pistols inside their holsters.

Garcia Perez is one of the most honored cops in Philadelphia. He has guts, and he is smart. Very smart.

For Perez, the job at Second and Cambria requires two sets of priorities. He must assemble the facts for the official record, and he must cover his own ass. He speaks again, then goes quiet.

"Oh my God, please get me some . . ." The dead air is frightening in the crowded radio room at police headquarters on Race Street, where the radio dispatchers listen to the voice of a man in distress.

"Get me some help . . . fast . . . a rescue squad . . . shit . . . it may be too late. I think it is. Oh, Mama, this is deep shit here."

Perez has seen victims before, but never like this. As far as he knows, there never has been anything like this. He looks down at the men. They are bleeding out. The man on the left is also choking, his eyes bright with alarm. The blood is dripping down over his chin. Every time he regurgitates, it is blood that seeps from his mouth.

"Get rescue in fast," Perez calls. "I'm at Second and Cambria."

The first on the scene of any crime is one lonely cop. Victims may still be breathing. Chances of saving them are bad to nothing. What he sees might cause palpitations of the heart or worse among those who are untrained and unprepared to watch death. At Second and Cambria, the blood is flowing from various bullet holes in the two bodies, emptying onto the pavement and winding in small pools till it runs over the curb and into the street. But cops are used to seeing blood, so what is it that freaks Perez out? Is it the path he has chosen?

Perez tries to avoid the faces of the victims. Instead, his eyes focus on the street signs, then move quickly to a mural on the side of an abandoned building. Murals are a big deal in Philadelphia, and this one has Julius Erving, Dr. J, driving in, his legs three feet off the ground, making a lay-up for the Sixers. With his eyes on Dr. J, Garcia reaches into a pouch. He looks away from the mural art and back to the dying men. Carefully, he puts the plastic gloves on his hands. He drops the small pistol, the Beretta, into the pouch. The service revolver remains in the holster.

With the backup gun safely stored in the pouch, Perez picks up the microphone again.

"This one guy is bleeding to death," he continues. "There's something really strange. Oh, God . . . I don't believe what I'm lookin' at. I'm gonna be sick."

Perez pauses to recover, then grabs a handkerchief from his pocket and knots it. He places it in one of the wounds of the man wearing the Phillies jacket. He needs to make it look like he's helping, but he also needs the men to die before the first medics arrive. The victim's eyes are glazed. The other man is coughing, suffocating in his own blood. The purplish, fresh blood of the wound starts spreading over the officer's fingers. The blood quickly spreads, covering the glove.

He takes his hand away and lets it hang in the air, holding the bloody handkerchief. Stinging from the cold wind and the sight of the carnage, he feels the nausea grow in his stomach.

Parts of the bodies are lying alongside the men. Crime scenes are routine to police officers, but a moment like this, with all these screwed-up emotions, is something they never train you for at the police academy. He puts the essential tools from his emergency medical kit back in the pouch that he wears around his waist. Slowly, he picks up the disconnected parts and wraps them in plastic. Like critical evidence, the pieces of the mystery are slipped into the pouch.

Tears form in Perez's eyes. He hears the wailing sirens of his reinforcements, but the pounding of his heart seems even louder. Within minutes, he knows, both of these men will be dead. He could force it, but he also understands the delicate nuances and finite work of medical examiners who miss nothing. As he carefully walks around the bodies, he wonders if this crime will take him to the path of redemption, and if the boss will allow him to reach closure. "God's will," he thinks. God's will can guide him to the finish.

CHANNEL FIVE NEWSROOM

My late friend Ron T. was a fighter for ethics in the news. We came from the era of "yellow journalism," the tabloid exploitation of sensationalism. We tried to be better, but it didn't always work out. Ron, mimicking a toothpaste commercial, always said, "I wonder where the yellow went." "Yellow journalism" meant reporting without responsibility. Ron, if you're listening, I know where the yellow went. It's right here in this goddamned newsroom. Channel Five in Philadelphia—always first and sometimes wrong. Right now, we are not first, or second. We are not *there,* or at least it appears that we are missing the story.

We are summoned to the rectangular meeting desk in the southwest corner of the room. Seven chairs are filled for the three o'clock meeting. The rest of the gang stands. A bowl of candy sits at the center of the table. Barb, finished with the stale danish, reaches over and grabs a Goldenberg's Peanut Chew. It's a Philly specialty, and the dentists love it. Barb is amazingly thin, considering all the newsroom crap she ingests. As she chews the candy, she opens her mouth to speak.

"Let's move it and shake it. We're two weeks into the rating book, and we're in deep shit. Channel Seven is kicking our butts. Even Diana Hong over at Channel Nine is moving up. That broad is good. I worry about her. She's a looker, but she's got brains. Has anyone met her? Hong and the also-rans at Channel Nine are knocking at our door. Any smart-ass ideas for tonight?"

"The shooting of two men is a smart-ass idea," I say. "Are you listening, Barb, or are you brain dead?"

"Fuck you."

The truth is that plunging ratings are making Barb into a callous, hypocritical fearmonger whose purpose is to get a news audience any way she can. But to be honest, she has never really cared. She is an honored graduate of the class of shame, circa 1990, when the people in local news started heaving into the trash bin of filth. Barb cares little about the public interest, just her own survival and mind-screwing her staff enough to keep them off-guard, insecure and screwed up so badly that they fear for their jobs more than they care about the damn truth.

She says it again. "Fuck you."

"I'm calling human resources," I answer.

"Go piss up a rope," she says. The first time I heard "go piss up a rope" was in basic training in the Air Force. Barb never served her country, but she loves the expression.

She unmasked her style when she told me once, "Listen, I don't want anyone to know how I feel about them. That way they are like little puppets and I can hold the string on their balls, if you know what I mean, Mikey."

Yeah, Barb. I know what you mean. Barb's style of management is a blueprint for failure. And we are failing—I mean, our skills are falling—off a cliff. And so are the damn ratings.

You want to get the picture? Look at the stories we covered last night at eleven. We led the show with the story of a hooker ring broken up in Kensington. I don't mean London; there's a Kensington in Philadelphia. Our other stories included video of a new mega-drugstore in the center of the city. We followed that with a domestic killing in Camden, New Jersey, three accidents on two of our fabulous crawlways, and a mayoral proclamation honoring Buster Bortman, a philanthropist who was recently released from the Federal pen at Lewisburg after serving one year for tax fraud. The increasing death toll in Iraq and the staggering stock market were relegated to the second fifteen minutes of the show, when most people are brushing their teeth or hoping for bodily contact.

The November sun is moving quickly now over the office buildings to our west. As darkness falls, a double murder is unfolding. The boss is in a state of nervousness, accented by the cigarette she lights in the middle of the newsroom.

"Barb, I'm calling the Fire Marshall," I say.

"Call the Fire Marshall, call Human Resources. Take a car to the fricken murder and get your rocks off, Mikey. I'm ready for real news." She looks at me in that wily, weird way of hers and says, "Let's cover the school board hearings on the new Holocaust curriculum."

"Now that's a story," I say.

"You like it, Mikey?"

"I like it, Barbie."

"Then let's pass." She looks at the story proposals. "Here's a good one. An abused puppy is rescued by some kids in Allentown."

I love pets, but it's all about sex, babies, pets and vets in this newsroom. The heart tuggers. Some people care more about abused pets than abused people. But it is a great story.

"Okay," I say.

"Good, we'll cover that. And how about we send a crew to the Thanksgiving party hosted by Angel Esperanza. He's been doing it for twenty-five years."

Bob Harris says, "Why don't we get to the Cambria murders now." It's a ruse because Bob knows damn well that he's got a shooter headed to the scene.

"Forget Cambria already. You are ticking me off, Bob. Move on!"

"Okay, why don't we cover the controversy in Yeadon? A principal there wants to ban all classroom teaching of Darwinism."

"What? Have you lost your fuckin' mind, Bob?" Barb looks at him with a face of terror. "Do you think there is any way our audience knows the difference between Darwin and dick?"

For my part, I'm getting a headache. This is not just a content problem. Recently, Pierce has lost her groove. She stereotypes the viewer. She seeks an audience with phony premises: If it bleeds, it leads; if there's flesh, you've got an audience.

But her point of view does hold some truth. After all, as the men on Cambria Street gasp their final breaths, Barb knows that most viewers in the suburbs, the whites in the twenty-five to fifty-four age range that advertisers prefer, care little about the city, except for its theaters and swank restaurants. For suburbanites, the path is simple—drive in, have a valet park your car, eat and be entertained, and after you're done, get the hell out of Dodge. Barb is first and foremost, she believes, a realist.

Keith Byrne is sitting across from me at the meeting desk, and I can feel his impatience. His blue eyes are barely visible, staring as he does out the picture window, then turning as he gives Barb the big squint. He says, "Cover the damn story, Barbara. It's a two-fer. Two may be dead. C'mon, Barb, let's rock."

Keith Byrne, my friend and future draft pick in the anchor sweepstakes, is hungry, but not for food. He is breathing heavily because he wants news. After listening to the boss, Byrne opens the top drawer of the supply cabinet, grabs two pencils, and walks over to the electronic pencil sharpener bolted to the wall of the assignment desk next to the maps. I have to hold back a smile. Every time Byrne gets tense, he inserts a pencil in sharpener. He seems calmed by the sound of the machine slicing through the wood and the lead, the buzz of that little saw inside the machine.

Byrne is frustrated, not only by the agony of trying to get the real news covered but also by another distraction. Byrne, who for some reason views me as a mentor, is still looking in the wrong places for the right woman. Keith is currently obsessed with Suzie

Berman, who was just brought up as a reporter from the company station in Kansas City.

Suzie is a looker, but not a zipper hire. A zipper hire is a reporter hired because a general manager likes her so much that he wants to open his zipper and let his feelings hang out. In our station that is a real possibility because the general manager is a woman, a woman who also connects to female passion. I think Keith Byrne likes Suzie for two reasons. One, she is a news junkie. Two, Keith is crazy about her face, her arms, her legs and the way she walks. He talks about her fingers, how delicate they are. The way I figure it, if a guy is hot about a woman's fingers, he must either be a QVC fan or crazy, at least about her. I can tell you that when I first met my wife, Rebecca, back in the day, *I did not look at her fingers.*

Is the pencil inside the sharpener a symbol of where he wants to be? Maybe he is sharpening his act in hopes of finding true love, or something close to it, with Suzie.

At this moment, Keith Byrne looks like he's going to explode. He is an award-winning writer who is never appreciated by his boss. If you want great journalism, exclusive reports, a breed above the rest, he is the go-to guy.

Go-to-guy is tall and handsome, with a dark head of hair so full he could be a model. His face is chiseled, dimples crease his cheeks every time he smiles, and he has the all-American blue eyes of a movie star and an Einstein brain. I hate him for his looks, but I love him for what's between the ears. I mean, Keith is from central casting for women who like hunks.

I am the reverse; I'm what they call ethnic. My nose is long; my hands wander in the air when I talk. My smile is crooked. So Byrne and I look different. But we have shared values. Keith knows the difference between news and bullshit. The day of Lakeview, he saved the day by being smart. After all, who knew what the Lakeview High trouble was until Keith cut through the bullshit? Even the cops were confused.

Go-to guy is pissed off. And as Barb looks at him with scorn, he is getting more pissed off.

"Wait a minute," he screams. His shout-out briefly outdoes the volume of the pencil sharpener, which keeps buzzing and cutting. Finally, he collects the sharpened pencils in his fist and walks quickly toward the news director.

"Go to hell," she yells back.

"Hold on," he says. "They are *people* at that crime scene. God dammit, Barb, you are so full of shit they would need a landfill to empty you."

Pierce's dark eyes dart from side to side. Then she looks straight at Keith like he is a dead-on-the-dock, limp fish.

"Don't you ever embarrass me again, you no-talent, under-qualified pain in the ass. You belong in fucking Clovis, New Mexico, you dick-dangling disaster."

Not trying too hard to disguise his contempt for her decision, Byrne blows her a kiss with the middle finger of his right hand and says, "Love you, babe."

Barbara Pierce is not a babe. She is the most profane, frightening, and demented news boss Byrne has ever had. Tall and lurking, Barb is imposing in a Hulk Hogan sort of a way. Her face has rugged lines. Her eyes are deep set. She wears long skirts , and high heels, and her eyes are surrounded by blue circles. Sleep is not her friend. Pierce began as a proud, fact-finding journalist. But now, Barb will not let facts or accuracy get in the way of a story. Survival of the fittest. That's what this game is all about.

Still, despite her toughness, she does have rare moments of feelings. She thinks of other people's feelings, on average, about once a year. I stand up, walk around the table, and put my arm on Byrne's shoulder. "Take it easy, man," I tell him.

"Mike, how can I?"

"Just cool it." I believe Keith will be my successor some day. So I always try hard to counsel him to be patient and stick to his convictions.

He looks up, the creases of his forehead strained in anguish. "In our newsroom," he says, "memories fade until the next fuckup." Keith swivels in his chair and looks at me. I look back. I know what I have to do. In pompous-ass mode, I often say, "It's getting the news that counts, stupid." So I say it again. Keith says, "Right, Mike, but if you get it, they have to let you report it. Otherwise, man, it's only news to us."

I nod. Then a dramatic, fear-stirred voice on the police radio cuts through, telling us that the bodies are still on the scene at Second and Cambria. If Barb doesn't decide to cover this, we will be clobbered by Channel Seven, WTVX, our main competitor and the market leader. I can't let this happen. I motion to the news director to come into my office for a moment. The staff sits in silence as we walk away.

My desk area is small. But the view is perfect, a panorama of Philadelphia. I mean, Old Ben once walked here. Tom Jefferson told the British to go to hell. John Adams risked his life to save the damn country. And I'm sitting in my desk chair, about to start arguing with a malcontent boss on how to cover a double murder. This *is* America.

She walks after me, eyes glaring. "What's up, Mikey?"

"Barbara," I say, "don't call me Mikey."

"Shit, I'm sorry, but . . ."

"It's disrespectful. I was doing news when your mother was nursing you. Listen, you can't just walk away from a double homicide because the victims are black."

"Bullshit," she replies. "The news is what I say it is. If it happens in the suburbs, it's real big. Mikey, I mean Michael?"

"Yes?"

"I mean Michael, the only way we win, babe, is to think white. These crap-ass killings are just a way of life in the badlands of Philadelphia. A dime a fucking dozen. As I see it, in *those* neighborhoods, death by gunshot or even by knife is part of the damn quality of life."

"Let me make something clear," I tell her. "Byrne is right on. A double murder is a double murder, no matter where it happens. This could lead to a bigger story. You've got to cover it."

"I got to do nothing," she says. She stands up. She puts her face in her hands, then raises her head and moves her hands into a vice-like grip. She looks disgusted.

"Time was when you ran this place, Mikey. But those days are over. I got to deal with you because you are a fixture, but fixtures fall just like anchors sink to the bottom."

"Get the hell out of here," I answer. "You are a poor excuse for a news boss."

She looks at me, kicks a chair, and says, "You're right, you bastard, you always are, but . . ."

"Yes?" I say.

She grins ear to ear, and in a whisper she says, "I am not going to cover the fucking story. You can yell at me till the cows come home."

With that, she walks out to the center of the newsroom, unwraps a small package, and devours two Goldenberg's chews. She doesn't even chew them. It is amazing she doesn't choke. I stare across the room. I am pissed and in a rage, and I can feel the veins trying to explode through my forehead. I get even crazier when, rather indelicately, she blows a kiss at me, crumbs seeping out the side of her mouth.

More sounds erupt from the scanners. This time, the trembling voice is a man's. He's one of ours, our cameraman.

CRIME SCENE—SECOND AND CAMBRIA

Garcia Perez runs to his car, opens the trunk, and throws the pouch into the rear of the compartment near the automatic rifle box. Time is running out. He needs to dispose of the latex gloves before reinforcements come in. He looks around. He feels someone close. Behind him is a man with a camera. He takes the gloves off anyway and stuffs them into the cargo pocket on his left trouser. The camera guy is taking video of him. Did he see him slip the gloves away? Perez doesn't care. But he senses a need to look like he's suffering. Perez kneels on the ground. On his knees, he wraps his head in his hands and covers his eyes. The cameraman looks familiar, Perez thinks. The cameraman puts down his camera. He says, "You okay, man?"

Perez answers, his voice muffled by his hands still gripping his forehead. "I just never get used to this shit. Been doin' it for years. Never get used to it."

The cameraman looks at Perez with sympathy and concern. Then he moves back and focuses his camera on the bloody remains. While the cameraman stands directly over the bodies, Perez, now out of view, crawls on the ground, as if he is sick, but he is really searching for any residue, anything that might have fallen from his double-layered belt, the outside pure leather, the inside a Velcro-locked compartment for storage of bullets, tools of the trade, or even small knives. Very quickly, he grabs the rubber cover from each of his shoes and stuffs them in the rear of his trousers, where, hopefully, they will stay until he can hide them away alongside the fingers, the toes, and the teeth.

CHANNEL FIVE NEWSROOM

"I got a twenty at Second and Cambria," says our cameraman, Jimmy Manstein. Then, "Oh my God . . . Mother Mary . . . Mother Mary."

"A twenty" means the exact site he's calling from. Manstein is the greatest cameraman in the history of Philadelphia television news. I mean, Manstein walks through fire and lives to show the story. He deftly maneuvers through a horde of Secret Service agents to get footage for our station. His video of the funeral of

Princess Grace of Monaco, Philadelphia's only royalty, was breathtaking and up close. He is the man. He doesn't just take pictures. His eyes see news unfolding. He is tall, with the grace of a ballerina and the disposition of a Marine, which he was in Gulf War number one. But at this moment, standing at Second and Cambria, he is scared shitless. Believe me when I tell you that fear is not usually a part of his makeup.

"This is Manstein," he continues. "Got two dead men, shot a few times, dead I think just a few minutes. Both of these men have no . . . Oh my god. I . . . I can't believe this." His voice gets higher. "I. . . uh . . . I . . . do not . . . see any fingers. No toes. No teeth."

Then he screams into the microphone, "One guy has a blood-soaked map on his chest with arrows pointing toward Valley Forge. Cop says no big deal. Anything going on in Valley Forge?"

When the radio crackles, Bob Harris rushes over to the middle of the assignment area. He asks, "You still there, Jimmy?"

"Yeah, I'm looking at the bullet holes. I'm looking for the fingers. One cop here. Rescue units One and Two. These guys are deader than dead. They bled out. No fingers, toes, teeth. I gotta go . . . The smell. The blood is on my shoes. I gotta go."

At the news assignment desk, Bob picks up the microphone and says, "Bring the video back. We're not covering it."

"Why the hell not?" Manstein roars back.

"Because," Bob replies with a mixture of sadness and sarcasm, "because the boss says that we—uh—are not covering it."

Pierce hears the exchange. Her heels the floor, she grabs Bob by his hair, and she yells.

"Why the hell is Manstein there? I told you I didn't want to cover this fucking story, goddamit! Bobby, what the hell is wrong?"

Harris says, "Get your hands off my hair. I sent him there. You said to whack it and track it. No reporter. Just video."

"Did I tell you to do that?"

"Yes, you did, Barb."

"Well, get him the hell out of there."

I feel utter disgust. We are walking away from serious news. Why is a murder victim carrying a map to Valley Forge? And who has the fingers, the toes, the teeth?

My desk phone rings. I pick it up. Civic leader Angel Esperanza says, "Marone, get Newsboy on the phone." I motion to Keith. He's in my office in a few seconds. I activate the speaker phone.

Esperanza continues. "Newsboy, I've got a lead for you. It's a story that will shake the foundations of City Hall. Call me on the cell in five. Get a pencil. But don't sharpen it first. This is a mini-bombshell."

DILWORTH ARMS CONDOS, 3924 CHESTNUT STREET

"Yikes. This is so hot. Like you, you little basket of sunshine."

Harvey Hopkins is sipping from a cup of black coffee, and some of the liquid is dripping from his lips to his chin and falling to the knot of his tie. He uses the coffee to balance the alcohol, but it never really works. On this day, as the gunfire rings out on Cambria Street, Hopkins is knee deep in vodka and being embraced by the perfumed being of Ann Marie Hartz, the weekend weather person for Channel Five. According to Harvey, Ann Marie gives great forecast, and great highs and lows.

Love is not the mission of the legendary anchorman. All people grow old, but anchors, larger than life on the small screen, grow older in front of thousands who remember them when. More than the thinning grey hair, more than a sagging face, he needs reaffirmation. His affair with Ann Marie is an emotional tonic meant to relieve him of the aging process.

Anne Marie is naked, her body draped across Hopkins's bulging stomach. She lifts her neck up and says, "Honey, you gotta lay off the sauce." Ann Marie moves off his body, gets up on her hands and knees, and moves her face to his neck, where she offers a soft kiss and whispers in his ear. "Baby, I'm so into you. I worry about you. Please sweetie, lay off the sauce and the other shit."

Hopkins looks at her. "I know, but yikes, sweetie—oh, shit. I can't stop it. It makes me feel good. Actually, it makes me feel—nothing. I love that." Harvey rests his head on the soft pillow and puts his right arm over her naked back. He glances over at the clock on the nightstand at her side of the bed. The bedroom is furnished with the narcissistic accoutrements of his reckless career. On the top of the armoire facing the bed are three gold statuettes, local Emmy awards from his lead-anchor days in Pittsburgh. The wall, papered in a dark beige, is filled with a blend of plaques and pictures from the groups that have honored him. In the far corner, on the wall near the window, is a framed picture, in color, of a little boy. The child's eyes are filled with hope. He thinks of Tommy all the time. Tommy, the ghost of Harvey's past, was just three when the leukemia arrived. After Tommy's passing, Harvey and his only wife, Teresa, divorced. Since Tommy's demise, love, real love, has never visited Harvey.

Harvey slips out of Ann Marie's arms and stands up, putting the coffee down on the nightstand. His legs shake as he lifts them one at a time to put on his trousers. He zips his fly and prepares to go down the freight elevator, as he does every day. From the ground floor he will enter the cab waiting to drive him to the station. The six o'clock broadcast will start in two hours, which leaves him just enough time to wash up, apply his makeup and, in the final moments before air, sniff the white powder tucked away in his briefcase.

He gives Ann Marie a goodbye peck, then goes down to his waiting cab. He wouldn't dare drive drunk. He peers out the window. "The Big Gray Lady," as he calls Philadelphia, is dark and lonely in the middle of November, the people wrapped in their coats walking quickly in the high winds. He wonders how they would react if they knew that one of their favorite news anchors was in the cab. Eyeing them one by one as the cab rounds City Hall, he gets the usual anxiety about going on the air. And he wonders how much more time he'll have on the air, and how much longer the weather babe will meet him for afternoon delight. "Here I am," he thinks. "I'm a fifty-nine-year-old drunk, yikes, and I'm still hard as a rock."

Just about the time the two bodies are being loaded into the medical examiner's truck at Second and Cambria, Harvey Hopkins arrives at the Channel Five studios. He emerges from the cab and is so drunk that he asks the driver to help him through the door, where he complains to the receptionist that he has a "touch of the flu."

Harvey takes the elevator to the third floor, avoiding the stairway. He walks to his cubicle, which faces the waterfront side of the panoramic window. Barb Pierce walks up.

"Hi, Harv. You're going to whack and track a double murder in the 'hood." That means that he will "front" the double murder story, since there is no reporter on the scene. He will be given the facts, look at the video, and write a short report. He will report the story from the set, but the viewers will think he went to the scene to get the facts. This deception is standard practice at our place. It's been a long time since Barb has allowed her backup anchor to go to a crime scene. Barb walks out.

"Yikes, sounds like a gruesome fucking story," Harvey calls out across the wall to Keith Byrne, who is staring at his computer terminal in the adjacent cubicle. Keith nods.

"I'll have more info for you shortly," calls the production assistant, Ronnie Pulaski, from across the room.

"Yeah," says Harvey. "Like to know who those suckers are. Any video?"

"Yeah," the drowsy video editor answers. "We need some pictures to make it happen."

The production assistant calls to Harvey. "Come on in." She gestures toward the edit booth and hands him a small cartridge of videotape. Hopkins sits in the edit booth alongside the editor. The production assistant watches, leaning on the sliding-glass door of the booth. Hopkins presses "play" on the digital control board.

On the screen is Manstein's video. At first, the camera is a bit shaky. In about thirty seconds, the zoom lens takes us to the face of one victim. There is a single bullet hole above his right eye. The skull has collapsed, so it appears that his face is resting flatly on the concrete. There is no head to the head. The camera moves down to the arms and hands. What's left of the hands is soaked with blood. As a police officer kneels by the second body, the cameraman goes wide. The officer is checking the second victim's neck. He is seeking a pulse. The second victim wears a Phillies jacket. Watching the video, it is hard to see where the red of the coat ends and the blood begins. The cameraman zooms wide to show the arriving medical crews and crime-scene investigators. Quickly the scene transforms from the lonely visual of two men dying in the cold to a maze of blinding lights and the sounds of wailing sirens.

Barb is looking in at the door of the edit booth.

"Should we kill or black out some of the grisly shit from there?" she calls to Harvey.

"Why?" says Hopkins, his eyes still glazed from his medicated afternoon.

"Because it's dinner hour soon. I don't want our viewers puking to death."

"Why not?" Hopkins inquires. "These are great fucking movies. I can't wait. Man. Yikes. This is great stuff." Some news people actually delight in bad news. Harvey is one of them. It helps him deflect thoughts about his own sack of shit.

In the small edit booth, Hopkins says to the videotape editor, "Back it up. Go back. Now. Okay. Stop it."

He gets up and walks closer to the screen. There, in slow motion, a Philadelphia police officer with his head drooped is walking away from the scene. His face is grim. But Hopkins has noticed something: The cop has on latex gloves. Hopkins watches as the cop slips them off and tucks them in a pouch in his pants. "Yikes," he thinks.

Hopkins walks over to the desk of Wally Tracker, the station's crime reporter. Tracker is disgusted. He is the journalist here, and instead of letting him write a substantial piece on a double murder, "the lunatic," as he calls the news director, has assigned the story to the man with the habit.

Hopkins says, "Wally, are detectives the only ones who wear gloves at crime scenes?"

"Yes, Harvey, just detectives. They don't want their prints to get confused with any other findings."

"Thanks, sir."

Hopkins returns to his desk. The blood is flowing to his brain. He knows something is up. And even the slightest deviation from normalcy can bring Harvey to the threshold of personal destruction.

Very calmly, he reaches into his briefcase, grabs a leather pouch and places it in the bottom left drawer of the desk. He locks the desk with the small key he keeps in his briefcase. The coke is safe. He believes that. He really believes that. He thinks of his next date with his weather honey, but he has no idea just yet of his date with destiny.

CHANNEL FIVE EXECUTIVE CONFERENCE ROOM

It is 5 P.M. and Keith Byrne has no story. He watches Harvey slap his makeup on while looking in a small mirror on his desk. Keith hates Harvey.

Keith has a nasty case of anchor envy, the most sordid, insidious envy there is, a fear and loathing laced with jealousy and firmly rooted in insecurity. I know about anchor envy. I used to have it until I got the main job. I can tell you that it is a sickness that spreads like a cancer through Keith Byrne's insides every time he looks at my backup, Hopkins, and thinks that he would make a better anchorman, even though Keith knows he isn't really ready, not yet. Harvey is a pro. He is out of control and personally corrupt, but he is a dramatic communicator. The people have no idea that he is a drunken low-life, not yet. They also don't know that, in the stupor of drink and drugs, Harvey has turned into a mean bastard.

Last August, I was on vacation, so Harvey was anchor. Keith arrived on the set to do a story. Harvey looked over.

He said, "Byrne, you've gained some weight. You okay, man?" Keith sat there. He told me that tears welled up in his eyes. He was angry, he was sad, but ultimately he was envious. The man had slimed him, and although Hopkins doesn't have a journalistic gene in his body, Keith knows that Hopkins is a better anchor. He is smooth, relaxed and warm.

Anchor envy, mixed with a blurred and bloated vision of your own ability, is a recipe for a lifetime of misery. The jealousy gives you pain and anxiety. Pain and anxiety cause irrational behavior.

On this day, Keith has no story for the newscast, but there could be one on the way. He dials Esparanza's cell.

"Hello, Angel."

"Hi, Newsboy."

"What's up?"

"What's up is that police will raid home of Sammy the Salami, aka Sammy the Shit, tomorrow morning at 7:30, 424 Reid Street. Be there. It will be the largest grab of coke in twenty years. And Sammy, who will be sleeping with his boyfriend, will be totally surprised."

"How did the cops find out?"

"I told them."

"But how did you find out?"

"When it comes to drug dealers and corrupt newspeople, I am what the kids would call 'the bomb.' Got it, Newsboy? And one more thing. Sammy gave five grand to the campaign of City Councilman Bertram Gerard. That revelation will totally screw up Gerard's bid for mayor."

"Why?"

"Because Bertie Girard is under investigation by the Feds for buying coke from Sammy the Salami. Go for the story, Keith. And remember who gave it to you."

"Thanks, Angel."

Click.

No story today, but a good one coming tomorrow.

CHANNEL FIVE NEWSROOM

Bobby Harris collects all the paper trash on his circular desk in his arms, walks over to the big recycling bin near the elevator and dumps in the remains of the day. He looks back at the room and sees Harvey primping himself and the production assistants running back and forth with scripts. As Bobby prepares to go home for the night, he feels chills and heat building in his body. He goes back to the desk, grabs his briefcase, and comes over to me.

"I'm sorry, Mike. I'm really sorry. I should have fought harder to get there faster. I feel like I really fucked up."

His eyes are red, and small tears are forming. Now the tears are trickling down his cheeks. I know this is more than the story. I know exactly what it is.

"Look," I say. "Look at reality. She just doesn't get it. You should be angry, not hurt."

"But I am hurt, Mike. I can't stand it. I grew up near Second and Cambria. Every time I challenge her, she looks back at me with those angry, staring eyes, like the only reason I care is because I'm black."

"I know," I say.

"Mike, it is not the color of a murder victim's skin that makes me care. But the fact is that some people care more about a murder in a classy suburb like Bryn Mawr than one in Philadelphia. They feel utter disrespect toward the people who were killed. Honestly, I *am* angry."

He reached for a handkerchief and wiped his eyes. Then he waved goodbye, and his head slumped down over his chest as he walked slowly toward the elevator. I think we're both wondering when Barb's bad judgment will come with a price she'll never forget. I just hope she doesn't take the lives of innocent victims when she takes that big fall someday.

SHOWDOWN—CHANNEL FIVE

Keith Byrne takes the stairs to the second floor, where he has to give a deposition in a case filed by a desperate, angry plaintiff.

Byrne anchored a weekend newscast last month. Channel Five reported the name of a teenager, Jimmy Burget, who was killed on the railroad tracks by a commuter train. The story was right on, but unfortunately, the station broadcasted the name of the victim before investigators had a chance to notify his next of kin, a widowed mother with congenital heart disease. The woman, a Channel Five Pulse Report viewer, collapsed in her living room when she learned her son's fate and teetered on the brink of death for days. She survived to bury her son, but she will not forget. I mean, can you blame her?

Her name is Stella Burget. She is an angry woman. The other night, I picked up the phone, and it was Stella. She said, "Marone, you bastard. My son dies. I find out from you guys, you bastards. You and the bastards who screwed up the Lakeview story. You are a bunch of sorry bastards."

Byrne walks into the conference room on the executive floor. Stella Burget is flanked by her lawyers. Byrne sits next to the three members of the company legal team. He has been well rehearsed for the deposition.

He says, "Hello, Mrs. Burget."

Stella, a stout woman in her forties, gets up from her chair. She says, "Hello, Mr. Byrne, you rotten bastard. You have no idea what it's like to lose a kid, you rich moron." Keith is shaken. He looks away, glances at the court reporter, and fidgets with his hands and with the Dixon Oriole 267 Number Two, his pencil of choice. He knows the news team didn't kill her son; we just broke her heart by prematurely announcing his death to her and three hundred thousand other viewers. In some newsrooms, being first is more important than doing right. In the Channel Five newsroom, as Byrne has lamented to me every day since, the episode was quickly forgotten by our boss, as most mistakes are.

The plaintiff's lawyer, Peter Remick, clears his throat. Remick is wearing a bow tie with white polka dots on a field of blue. He gazes over to Stella and nods his head with a look of comfort. Then Remick stares at Byrne.

"Mr. Byrne, when you reported the tragic death, did your news operation know that Stella Burget did not know that her son was dead?"

"No."

"So you reported this life-changing story with no knowledge that the next-of-kin wasn't notified."

"Yes." Byrne fidgets with the pencil.

"Do you understand the power of television?"

"Of course. What are you getting at?"

Company attorney Gloria Disenfelt looks nervous.

"I'll tell you what I'm getting at. You and that irresponsible bunch of news knuckleheads at Channel Five didn't even bother to find out if the family was notified."

"No, we didn't, but we didn't kill Jimmy, either."

"No, you did not. But you sent Ms. Burget into a near collapse. She had heart palpitations. And by the time they got her to the hospital, she was in cardiac arrest. With her precondition, she neared the edge of death. You didn't kill the boy, but you almost killed the mother."

"I'm sorry."

"That's not enough."

Disinfelt breaks in. "That's enough for now. We're through here." The network lawyer grabs Byrne by the arm. They leave the room.

As they walk down the fire stairwell to the news floor, Byrne says, "I'm sorry."

"Nothing to be sorry about, Keith. We screwed up. I'll tell New York to settle. Tell me something, though?"

"What's that?"

"Does your lunatic news director have any control over that place?"

"No, Gloria. She thinks she does. But the decisions are flawed. Let me tell you, Gloria. Barb is the conductor of a train wreck waiting to happen."

CHAPTER TWO: **THE COP'S NIGHTMARE**

In the blur I see what could be a dog and a cop. Yes, and behind the cop is someone with green pants. I'm moving fast now. Corridor walls are passing me by. Why is Mr. Green Pants following me? Why is he carrying an M-16? I hear a few mumbled words. Something like "bleed out." I can hear in only one ear. Green Pants looks down at me and says, "It's him, goddamit." Another voice, maybe that of a nurse, says, "Get the hell out of my way." The man says, "I've got orders." The other voice says, "Get the hell out of here, or in a few minutes you'll be protecting a corpse." They're talking about me.

6220 BUIST AVENUE, SOUTHWEST PHILADELPHIA
HOME OF GARCIA PEREZ

Perez returns home late, after the report is filed and the interviews are over. He removes his clothes and gets in the shower. Over and over, he tries to cleanse himself of the stains of the day. He remains in the shower a long time. Maria shivers in bed. She waits and wonders what's taking him so long. He scrubs hard. He knows this is a form of purification. He scrubs more, then uses a brush to clean the blood off his fingernails. He is immaculate. He has done this before.

"I love you, Maria," he says when he finally comes into the room. "I love you more than I did yesterday and the day before yesterday."

Garcia Perez lowers his head into his pillow. His wife lies beside him, reading the *Philadelphia Inquirer*. Fear and pride grip him as the crime scene comes back into his mind, along with visions of the blood, the despair, the feelings that have so often threatened his sanity. Witnessing violence sparks the worst fears within him, and the day's work has brought his son Tony's destiny back to life. No day passes without a memory of his son.

For Maria the memories include, in bittersweet flashbacks, recollections of the music her son loved.

Maria clasps Garcia's hand in hers as she turns to face him in the bed, swaying slightly to the music in her head.

Tony Perez had loved music. His body moved easily and smoothly at the church dances at St. Barnabas. That vision will remain with Maria till her own last breath.

Garcia looks at her. Maria is perfect, not a blemish in the bronze skin. Her eyes are deep brown. Her lips are seductive and open. Yet the woman he loves, a beauty inside and out, remains in a state of grief. Tony was an only child, a star student at Temple University, a loving young man who would do anything for anyone. And now his mother's existence is endangered by dark thoughts of how one act can destroy a life, the life of a loved one, and create scars in those who lived. To her husband, the highly decorated Garcia Perez, the death is not just an event, but a dark act of the human spirit, an act with consequences. Perez has transformed his indescribable grief into a fierce determination to do "God's will."

He thinks it again as he lies next to Maria and hopes a dream will take him away from his anguish. He tries to breathe slowly to calm the beating of his heart. He grabs for the TV remote, hoping the sound of TV will calm him. He hears a familiar voice.

"Good evening, I'm Danny Caldwell, and the top story on Channel Seven Newswatch at 11 is the six-alarm fire now ravaging an abandoned factory at Third and American Streets."

A six-alarm fire with no injuries or risk of injuries instead of a bizarre double murder? Garcia lowers the volume on the remote and whispers to Maria, "I wonder if Seven will even run the damn story. I know Channel Five was there, and the shooter said his crazy news director passed on it."

"Garci, it don't matter to some people, especially Caldwell," she answers. "The blood is all over him and his newsroom buddies."

Perez strokes her hair. "I still don't get the missing parts. Who the hell would do that? What happened?" Perez hates hiding any aspect of his job, but God's will be done, he thinks. But was it God's will that broke their lives in two like an axe slamming into a piece of wood?

"Garci," Maria says. "Stop being a cop for a minute and go to sleep."

On the small screen, Danny Caldwell's thick eyebrows jump up and down, and his lips widen and then purse in smiles and grimaces. He reads a series of stories: a riot at Central High, a breakdown in the subway, a "live" hit from reporter Vivian Edwards at the Philadelphia Flower Show, and then, finally, the carnage.

Garcia and Maria are beginning to find sleep even as Caldwell tells the awful story. Garcia props his pillow up and glances at the screen.

"Two men in their thirties were found shot to death at the corner of Second and Cambria. The men remain unidentified." Caldwell, his eyebrows tilted higher to emphasize his eyeballs, pauses just before the graphic video hits the air, then says, "Detectives believe the men were victims of a drug-related shooting."

"Drugs, my ass," says Perez, lifting his head up from the pillow a little. "Those guys were murdered twice. What's the rest of the story?"

Maria curls against the backside of her heroic and deceptive husband, her neck straining over to glance at the video of the murder victims. The pictures on the tube are graphic. The camera zooms into the bodies covered in white sheets, blood stains seeping through the material, the sheets covering the savage cuts on their extremities.

As Garcia drifts into sleep, his dream begins with a picture of the crime scene. The bodies are being carried away. The medical examiner's officers are grimly carrying the dark body bags. He hears laughter. A tall, graying man is standing on the sidewalk, giggling uncontrollably, clapping his hands as though the home team has just won the game. The man wears the tattered clothing of the homeless. He looks down at Garcia Perez and what remains of the two murdered men.

Grimacing, the man says, "So what's up with the chop shop? What are you doing with those spare parts? Tell me, Perez, why don't you become a real surgeon? You could make a fucking fortune with those pliers."

The face belongs to the franchise anchor of the city's number one station, Danny Caldwell, though the voice isn't his. He stares at Perez with cold blue eyes. In his arms he carries a body draped in a red-and-white blanket, a blanket bearing the colors of Temple University. The blanket is wrapped carefully over the body of Tony Perez. Caldwell is now shrouded in a gown with a halo around his head. He holds Tony out as an offering, then launches the boy on his ascension to heaven. Caldwell says to the cop, "We have secrets. You know mine, I know yours. And Perez, you moron, I don't have one fucking regret."

Soon, Perez dreams, Caldwell will trip into a crevice in the ground. He will be sucked into the quicksand of inner earth on his tortuous descent into hell.

CHANNEL FIVE NEWSROOM

The full story of the Cambria murders never makes it to air at Channel Five. Instead, we have Voice-Over Plenty–a sequence of news stories with brief videos of the scenes, accompanied by short bursts of information read by the anchor. VO Plenty gives the impression that a TV station's reporters manage to be everywhere. In reality, meaningful information never reaches the viewer. VO Plenty is a fraudulent form of news with no or little value. My co-anchor Veronica Victor and I present accidents, a robbery at St. Katherine's Church on Belgrade Street, and two stories about Britney Spears being found half-naked in a car parked at a strip joint in L.A. The program opens with an emergency snow warning for Altoona, Pennsylvania, 350 miles west of our coverage area. And Harvey appears in a short, on-set wraparound of the Cambria killings that gives it the appearance of a minor story.

After the show, I head for the green room, the waiting area with its small sink and mirror. Veronica, who is there when I arrive, pauses just a moment from wiping her makeup off with a moist towel. She whispers in my ear, "Mike, did we suck tonight or what?"

I answer, "We have an integrity crisis. We didn't give that double killing the coverage it deserved."

She replies, "I'm really worried about something."

"What's that?" I ask. "There will be other nights, other stories."

Grimly she answers, "I really hope the viewers don't hate me because of my looks."

I can't believe it. We got a double killing. Two lives have been snuffed out. God knows why? We are living under the cloud of a lawsuit from a mother who got the death notice from us. And V, as we call her, is worried that her good looks will kill her career. I can't believe it, but let me tell you, there is a reason for this behavior, and it is really not her fault. They say in our modern media world that perception is reality. It is not just vanity that runs through the mind; it's the lousy standards of this business.

"V," I say. "Get over this beauty kick. They like you because you tell stories well. Some people like you because you are very beautiful. The only people who would hate you because you are beautiful are jealous idiots who can't see the brains through the beauty."

I'm lying. Just a little. Some viewers see Veronica as hot. Others can figure it out that she's got the goods when it comes to writing and pursuing news. The truth is that Veronica is not just a looker, a beauty without a brain. As I wash the oily makeup from my face, I glance over at Veronica. She is holding a towel, drying her face off. She looks so sad. Sadness, unfortunately, goes with the territory, along with the fame and the fortune. You reach a point when you realize, perhaps too late, that the ego and the blurred vision of reality is just so much bullshit. When you reach that point, you hate yourself, and you are sad. I've been there, too many times. I also think Veronica is unhappy. She talks about "getting a life." She keeps her personal life private, but I sense she's dating someone high profile. Why has she never introduced me to anyone, and why does she always come alone to the dinners that Rebecca and I invite her to? I also wonder how she is so connected to inside political information. Like all of us, she protects her sources. But I'm intrigued by how well she is wired.

Anchors come and anchors go. Most of them don't last long in Philadelphia, or for that matter in most big media markets in America. Of course, appearances can be everything, but I must admit that the real reason for the revolving-door nature of Anchorville is the egomaniacal decision-making process of some of the fools who hire anchors. I once told the general manager of our station, Cynthia Cavanaugh, that substance is the key.

"In this town," I said, "you can be pretty, but you have to be gritty."

She disagreed. "First of all, Michael, give me a chick men want to do, if you know what I mean, and she'll bring 'em in, just like bait on a fish hook. Show me a guy who tickles the fancy of women eighteen to fifty-four years old, and I'll show you a damn winner. Look, even you looked good way back then."

Cheap shot. Probably true. I put the ageism out of mind. What else can I do? The boy wonder in me vanished years ago, along with the brown hair. But I still have my principles.

"You're so wrong, Cynthia. It's all about the news. Even slush man Harvey Hopkins has some texture and competence. Not a lot, mind you, but he's good."

She replied, "Do you think Veronica is good because she can wing it without copy? No. She is just so delicious to look at."

"Coming from you, a closet lesbian, I would have to consider that a sexist remark."

"Well," she said, "I do get turned on by the way she walks, not by the way she talks."

Cynthia and scores of other bosses have made zipper hires. Few of these hires stay, but Veronica has. She defies the stereotype.

What is it like to sit next to a beautiful woman every night? That's a common question at my gym. My answer is always the same; I assume they're talking about my wife.

"Rebecca," I say, "has been my wife for forty years, and I still stare in wonder at her. That's what it's like to sit next to a beautiful women every night."

That is not, by the way, a devious answer. My wife is a knock-out. Lights out, believe me. But on the work end, when you share a desk with a woman as beautiful as Veronica, you really don't see her as others do, because you know the person, not the face. Veronica is not your ordinary zipper hire. She's got nerve.

One night there was what we call a perp walk down at the Nineteenth District Police Headquarters. The cops, trying to satisfy the video needs of a reporter, told the perp, "Get up off your ass and go to the john." The camera man filmed the criminal walking, and that was a perp walk. That night, however, the handcuffed suspect looked over at Veronica, stuck his tongue in and out of his mouth, and yelled, "Yo, bitch, I'd like to bite you." It was gross, to say the least, even to the veteran cops watching with amusement.

Veronica moved close to the prisoner, even closer than the cameraman. Her face was inches away from his, close enough to see the scars from his purported lifetime of crime. Then, in a sultry voice, she whispered, "Dream on, big boy. Where you're going, it's your roommates who'll be doing the biting. Send me a postcard from hell, won't you, asshole?"

To hear such words from such an angelic face was even shocking to the police on hand. But that is what my friend and compatriot in news, Veronica Victor, is all about—straightforward, no bullshit.

It would be nice to report that she is Ivy-League educated and brilliant. The brilliance is there; I've watched it every night for ten years. But Veronica is a proud graduate of Montgomery County Community College and Temple University. She grew up in a lower-middle-class home in Richmond, Virginia. She came north for college. She is self-made in every sense of the word.

Veronica is tall, so tall that the bosses pressure me to sit on a phone book so I won't look like a dwarf next to her. I don't do that; I'm not that vain. Veronica has long blond hair that she controls by using three tall cans of hair spray a week. Veronica is a threat to the ozone layer. She sprays so much that the sweet-scented spray permeates the studio. She is fair-skinned. The nose is perfect, the teeth are white, the figure is full-bodied. And she is also a great newsperson. V has the instincts of a tiger waiting in the grass, ready to pounce on the latest piece of information coming her way.

To the envious members of the TV writing press corps, V will never be more than a babe, because they can't see the talent through the cosmetic haze. This is sad, but in a way she brought this on herself.

When she arrived as a young anchor in 1997, she faced the press. Aware that her looks always overshadowed her ability, she tried too hard to compensate. The transcript of her first interview is still available, which is unfortunate. Here is an excerpt:

"INTERVIEW WITH V. VICTOR, ANCHORPERSON, WGET TV" PHILADELPHIA INQUIRER, AUGUST 14, 1997

Reporter Ned Howlston: Welcome to Philadelphia, Veronica. What do you expect to bring to the station?
V. Victor: I want to cover more political news and try to have less glam and trash. I like news, period. That's it.
Reporter: But you yourself are a glamorous woman. How do you get away from that?
V. Victor: I can't help how people see me. All I can say to the people of this region is, please don't hate me because I'm beautiful.

The line was a mistake. It made front-page news in Philly and even in New York: the *New York Post* plastered the headline "SEXY PHILLY ANCHOR RUBS VIEWERS WRONG WAY." The *Daily Philly* in Philadelphia featured a picture of my new co-anchor on the front page with the headline "BEAUTY AND THE LEAST."

I feel for her, but frankly, I'm tired. All this arguing about the Cambria killings has taken the energy out of me. Besides, I want to catch up so I can get a bite and start getting ready for the eleven o'clock news. Contrary to general consensus, anchors, or at least the ones who get it, don't arrive a few minutes before the show, spray their hair and read the news. I move fast to leave the green room and head to my desk. I can't put the murder out of my head. Engaging in my usual post-show routine, I check my bookmarks on the web. On the home page of the Philadelphia Inquirer, the headline stands out.

"DECORATED OFFICER DESCRIBES MURDER SCENE"

Twice-decorated Philadelphia Police officer Garcia Perez describes the scene of this afternoon's double murder at Second and Cambria.

"I get there about 3:10. The two men, they look Hispanic, lie on the ground. Bullet holes in the bodies. One was shot in the neck. When he breathes, blood comes out. I tell you, it was sickening, but for me, it got worse when I saw their extremities cut off, severed, and their cheeks are collapsed. There were no teeth. Whoever did this deed is a sicko, man. I see bodies all the time, but this was mutilation. They died in front of me. I think they were shot, then cut. By the time I got there, it was over for them."

The description is graphic. But he left some things out. He said nothing about the blood-stained map with the arrows pointing to Valley Forge, the map that Jimmy Manstein noticed as he videotaped the crime scene. He said nothing about the plastic gloves, and the pouch that Hopkins told me he noticed when he went over the videotape.

Missing body parts. Missing information. Was it just another savage murder?

CHAPTER THREE: **DEATH BY REMOTE**

My arms and legs are confined close to my body. My body hurts so badly that my eyes keep closing. This place smells like antiseptic and gauze and the repulsive odor of waste.

I glance over to a chair. The man in the fatigues sits on it, his weapon balanced against the wall. He's talking on a cell phone. "No way, that many?" he says. "No fucking way. I have to call home. My God, I hope the kids made it back okay." What is he talking about?

REWIND
SEVEN MONTHS EARLIER, LAKEVIEW HIGH SCHOOL
FEBRUARY 12, 2007

Lunch time in east-coast America. The Glock 17 pistol the student was waving around is now on the ground near his head, which is saturated with blood. Herbert Hornman will be dead in seconds. The other students gather around in silence, some comforted by the fact that they are alive, others shocked, stunned, nausea welling up from their stomachs. One student, a young man, kneels to the ground. He starts performing CPR on Hornman. But there's no use. In a little over thirty seconds, he knows that Hornman is dead.

Back at in the newsroom, seven minutes after the shooting, Producer Kenny Abdul screams so loud that I flinch. "We've got gunfire at Lakeview High! Three shots fired."

I run from my desk to Kenny's, which is across from Keith Byrne's cubicle. Kenny looks crazed. Kenny never looks crazed. He was even cool as a kid, on the day he walked through a phalanx of state troopers to become the first black student to attend Girard College. Girard is a school for fatherless boys, but in the early days of this country, Stephen Girard declared that the school would be endowed for admission of only "white" orphans. Kenny broke the barrier. He is a winner. In 1972, he was the first black local news producer in America. He is confident and together. But not today. Today he is gripped by fear. Kenny has two sons at Cheltenham High School, a school in a leafy, middle-class suburb of Montgomery County, not far from Lakeview. Kenny needs to know that his own children are far from danger.

"Bob," he says to Assignment Manager Bob Harris. "Get every available crew in. I want Suzie Berman on lead. Find Byrne. Find him fast. I want him to field anchor. All hands on deck. We've got a shooting in a fucking suburban high school. And another thing. No information, not one piece of information, until it is confirmed. Understand?"

Bob says, "Of course."

Kenny and Bob are part of the quartet of reason at the news operation. Together with Archer McDonald and Quinn Michaels, they keep the fire of ethics enforcement burning. In the old days, you checked your facts. You checked again. In the new era, some producers don't give a shit about information, as long as they get it on the air and get "movies," the slang for video.

Managing Editor Archer McDonald is a tall, thin man with jet-black hair, a pencil in his ear, and a hunger for information. The fourth member of the off-air truth squad is Senior Writer Quinn Michaels, who is also the union shop steward. Quinn has never met a real story he doesn't like. He is fifty-nine years old and has never missed a day of work. If he ever gets sick, he hides the weakness the way a washed-up anchorwoman would hide her tattered press clippings in a purse.

Every day, Quinn yells across the room, "Listen up. When in doubt, don't. Ya hear me? If in doubt, don't." He means that if you don't have the facts, blow the story out. Quinn would take half the pay to do his job. And at Channel Five, Quinn, Archer, Bob and Kenny are the last lines of defense against a complete loss of ethics. Today, the four of them are getting the wheels in motion for afternoon and evening coverage.

At 2:45, a tipster calls. In her seat at the assignment desk, Temple University intern Gail O'Brien takes the call. She writes quickly on the lined yellow pad. She gets up and hands the note paper to Bob. Grimly he reads the note: "Student kills two students in a hallway at Lakeview High."

Kenny and Archer start working the phones. Archer dials the Lakeview Police Department. While he's talking, intern O'Brien points to the row of monitors. Danny Caldwell is interrupting a soap opera on Channel Seven with a "this just in" announcement, saying that two students have been murdered at Lakeview High by a lone gunman.

Barb walks in after taking her lunch break and asks for a briefing. Kenny issues a warning from his chair at the assignment desk. His voice is clear and his mood is stern as he speaks to anyone within earshot.

"Nothing is confirmed. I repeat, nothing is confirmed."

"Then why the hell are we not breaking in and saying that?" Barb asks. "Is Chopper Five over the scene?"

"No. ETA about forty-five seconds."

"Marone," Kenny yells so loud that I get startled. He is working at the assignment desk. "Get into the studio. As soon as we confirm, we'll get you the info for a break in."

"Okay. I'll head right down," I answer. But I offer a caution on the way out to the elevator. "Hey, remember this, though. There are three Lakeview Townships. One in Montgomery County, one in Bucks, and one in Salem County, New Jersey."

"Good point," Archer replies.

Barb follows me to the studio. On the set, she sits in the co-anchor chair, waiting for the call from the newsroom. On the monitor, Caldwell is back on air. There is no sound. We can only read his lips.

Barb says, "Michael, what do you think?" It is a rare request for input. Is she going soft?

"I think we need information before we go on."

"But the damn chopper is on the scene, and we know there's a shooting. Caldwell says two dead. We are still not on air."

"Barb, we are still not on air because we have shit. We need information, fast." I just broke my rule about bad language on the set. I'm usually very careful, because it just takes one open mike to destroy you. I feel guilty. You just never say "shit" while wearing a microphone.

Time passes. My stomach is a mess. I fear death by deadline. Death by deadline has two meanings: a career-killing broadcast that has bad information, or a bogus story that could, by its gross misinformation, kill someone. I know that Channel Nine, led by News Director Dan Hurley, always opts to be careful. Phil's anchor, Diana Hong, is always careful. I wish we were.

Barb climbs into the set and stands behind me, reaching over for the phone. She calls Kenny, then turns to me. "The copy has already been filed from Kenny's computer to the teleprompter," she says. "Break in now." She looks mean.

The BREAKING NEWS graphic emerges behind me. The copy is there, and I can see video of the school from our chopper. The parking lot is filled with evacuated students, surrounded by black-shirted SWAT teams and ambulances. It's time to go on.

"Good afternoon, everyone. I'm Michael Marone, and this is breaking news from the Channel Five News Pulse. As you can see, swarms of police are surrounding Lakeview High School in central Montgomery County. Channel Five has learned that a member of the junior class has shot and killed himself. The public suicide took place as classes were letting out. There were no other injuries, and despite reports on another station, students were not attacked by the gunman. Once again, this is Lakeview High in Montgomery County. All the students are safe, and the only victim is the student who committed suicide.

"I'm Michael Marone. We'll have more information as it becomes available."

I return to the newsroom. Barb wraps her arms around me. Archer, Quinn, and Kenny form a circle of hugs.

"Thank God," Barb says. "We did right, but Cavanaugh is so pissed at me. She wants to whack me on the spot."

"Yeah, but we got it right," retorts Archer.

"We got it right, but Danny was first on," she replied.

"With bad information. That guy is poison," I said.

The fact that General Manager Cynthia Cavanaugh was pushing Barb to take air without confirming the facts of the story is an outrage. But the episode passes. There is no postmortem, the TV news term for an analysis of what could have gone wrong or did go wrong. We dodged the bullet, but barely.

I can't say the same for daring Danny Caldwell and the scare boys at Channel Seven. His premature report on the "murders" scared the hell out of people in all three Lakeview communities. Parents were scared to death, in one case literally. In Salem County, New Jersey, fifty-one-year-old Salvatore Gregoria, a dairy farmer, went into cardiac arrest when he heard Caldwell report that two kids were murdered at Lakeview High. The Lakeview High where the suicide occurred is sixty-three miles away, in Pennsylvania.

Mr. Gregoria died on arrival at Cumberland County Medical Center. When *we* find this out, his son, Armand, a senior at the New Jersey Lakeview High, is finishing up the day in English class. Armand is having a normal day until he discovers that his dad died.

Caldwell apologizes for the bad information and blames it on a member of his staff. The *Philadelphia Daily Philly* headlines the gaffe: "CALDWELL SAYS SORRY FOR BAD REPORT."

How many suffered because of this TV cartoon cowboy, the great pretender? Thousands of students and teachers, families of students and teachers, families of school employees, and many others in the two Lakeview communities that were *not* involved. Of course the one man who didn't make it suffered most of all. The death certificate of Armand Gregoria should read, *"Cause of death: Uninformed, ambitious, lunatic anchorman who puts winning the news competition before public safety."*

In our newsroom, it is a lesson learned. But General Manager Cynthia Cavanaugh is still under pressure to hike up the ratings. She is still pissed that we didn't break in, even with bad information. Cynthia will never understand the purpose of being correct rather than being first.

Neither does Bernie, who owns the station. Bernie makes Cynthia crazy. Then she makes Barb crazy, and Barb drives us crazy. Every day we dodge the potential consequences of sloppy work.

When I return to my desk, I find a pink phone-message slip. I dial the number.

"Hi, how's the king of news?" the man asks me.

"Feeling like I just escaped the executioner."

"I watched with interest," says Angel Esperanza. "You guys did the right thing. That asshole Caldwell . . . well, he doesn't give a shit, does he?"

"What's on your mind, Angel?"

"I was curious, Mike."

"Yes?"

"I'm delivering a speech to the Chamber of Commerce on Monday. It's a bit critical of local news and the state of it. I'm going to do some media bashing, and I might take a shot at Caldwell. Tell me, how many sources does it require for you to report a hot, breaking story?"

Esperanza is our number one tipster.

"Angel, when it's you, there are no other sources needed. You are a sub-rosa primary source. But when it comes to people we don't know, we look for at least two bona fide primary sources."

"Thanks, Mike. That is very helpful. Say hello to Rebecca."

"Take care," I say, ending the conversation. I hang up the phone.

Why did Angel ask that question? Maybe he's building his case, attempting to try Caldwell or some other news goon on charges of moral turpitude. Then again, maybe I'm making too much of his question. But why would one of the most powerful men in Philadelphia want to know when we feel we've got enough "reliable sources"? Something is up. No question. I feel uneasy.

CHAPTER FOUR: "SOMETIN' STINKS IN DE NAYBOHOOD"

I'm still in the bed. The room is dimly lit, and the pain is gone for now. I hear sobbing. It is not coming from M-16 man. He just sits there, talking on his cell phone. He looks grim. So do the cops. I guess I'm in an ICU room. I see Rebecca sitting not far from me, and she's sobbing. "I'm staying with you," she tells me. "Can't get home anyway. The roads are still a mess." Still a mess from what? The cop looks at me. Is he angry at me? The guy with the M-16 talks into the cell phone and then looks at his watch.

TIOGA MARINE TERMINAL

Bobby Alvinato adores the waterfront. The gentle breeze sends a chill to his cheeks. Alvinato is fifty-five years old. His hair is wavy, with an old-fashioned pompadour in the front. He is proud not to have a speck of gray. He is wearing a brown leather coat. He feels his biceps pressing from the inside out. There is no midlife crisis for the leader of the South Philly mob. That's because Alvinato has the steel-trap mind of an accountant and the hard body of a natural-born killer. On this November night, a few days after the grisly double murder on Cambria, he shows up at the dock where the freighter *Caracas* is berthed.

A week ago, Alvinato brought the two illegals into America on this very dock. Now he has a job: to tell the captain that the men are not coming back.

Alvinato is possessed by the thrill of power, and he knows that information is power. But this time, as he walks along the Delaware River with Teddy Vitaliano, his aide de camp, he is dumbfounded about what happened to the two men. Alvinato does not relish being kept in the dark. The Venezuelans were killed on the streets of his city, yet the man who deftly controls the invisible economy of Philadelphia knows little. His mind races, but his words are measured.

"Something stinks," he tells Vitaliano. "The stink is so heavy. I want to know what happened."

The two walk the promenade on Penn's Landing, the site of William Penn's landing in the fall of 1862. Penn, a Quaker, was seeking freedom of religion. Penn designed early Philadelphia and was the founder of Pennsylvania. He moved quickly to consolidate his power, but it took the city 320 years to finish the waterfront development named for him. Today, the part of the waterfront that runs from Penn's Landing south to the Walt Whitman Bridge is run by a city agency, but its real owner is Bobby Alvinato.

Vitaliano is part of the new generation of rulers, a businessman to the core. He manages the business end for Alvinato. He is known as "the insider." Nothing escapes his curiosity. But his friends near the top are silent on the double murders.

"Bobby, I've tried everyone. Peacemaker won't talk. Louie the Lip can't find a damn thing. Even Hopkins over at Channel Five doesn't know a thing. The MO is crazy. Fingers, toes, teeth. Where the fuck is this going?"

"Funny you should mention Hopkins." Alvinato holds the railing to the gangway that will take him on board the freighter and stares into Vitaliano's eyes. "Let me tell you, that Hopkins asshole is in deep trouble. That bastard owes so much money for the white stuff. He knows we don't do drugs, so he does business with slime. Bastardo, the creep who owns the new beer joint on Girard Avenue, is after Hopkins's ass. He's down about ten grand to Bastardo, and Bastardo will fucking filet him with a carving knife if he doesn't pay up. You tell Hopkins I need to know what the news people know," Alvinato says. "And maybe I'll cover his bill."

"You'll pay his bill?"

"In a second. I want the goods."

Vitaliano's eyes light up. "Want me to work over Hopkins? I'll beat him to a pulp and come back with the skinny."

"No," Alvinato replies. "Louie the Lip really says nothing?"

"No. And Louie is plugged into every police district in the city." Vitaliano sits on a bench on the dock across from the gangway and ponders his boss.

Alvinato's world is bottom-lined by loan-sharking, food distribution, and trash collection. He stays clear of drugs. He hates the drug trade and is known as the drug-free boss, much to the dismay of the Irish mob in Boston, the Russian mob in Brooklyn, and his fellow mafia men in New Jersey. But even if he wanted to deal in drugs, the "boss" would never allow it.

"Bobby," Vitaliano asks, "what do you know about these dudes?"

Alvinato reaches into the side pocket of the jacket. He pulls out a cigar, which was lodged next to a pistol. He cuts the tip of the cigar with the small switchblade that is housed in a mini holster attached to the right inner pocket of the jacket. Pausing a moment, he places the cigar in the right side of his mouth and lights up with a stick match. He got the match from the emergency kit housed in a small canvas gun holster with a Velcro finish strapped to his left ankle. In a city where seven mob leaders have been murdered in three years, a man can't be too prepared.

Alvinato enjoys the smell and the smoke of the cigar and looks across the river at the Camden Aquarium, pondering the murder victims. "Teddy, I know our old friend brought them here for a job that was gonna hit in a couple of months. They were from Venezuela. That commie punk Chavez let them out of prison on a contract deal. When I met them, I gave them five thousand dollars each. I told them to get some rooms, get lost, and wait for instructions and training. Now they are news. I hope to hell that no sharp young detective dick finds out that we brought them in. I am *pissed*."

He walks up the gangway alongside Teddy. He turns around to look at the glistening skyline of the city. Somewhere out there, he knows, sits a gruesome killer. That he can deal with. But he also clearly understands that, beneath the bright lights, a gifted liar, his boss, is playing with his head.

Alvinato's biggest fear is the boss. What does the man know, and why is he keeping it secret? That's the worst rub, knowing that the boss, his excellency, the number one friend, leader, and affectionate prick that he is, is playing a game of silence.

THE GRILL, NORTH FOURTH STREET, PHILADELPHIA

"So, was there a lot of blood?" the boss asks.

"Do you want to talk about this over dinner?"

"Why not?" The two men sit across from each other in a comfortable booth on the second floor of the Grill, a room filled with white wood tables and gaslight lamps. It is a charming enough place to bring the kids, and innocent-looking enough to sit down in and have a bite while recapping a double murder.

"So tell me, where did you put the pieces at the end of the day?" the boss whispers.

The other man answers, his eyes blinking rapidly. "I put them in a pouch. I took the pouch to my fireplace. When the fire was going, I burned the forty fingers and toes. I took the charred stuff, along with the teeth, and put them away in the garage. Next morning, I grabbed the stuff and gave it to my brother, who ground it to a pulp with a pile driver. Ashes were left. I took the ashes and put them in the mulch around my cherry tree. A proper burial for two assholes. That's it."

The boss can't let it go. "Tell me. Do you know why you killed them?"

"No," his friend says. "But I would like to find out."

"Let's just say that these two desperados decided to entertain themselves by freelancing. Can you imagine? They cut and run at a mom-and-pop store. The idiots ripped off a vending machine. I will now have to plan our next move without them. My friend, we'll need the TV news people to make it happen. Isn't it amazing? These college-educated elitists are just puppets waiting to be led. How and where we lead them will determine whether our dreams come true.

"Your dream," the boss continues, "will join with mine. Just wait and see. Load the gun, but hold the trigger."

CHANNEL NINE NEWSROOM

The librarian has worked at WPHI, Channel Nine, for over three decades. A pillar of strength, a genius of the search, Charley Bergman is the glue of the city's most trusted operation. As Charley says in his Boston accent, "We are yunga. We are tuffa. We have ethics, journalism, and no ratings." And then he laughs, with the proud laugh of a veteran who stands for something.

Charley is a real Philadelphia character, even though he never lost his native Boston accent. He's diminutive, only about five feet tall, but as the Philadelphia *Daily Philly* recently called him in its "Legends of Philly" column, he's a "certifiable giant." Charley's voice, a high-pitched monotone, is known in every police department in the area.

He walks through the Channel Nine newsroom like a little king with a big sense of humor. Dressed in his mainstay, a black and green Eagles hat, denim jeans, and a Sixer's hoodie, Charley is not shy. On the day of the Cambria murders he yells out in a carnival barker's voice, "Yo, people of Channel Nine. Sometin' stinks in de naybohood. And it ain't stinky wahta. This ain't Kosha. I rung up the medical examinawh, and he says, 'Charley, keep an eye out. There's bag of finga pahts, and who has it? Now Chahley, that's the question." Reminds me of de twin snuffs at Seventeenth and Diamond. That, if I recawhl, was in 1979, May 13, at 8 P.M. eastawn delight time."

Charley is a walking encyclopedia. He remembers the dates and times of murders, elections, fires and all kinds of happenings. His mind is a breathing almanac of the thirty-two years he's been at Channel Nine.

Channel Nine is number three, but that will soon change. The anchor, Diana Hong, is dazzling. She is also the brightest mind on the scene since young Colleen Brown became the first female star in 1973. Yes, Diana is a comer, or as Charlie would say, "a cumma."

In the dog days of Channel Nine, which means most of the last thirty years, anchors have played musical chairs. But now the new woman on the block is staying put. She is the buzz.

The esteemed news director of competitor Channel Five, Barb, loves to hear herself talk about what makes or breaks you in the big city. Barb says, among other things, "People don't make passes at anchors who wear glasses."

Diana Hong wears glasses. Some days.

"In this town," says Barb, "being pretty can be deadly. Getting smudge on your face . . . now that is a winner."

Diana Hong is not afraid of getting dirty to get news. She is of the people and always appears to be with them. And Diana is deeply affected by the librarian's pursuit of news. Charley Bergman is always searching for information, uncovering the covered.

It is 3 P.M. The afternoon meeting at Channel Nine is being led by Charley. Charley seems to explode with excitement. His face is flushed red, his hands are in the air. He is ready.

"I have searched the files for a similah double snuffing, and I gaht it, I mean right awhn. You guys won't believe it. On July 7, 1894, that's when. It's in da *Public Ledger* newspaper. Two men found dead in Nawth Philly. Same thing. Teeth, toes, fingers, gawhn. The papeh called the poip 'the heinous killah.' No clues, nothin'."

"Was the case ever closed?" Diana asks.

"Yes. Yes. They linked the killings to Theodore Penridge. Theodore owned a fahm in Vineland, New Joisey. Turns out he brought them here from Ahgentina. But in his signed confession, Penridge said they wah highway robbas. He found out. He was afraid of getting the rap for havin' aliens, so he takes them out. The cops had one clue. Fertilizer stink on the bahdies. They traced it to a store, then to the fahm.

"So," he continues. "These two men appeah to be Latin. Was theah somebody so 'fraid about why they heah that they decided to blow them off and take the bahdy pawhts?"

Diana, feverishly taking notes, stands up at her seat. "I'm calling Homeland Security. I want to know what these guys were doing. My sources tell me that the cops found a blood-soaked map with an arrow pointing to Valley Forge."

Bergman looks at her. "What did you say?"

"A blood-soaked map."

"Are you shawh?"

"Charlie, the tipster is never wrong. Never."

CHAPTER FIVE: **TIPSTER, INC.**

*E*ven with the meds, the pain is unbearable. How many people are dead, besides those I saw at the bypass? Rebecca won't say anything. The world is timeless to me now. Can't keep track of the visitors. But I think I recognize the man in the dark suit who's coming in the door. He walks in after the man with the lapel pin. Can it be him? Yes. In my hospital room stands the U.S. Secretary of Homeland Security.

WHITPAIN TOWNSHIP, PA.

"I think it takes a lot of chootspah. Do ya know what that means? Sorta like nerve."

Charles "Buddy" Lewis looked at his friend Peter. They are sitting in the close quarters of Pennsylvania's Montgomery County radio room in Whitpain. The room is one of two housed in a small concrete structure that resembles an above-ground bunker. The second room is a bathroom, where Peter, a combination cleaning man and part-time dispatcher, has just tidied up. The smell of citrus cleaner fills the building.

Peter, incredulous but hesitant to make Buddy look incapable, decides on a helpful, almost affectionate answer.

"Chootspah? No. It's with an 'H.' Hoots-pah."

"No, it's chootspah," Buddy roars back.

Peter, a kind and usually quiet man, loses his patience. "Are you fuckin' crazy?"

"Crazy like a fox, yesiree, Petee." Buddy was trying not to look at the little slip of paper Peter had just handed him. Finally, Buddy read the message: "Buddy, you bastard, call me right away or your redneck ass is grass. Danny Caldwell."

He crumpled up the paper. As he lobbed it into the trash can already containing a half-eaten Big Mac with cheese and bacon, Buddy looked over at Peter.

"Yesiree, Peter. That Caldwell is some bastard. Let me tell you, I've been feedin' him stories for years, and the fucker thinks he owns me. Which, I've gotta tell you, he does. He owns me, but in the end, I'll have his sorry ass. Yesiree."

Pete watches as Buddy dials his cell phone. The voice on the other end resonates with the deep tones of Philadelphia's most famous anchorman.

"Danny here."

"Mr. Caldwell, this is Buddy."

"Buddy."

"How are you, Mr. Caldwell?"

"Pissed."

"Why? What's wrong?" Buddy squeals. Buddy's voice goes to a higher pitch when he's nervous.

"What's wrong? I'll tell you what's wrong. You're wrong, Buddy. How many cases of liquor have I sent you? How many Christmas parties at Channel Seven have I invited you to? How many times have I made your white-trash ass golden? What do you think I paid for that 42-inch LCD TV that you and your babe use to watch those fuck movies at night?"

"What did I do?"

"What did poor Buddy do? I'll tell you. Channel Five beat the shit out of us on the Lower Merion house invasion. They cleaned our clocks. And *you* know why. Because, you illiterate son of a bitch, you didn't call us."

"Mr. Caldwell, I forgot. Yesiree sir, I forgot. Makes me sick, you know." Buddy winks at Peter. "Can't sleep at night over it."

"Makes *you* sick? Makes me re-think how I take care of you, Buddy."

"It won't happen again."

"Yeah, go blow, you moron. And call me when you get something."

The line goes silent. Buddy puts the cell phone in his shirt pocket and looks over at Peter. "Danny Caldwell thinks he walks on water," he says. "He's the baby Jesus of newscasters. Yesiree, Pete. I'm in his hip pocket, but you know, Judy says I've got Caldwell in my pocket. Judy, God bless her, says that I got the power. You watch, Pete. Someday I'm gonna give Mr. Caldwell a thumpin', a real thumpin'."

"You are one of the world's greatest double dippers," Peter says, "and for that, I can say you *are* the man." And, he thinks, I know you will screw Caldwell over one day.

Buddy is forty-one. On the surface, he appears to be a dud, but surface impressions can knock you for a loop. Since high school, Buddy has had a series of jobs. He clerked at Wal-Mart, ran a Jiffy Lube center for a year, and excelled at valet parking in Center City Philadelphia. Buddy hit the jackpot in 2006 when his friend Garcia Perez, his former teenage gang pal, helped him land the day dispatcher's job at Montgomery County Police radio. The job description was simple: Interconnect some of the twenty-seven police departments that do not have their own dispatchers. The second priority: Take phone calls from the media and pass them on to the right people. After two years, Buddy Lewis has become a bosom buddy of the most famous people in Philadelphia.

"Got a call yesterday from Keith Byrne," he boasts that night to his girlfriend, Judy.

"What a hunk. Just thinking about that guy makes me hot," she whispers.

"The one I like to talk to is Diana Hong. Man, that is a babe. Yes siree, mama," the boastful dispatcher says to Judy, his eyes wandering over her body like a lecher.

Buddy is legendary in the local media. Call him and he moves quickly. "Right, Mr. Caldwell. I'll get Lower Merion police to buzz you right away. Yes siree, sir."

"Miss Hong. Good to hear from you. Sure, I'll have Chief Melman call you right away."

Buddy has a chronic sexual appetite, and money is his second love. After he took the dispatcher job, he learned that information can be a lucrative commodity. Buddy quickly figured out that a tipster can double and even triple dip, satisfying everyone and greasing his palm by becoming a master dispenser of breaking news.

"I call the shots," he tells Judy. "When Buddy calls, those gorgeous, stuck-up anchor chicks and the anchor dicks, man, they get hot for facts. Yesiree. Who, what, when, and where. That's what I give 'em, and boy, do they give back. I mean, lunch with Diana Hong. That just makes me shiver."

"Shiver?" Judy looks disturbed, disappointed.

"Not like you make me shiver, babe," he adds quickly. "I like 'em American, like you. But Miss Hong, she just smells good."

"I don't?"

"Of course, honey. Yesiree. You are the chick I love."

"I should hope so," Judy retorts. "You keep flirting with them TV women and there will be no prize for you at the bottom of the Cracker Jack box, and I mean that!"

The dispatcher is entranced by TV's glamour. His big day at Channel Seven is always the day before Christmas. There he sits in the Ritz Carlton Hotel in Philadelphia, surrounded by Danny

Caldwell and the Channel Seven staff. Showered with booze and gifts, the dispatcher and Judy sit on a loveseat and take it in.

Caldwell says, "Buddy, you are the best. No Buddy, no suburban coverage. We love you, man. Remember, call us first."

The dispatcher is forbidden to call stations with news. He does anyway. He is especially kind to Channel Seven and Caldwell. Caldwell takes good care of him.

In the news business, finding tipsters is part of the game. Buddy plays the game well. Pitting one station against the other, he works the phone day and night with one powerful weapon: Buddy has access to all the police radios in the five-county area.

Keith Byrne and Diana Hong are gracious. Caldwell is, in Buddy's words, "a shit, a pure shit." But Buddy takes care of Channel Seven well because, at the end of the month, he always receives a plain brown envelope from Caldwell filled with cash. Buddy loves the smell of cash, even more than he revels in the perfumed skin of Judy.

Yesiree.

CHAPTER SIX: **GRENADES IN THE GARBAGE CANS**

*T*hey've transferred me to a burn center, which means my body must look barbecued. That's great. Burns on top of fractures on top of some brain damage, no doubt. The tall guy, the suit, towers over me, holding a yellow legal pad. The Homeland Security secretary has left after twenty-four hours of on-and-off questioning. What a waste of time. I know nothing, but obviously they think I know something. Are these guys crazy? Maybe I was too close to the action. Maybe they trust no one.

NOVEMBER 2007
CHANNEL NINE

What you see and hear on TV is not always real. This is especially true of the personality delivering the news. Faces are altered by cosmetics and lights. Voices are sometimes deepened, made unreal. Only in rare instances is the person you watch the genuine article. Such people are not products of celluloid spin. You, the viewer, know intuitively when the reporter or anchor looking into your eyes is sincere. That bond is intangible; no one can define what makes it happen. But when it happens, it is special, almost magical. And the words *special* and *magical* definitely apply to Diana Hong.

This woman takes the words of each day's news and says them as though she is sitting next to you on a couch, at a bar, on a train, or even in bed. Through the glass and steel and cable that bring her to you, you see and feel the intimacy.

Diana's path to this moment is cluttered with the debris of growing up in the American underclass. So when the bodies are found at Second and Cambria, Diana pauses. She always does when someone is murdered. Her mind flashes back to a time when the rules were clear: Fight and survive, or surrender and perish.

The evening anchor of Channel Nine is a dreamer. Always has been. Her experience of growing up was so horrible that to make it through she had to dream.

Diana is thirty-eight. Physically, she is thirty-eight going on twenty-one. No kidding. She looks striking on TV. Diana is about five foot seven. Her movements are supple, assured. She knows not how beautiful she is, which makes her all the more appealing. Her skin has the sheen of silk. Her eyes, small and deep brown, compel you to look even further into the soul. Her hair is a deep black and hangs over her shoulders. She dresses demurely, needing no fashion statement to accent her looks. Her voice is soothing but alert. She looks serious, and she is. But when the moment brings a smile, Diana's face morphs into a treasure of joy.

Emotionally, she is thirty-eight going on fifty-five. That's what happens when you see people and events differently than the ordinary person does. Combine her looks and the way she sees life and you have both real panache and a penetrating sincerity.

Diana was offered jobs at two networks. She turned them down. Her goal and passion is Philadelphia. And her new job makes Diana Hong the only solo female anchor in local television in the country. She is also the only Philadelphia-born anchor. Hometown kid, hometown knowledge.

The murders at Second and Cambria fascinate her, along with her talks with the librarian. What he says, along with the silence on the part of the police, bring her to the point of obsession. She thinks about the bodies. She thinks about the map.

"There is something more, Phil, believe me," she tells the station's news director, Phil Hurley.

Hurley is encouraging. Unlike most news bosses, he has total respect for his anchor. Most news directors enjoy pitting people against each other, weakening their souls, strengthening their own positions. Phil Hurley is a different sort of guy.

"Run a check on any similar murders over the last several years, here or anywhere," he says. "In fact, go back as far as you can. You never know."

"I do know," she says. And she tells him what the librarian told her.

"Amazing," he says. "That could come in handy, but let's not spread it yet. Call Marvin over at the FBI to see if there's anything new. Caldwell is on this over at Seven. Byrne is digging over at Five. So give it your best, and give me briefings on where you're headed. And Diana, get the staff moving on this. Don't be afraid to throw some grenades into the garbage cans." This is an expression that Phil uses often. The idea is to cause a little bit of chaos to wake the staff up. "Go splat," he tells her. "But in the end," he adds, "get it right. I would rather we got beaten by Byrne fair and square than be first and wrong, if you know what I mean."

Just the mention of Keith Byrne brings an adrenaline rush. She's never even met him. But watching him on TV brings her breathing to a stop. She's never been a groupie. A man's looks don't bring her to the edge of insanity. But she sees something in him. It happens every time she glances at the screen. There's something real about him, a vulnerability. And she likes the sound of his voice. Funny, she thinks, how two different feelings can bring on the same rush—passion and fear. Maybe, she thinks, they are interlocked.

Fear. She knows that feeling well, though she used to have it for different reasons. Diana grew up at Eighth and Diamond, on the fringe of the badlands of Philadelphia. Her parents, tortured by the Khmer Rouge in Cambodia, sought a fragile peace in the land of the free. They had one child and provided for her week to week through their small cleaning and maintenance business. Their daughter's childhood was sparse and frightening. She walked to school through an obstacle course of ethnic insults, flying fists, and the occasional sound of a Saturday-night special. She was a child afraid. But inside, her dreams persisted. She believed she would achieve. Fight and survive, surrender and perish. Diana had little. But she had loving parents and memories.

At the age of twelve, after entering the fenced-in schoolyard at Benjamin Rush Middle School, she saw a crowd encircling an object. She walked up. A pool of blood was flowing into the cracks of the concrete basketball court. A few feet away lay the lifeless form of one of her classmates, Shana Harrison. Shana would have lived if her bus hadn't been late that morning. The bus left her off at school in time for her to walk into a gun battle between rival gangs. The impression of this event—her classmate being the victim of someone else's rage, her body and life shattered—still lives in Diana.

At first, the academic phenomenon thought of law and justice. Then she found pleasure in writing. That and a curiosity for all things human brought her into the world of broadcast journalism. She loves the work and the hunt.

The lords of the press have followed her, examining her every move. Predators, they are, seeking dirt when there is none to be found.

"Marvin, this is Diana," she says into the mouthpiece of her desk telephone.

"What's up, kid?" Marvin Marzano is the longtime agent in charge of the Philadelphia-area FBI office. He rarely talks to the media. He talks to Diana because he knows she will not compromise him. The dreamer is also an honest information-seeker in a business of liars.

"Second and Cambria," she says. "Who are those men, and why is Angel Esperanza asking questions? Why the hell does he care?" Diana knows that Angel Esperanza is pressing his friends at Channels Five and Seven for information on the double murder and mutilation. Funny, she thinks. The tipster wants tips. Esperanza doesn't talk to Diana, but he talks to Librarian Charley Bergman. Everybody does.

The FBI man is curious. "Well, that's interesting. Why in the hell does Esperanza want the buzz on two killings? Is he on his damned high horse again?"

"I don't know, Marv. But I would like to know more about these killings. Frankly, the thing that bugs me—"

He interrupts. "The thing that bugs you is, there is no motive."

"Right," says Diana. "I mean Marv, this is not a vicious serial killing. We're not talking about human flesh eaters here, or people who get off on slicing and dicing. There's some reason that somebody cuts off fingers and toes. Yeah, I know it's all about hiding IDs, but why would you want to hide identities that badly? You could just weight them down in the river, or kill them and drive them out of town. I am crazed about this one." She cradles the phone between her neck and her right shoulder. "Marv, I need more. If you get anything, any morsel or tidbit, will you call me?"

"Of course I will. In a nanosecond, kid."

"Thanks," she says.

The FBI rarely lets out information. But Diana is trusted. Trust—conveying it, not betraying it—is everything in the pursuit of information. In 1997, during her first anchor job in Lancaster, a shooting was reported at an Amish-owned furniture factory in Intercourse, Pennsylvania. A phone tipster said that there were twenty dead. Diana refused to go on the air without police confirmation. Her instincts were dead on. In the end, the event was a domestic encounter in which one person died. The first report was wrong.

Diana's intuition about friends, too, especially men, is rarely wrong. The loves in her life have been brief, overwhelmed by her career pursuits. She wonders if that will change.

THE ROUNDHOUSE–POLICE HEADQUARTERS

Good, solid anchors hit the street, plain and simple. Others just show up at the station to go on air. As Barb Pierce says, "They're just phoning it in."

Diana arrives at police headquarters at Eighth and Race Streets at 7 P.M., a half hour after delivering the six o'clock news. The police commissioner's briefing on the Cambria murders is about to take place on the second floor of the building, known as the roundhouse. Round and contemporary, it looks more like a planetarium than a police headquarters. Diana is seated in the first row, a few feet from the wooden podium with the blue and gold seal of Philadelphia.

"You know, it's rare for the commissioner to comment on murder cases. That's why I'm here," she says to Channel Nine camerawoman Lauren Greenberg.

Greenberg nods. A ten-year veteran of the street, she sets up the microphone, places the Channel Nine microphone flag on the podium, and whispers to Diana, "The whole gang is here. Every damn station. Even star-man from Channel Five."

"Who?"

"Star-man. The hair apparent. Keith Byrne."

"You mean the *heir* apparent," Diana says.

"No, I mean the hair apparent. Have you ever seen a head of hair like that on a face like that on a frame like that? I mean, if I were ten years younger and I didn't have hips like a rhino, I would do that guy in a second."

Diana glances over sheepishly. Byrne is writing something on a notepad with a yellow pencil. He is looking down, very serious. There is no eye contact between them.

Police Commissioner Douglas Underwood walks to the podium. He begins, "Because of the bizarre nature of the crime, I thought it appropriate to explain the ongoing investigation." He reads from a prepared text. The cameras are rolling. "The murders at Second and Cambria are unusual, to say the least. The mutilation of the bodies is a clear indication that the perp or perps are trying to hide the identities of the victims. We believe the men are from somewhere in Central America. We are attempting to employ DNA studies, but it is difficult to make DNA matches with other countries. Citizens have been concerned that there might be a deranged killer among us. I want to assure the people of Philadelphia that we are working on every angle. A serial killer *is* a possibility, primarily because we see no motive. We are not ruling anything out. We ask for the public's help. If anyone knows who these victims are, please call our anonymous tip line. Any questions?"

"Commissioner," Diana calls out. While she is mid-word, Keith says strongly, "Commissioner!"

"Hold on a second," Diana says to Keith. "Don't be rude. We're not on deadline."

Keith looks over. He recognizes the face from TV, but she looks different, thinner.

Diana glowers at him. "Can I talk now?"

"Go ahead," he replies.

"Commissioner, we've heard that there was a map found on one of the victims, a map with an arrow pointing to Valley Forge. Can you confirm that?"

"No," he lies. "Other questions?"

Byrne says, "Commissioner, we have an eyewitness account that you have a blood-stained map with an arrow pointing to Valley Forge."

"Your eyewitness is a phantom, Mr. Byrne."

"Our cameraman saw it."

"Your cameraman must be smoking something. Where is he? I'll have him arrested for using mind-altering drugs!"

Diana retorted, "Commissioner, is there a reason you are covering this up?"

"I resent that, Miss Hong."

"But–"

"I also resent that you are trying to undermine the credibility of this office. Is that clear? This meeting is over."

The commissioner leaves the room. His news liaison, Captain Milton Ahmad, walks over to Diana.

"What the fuck are you trying to do? I'll get your card for this."

"Oh, go bag it, Milt," she replies. "You'll take my press card because I asked a question? What do you think this is, Germany in 1932? Get lost."

Keith walks over. He chimes in, "Milt, there's something missing here, and I'm not just talking fingers and toes and teeth. What the hell is going on?" Milton Ahmad walks out of the room.

"That was informative," Keith says.

"That was unfortunate," Diana responds.

"I'm Keith Byrne."

"Diana Hong."

They shake hands. Keith is awkward. He always is in nonprofessional situations.

"What do you think is going on here?" Diana asks.

"I don't mean to be petty, but if I knew, I wouldn't tell you," Keith says. He looks at her with determination, as if to say, "I'm in charge here, get it?" Then he adds rather meekly, "The truth is I really can't tell you anything, because if I did, back at my place, my ass would be grass."

"That was so well said, and that's just so nice of you to be so cooperative, Keith," she says with a sarcasm that's tempered by the sparkle in her eyes.

He feels like he looks, embarrassed. And he reaches for something to say. "We are competitors."

"True," she says. "But you have twice as many viewers as I do."

"Diana, with your talent, that won't last for long."

"Flattery will get you everywhere." She smiles. When she smiles that radiant, natural smile of hers, all rational reactions vanish. Keith smiles back. They shake hands again. He turns his back and walks away.

CHANNEL NINE NEWSROOM

Returning to her newsroom, Diana is intrigued. She senses a vulnerability behind the rugged face and the brashness. But she is still on the case. She gets back to the newsroom at 8:10 P.M. and visits with her favorite writer, Dana Birch.

"Dana, can you do me a favor? Look up any and all shopping centers, public buildings, libraries, and other significant locations within a twenty-mile radius of Valley Forge. Make me a list. Take your time."

Dana has deep respect for Diana. "I'll have it for you tomorrow."

"Thanks." Diana walks over to her desk. She goes to the search window on Yahoo. She types in the words "Keith Byrne + Television."

Sixteen blocks away, Byrne, unsettled, arrives back at Channel Five with the video of the news conference. He goes to the bathroom. When he returns, he gathers his yellow pencils and walks over to the electronic pencil sharpener.

CHAPTER SEVEN: **PEACEMAKER**

So much damn time to think. I think about my family, happy that everybody is whole. I think about all the newsmakers who are wondering whether I'm alive or dead. I also think about Peacemaker. Has he called? What does he know? And, with so much sadness, I think about the people who died. Who were they? Why was I spared? I would like to know. I wish I knew what the investigators think I do.

CITY HALL ANNEX

"You honor me with your support," says District Attorney Diane Isaacs to the giant of a man sitting across from her.

"This is what I love to do, as you know, Ms. District Attorney," the visitor replies. "The children of this city need safe neighborhoods. No request from your office or the police is too large. My job as a corporate leader is to supplement the good graces of government."

"As a member of the public sector, I appreciate that, Mr. Esperanza."

Angel reaches into side pocket of his gray, pinstriped suit and hands a folded slip of paper to the district attorney. The check is for $497,000.28 and is made out to "District Attorney's Anti-Crime Alliance."

"I hope this donation from the Corporate Leaders against Crime Crusade will do the trick," he says. "I know what it's like to be run down by thugs and punks. It's a crummy, godforsaken life."

"I promise you the funds will be well spent on programs for young people," Isaacs says. She looks at him. Handsome, well dressed. A pillar. A fellow lawyer. "How's your business?" she asks.

"Good. The firm is prospering. How is your work going?"

"Well, we've solved more crimes in this fiscal year than in any year since we began keeping records," she replies. "But we've got some problems. For one, the killings on Cambria. We've been working on the case for weeks, and still we're at a dead end. No names. No suspects. Not a damn clue for a brutal crime. Mr. Esperanza, this is not a drive-by or a drug kill. You've heard the grimy details?"

"I know," he says. "My sincere hope is that this money from the business community will help keep our city's fine young people engaged in fruitful and character-growing pursuits. Perhaps some day there will be fewer cases to prosecute."

She nods. "Are you ready for the picture?"

"Yes."

The door swings open at the press of a button on the right side of the D.A.'s big mahogany desk. A press photographer and two cameramen walk in. Two reporters follow: Artie O'Donnell, the journeyman from Channel Seven, and Harvey Hopkins of Channel Five.

The camera clicks. The video cameras roll. Esperanza stages the check presentation. Harvey Hopkins yells out, "So where is the money going?"

Isaacs says, "For young people. Safety programs. Crime prevention and education programs."

Hopkins adds, "Yikes. A bit too late for those mutilated men at Second and Cambria."

Isaacs winces. Esperanza recoils and tries to keep his cool.

"Mr. Hopkins," says Isaacs, "we are celebrating the business commitment to fighting crime. There will be another time to talk about that tragic murder."

"When?" Harvey asks. "After all, shit happens, and you're supposed to clean it up, Ms. D.A." It is 11 A.M., and Harvey is already drunk.

The photo session ends abruptly. Harvey waves at the D.A. and winks at Esperanza. The businessman ignores him at first, then winks back.

* * *

When the crowd leaves, Isaacs returns to her desk and dials the direct line to Barbara Pierce.

"Hello," Barb says.

"Barb, this is Diane Isaacs. I have some questions."

"Sure."

"When will you fire that drug-head asshole Hopkins? And question two: Until you kill him or he implodes, can you keep him out of my office?"

"Sure, Diane."

"Final question. Is Hopkins doing Angel Esperanza? The two of them winked at each other inside my office, in public. Do they know each other?"

"Beats me." But Barb knows full well that Esperanza is an extremely reliable news source to some of the most high-profile reporters in town.

LEFLER AND LEFLER LLC, 210 SOUTH BROAD STREET

Esperanza arrives back in his wood-paneled office at the law firm after his photo op with the D.A. Sitting in the big chair, he thumbs through his message slips. There are seventeen, four of them from Bobby Alvinato and marked "urgent." He dials the phone number.

"Hi, Bobby, this is the boss."

"Boss, Angel, I am pissed. I want to know who those two guys were from that freighter and why we chopped them up."

"Bobby, you know I'm secretive."

"Do I know! Sometimes, boss, you go batshit with secrets."

"Okay, Bobby. I brought them here to do a job, a diversion, so we could fulfill our passion to kill off the druggies, you know who I'm talking about."

"Sure," Bobby answers. "Like Bastardo and the others."

"Yes, but the two idiots strayed off the plan and I had to have them killed and mutilated. No chances. No traces. That's it, Bobby. But I have good news. I figured out how to do the whole trick without them or any other punks."

"What's the plan?" Bobby asks.

"Be patient, my friend. In due time, I will tell you."

"Gimme a break."

"Bobby, this is a work in progress. When I figure out what the hell is going to happen, you'll find out before anyone."

"Anyone?"

"I give you my word, as I did so many years ago when we began the games."

CHANNEL FIVE NEWSROOM

A news source takes years to develop. If a reporter burns a source with disclosure, he or she is screwed. And if the source gives the reporter bad information, game over.

Peacemaker, aka Angel Esperanza, is my number one source, so much so that I've turned him over to Keith Byrne to make sure the info will keep flowing when I decide to get out of the business.

Peacemaker is a moniker culled from the many editorials written about his community activism. He is, with the exception of the mayor, the leading community activist in Philadelphia. He has never failed me. Our conversations are direct, to the point, no nonsense.

Soon after Peacemaker leaves the D.A.'s office, my phone rings in the newsroom.

"Hello, Mike, this is Angel."

"Hi, what's up?"

"What's up is that embarrassment of a reporter, Hopkins. He was inappropriate, rude and silly at the D.A.'s office today. Can you tell him to stop that shit?"

"I'll try. Even the news director can't deal with him. The network is concerned about an age discrimination suit, so they put up with his crap. You know, Angel, they never go to court on those cases. They always settle. They are so chicken shit. We've got malcontents and news devils, people with not an ounce of credibility, working at stations around America, and they won't fire 'em."

"Well, try anyway," Esperanza answers.

I ask, "Anything new on the Second and Cambria murders?"

"How the hell should I know?"

Esperanza hangs up the phone. In his law office at Liberty Towers, he thinks, "Hopkins should die. He should get hit by a truck and never be seen again."

LEFLER AND LEFLER LLC

Magazine reporter Cheryl Tobias sits across from Esperanza, who wiggles in his chair in the boardroom. The windows stretching across his office give a panoramic view of downtown Philadelphia. Only the seventeenth-century desk, just a few feet of wood, lies between the reporter and her subject.

"Mr. Esperanza, what is your vision of Philadelphia?"

"When I look at the contours of this city, I think I could watch it forever. I love to look at the Schuylkill River. Look at it winding past the Art Museum. I love to watch traffic on the Ben Franklin Parkway flowing south straight to Logan Square, which as you know is really a circle. Go figure that. I'm not a sentimentalist, but I enjoy Philadelphia. And I love the people."

Tobias is impressed by the towering figure.

"But," she says, "the city has problems, crime and urban decay. Do they ever cause you to despair?"

"I know the dark sides. Imperfection is acceptable to me. But ignorance of the city's problems by government hacks is intolerable. Nothing is more dangerous than corrupt government lowlifes. And the drug trade. Oh my God. Nothing kills this town and the people like the flow of illegal junk."

"You perked up when you mentioned 'lowlifes.' Corruption really makes you crazy. But you have friends in high places who are not so clean, don't you?"

"What are you insinuating?"

"I'm insinuating, sir, that everybody has skeletons in their closets and bedrooms."

"My personal life is an open book. It's Darianna. Can't get enough of her."

"That's not what I hear."

"You know, that's what your magazine is about. Always accentuating the negative. At least Platt runs it now. I thought you guys were over the 'who do we get this month' phase. I challenge you, young lady. Scrape up the dirt. Look for the bones. You won't find a damn thing in my life. You are barking up the wrong tree. So quote me for the uninhibited giants of the Main Line who run this town, or think they do: You and they can go to hell in a hot air balloon."

What a performance, the reporter thinks, and what an impact that quote is going to have on her editor, Larry Platt, and on the

WASP leaders who so resent Esperanza's rise to fame and power. His is truly one of those only-in-America stories. And it began in the darkness and hopelessness of squalor.

Tall and wide, handsome and charismatic, Peacemaker was born out of wedlock and raised by his mother in the Nussbaum housing project. Though it has since been demolished, the Nussbaum development was a high-rise nightmare, a symbol of failed public housing. Its apartments were small, its plumbing was pitiful, and anyone who'd ever stepped foot inside would never forget the bullet casings on the steps and the pungent smell of urine in the corridors.

Peacemaker had been blessed with a mother who pushed him to academic excellence. While she offered the inspiration, she fought her own demonic battle. His mother was so dependent on drugs that she died an early and horrifying death. The day his bloated mother's corpse was delivered to the waiting medical examiner's truck, Angel, just twenty-three, was so stricken he could hardly talk. The cause of death was an overdose. The real cause, he would say later to anyone who would listen, was the insidious drug trade. Someday, he hoped to snuff it out.

His Dad? Dead from a cocaine overdose when Angel was three years old. Somehow, the doting mother and the hole in his life from his missing father pushed him to claw and fight his way through the projects. Bricks were his weapons. Books were his elixir. By his high-school graduation, he was determined to cross the boundary of his neighborhood, to overcome the limits placed on him by his origins. Harvard is considered unreachable for a poor, Latino kid from the projects, yet Peacemaker graduated with honors from the Ivy League bastion, attended Temple Law, and stunned his friends by taking an improbable career path. His mother never lived to see his success in business, but his thoughts rarely wavered from the woman, her hugs, her inspiration, her belief in his promise.

The reporter continues the interview, emboldened by his brashness. "How important is money to you?"

"Money is irrelevant to me," he replies. "I need little. But power is necessary. Power gives me the means to change people's lives, to alter the image of this community. I have seen the ravages of poverty and the injustices of city life, and I am convinced that life can be better. This is my town, and this is what I want to do."

Tobias nods. "What are the major forces in this town?" she asks.

"Well, there's the government. The business community. I don't think you can underestimate the power of community activist groups, and of course my business, the law."

"Is law a clean business?"

"Good question. Did you know that municipal bond deals for law firms are juicy? Law firms get flat fees for bond deals. No hourly fees there. That means there is a triangulation here, the trio of power. You got politics, law and government. If the right politician gets elected, he finds that government can be about big money. Where is the money? In those big shot muni bond deals. That's where the great profits are. Also, law is a big part of the economy. Twenty thousand people work in law in Philadelphia. Law is also the source of some of our great public servants."

"Like you?" she interrupts.

"I would have been committed to helping people if I was a plumber," he replies. "I just enjoy it. But law makes a difference here, until evil-ass lawyers with no talent pay to play. Some of them, I'm telling you, some of them would sell their kids for the right deal. Those are the poisonous bastards of law. They will bribe their way to success. I want the dirt out of our business, and you, young lady, should get the dirt out of yours."

"What do you mean?

"What I mean is that the media, especially the TV people, have their own problems. Some so-called reporters have been callous and unfeeling as they push their daily menu of negativity and sensationalism. They'd better clean up their act, or we'll push

Washington to clean up their act for them. The big companies in New York are allowing these stations to deteriorate."

"What do you mean?"

"Local TV news is out of control with innuendo, false reports, and a foggy version of the real world. I don't trust many of our reporters to tell us the truth. Too much tabloid, too little real news. In fact, you must be a graduate of TV news, because some of your questions are just plain bad. Where's the beef in your questioning, young lady?"

"Where's the beef? That won't work with me, Mr. Esperanza. I know your style. Slash and attack reporters to soften them up. You have no idea, sir, what my business is all about."

But he does. Esperanza is like a tiger waiting in the grass. While he publicly renounces a troubled industry, he knows that more leaks come from him than from a ruptured sewer system. He has a clear understanding of the routes to power–the regular ways and the alternate roads. They include utilizing his friends in the media. He has Danny Caldwell of Channel Seven in his hip pocket, but he detests Caldwell. He knows Caldwell cares for no genuine human cause. All plans need a backup, and that's why he is working an alternate route. His involvement with Keith Byrne is a project that will soon pay off.

Peacemaker hates the local media managers, especially the TV folks, with their jaded, biased view of the people of the city. But Byrne is different. With "Newsboy," as Peacemaker calls him, there is principle. Peacemaker is without question the most important source in Byrne's notebook, which is what he wants to be. In return, one day, Byrne might be the man who delivers the goods. Payback time will come.

"Would you like to see my picture album?" he asks her.

"Sure."

He opens up the brown leather album. Inside is a collage of pictures: Esperanza with Barack Obama, John McCain, the mayor. Esperanza smiles at the United Way dinner. He laughs at the annual Christmas Toy Appeal. As he turns the pages, reporter Tobias sees color photos of Angel in Israel at the Jaffa Gate of Jerusalem. In the middle of the book are photos taken throughout Philadelphia, and one in particular draws the reporter's attention. The civic leader and lawyer is imprisoned in the old Eastern State Penitentiary, handcuffed and smiling through the steel bars of the cell. He explains that the ploy was a part of a fundraising event. She laughs. He turns the page.

A half hour later, with the reporter gone from the office, Peacemaker opens up the album, rips out that picture, and places it into the office shredder. It's a picture that, even in jest, he doesn't want to look at or think about again. With the murders at Cambria and the unfolding events, the possibility of being behind bars for real is disconcerting, to say the least.

RITTENHOUSE PLAZA APARTMENTS

Byrne yawns and holds his head up with his right hand. He is a thirty-six-year-old with a sense of frustration, even desperation. On the shelf above him, overlooking the desk in his home office, sit two radios. One is a wide-band radio connected to the radio room at the Philadelphia Police Department. The older model on the right is a scanner that locates emergency calls in the thirteen-county suburban area. Between the radios and his notebook of 897 numbers, Byrne is plugged in to the region's breaking news. And his personal sources are in the hundreds, a testament to his dogged pursuit of information.

His mood is unsettled. The Cambria killings give him pause, and he thinks often of the chilling e-mail message sent to his private address on the night of the killings.

From: Peacemaker@widenet.com
To: Newsboy@home.com

Second and Cambria shooting more than it seems. Hands and teeth missing from victims. Toe prints not available. Believe hands blown off prior to shooting. Cavities stuffed with cocaine, marijuana, heroin. TV video doesn't show the real mess. Don't release yet. Something here. We'll find it. Stay close, Newsboy.

Byrne trashed the message. Now he remembers the adrenaline flowing that night. Hunting down a news story, clawing for the facts, making discoveries–these are the best diversions in a life of loneliness. With a source like Peacemaker, he is able to break big stories first. No one source, he thinks, has had the impact of Angel Esperanza on his reporting career. He accepts Esperanza's public blasts at the news media. What an incredible way, he thinks, to cover the fact that he is the leaker of all leakers.

He reaches over to his cup of coffee, brings it to his mouth, and sips. He wonders what to do with his night. He leans back in the chair and his eyes close. But in a few seconds, they open. His ears are filled with three loud beeps–the warning that a message is about to come through. In a second, a voice speaks on the radio.

"This is fire command. All available units, engines one to thirteen, ladders seven to nineteen, move with deliberate speed to Roosevelt Boulevard and Adams. Abandoned factory. Four alarms struck. Repeat, four alarms struck."

Keith picks up the phone and calls the newsroom. In a matter of ninety seconds, he gets out of his workout shorts, dives into his closet, puts his pants and shirt on, grabs a pad, and heads for his car in the garage.

While he's en route to the fire, his cell phone rings. He activates the speaker phone.

"Hello."

"Hello."

"Who is this?"

"Newsboy, where are you?"

"Headed to a fire."

"Fuck the fire. I've got some overnight breaking news that will rip your guts out and make you plead for more."

"I'll call you later, Angel. As soon as I get back."

THE HIDEAWAY

Peacemaker reaches for his reading glasses. The print is small in the *Intelligencer,* Philadelphia's legal newspaper.

"Jeter, Brown and Nathan is hereby awarded the responsibility of legal oversight for all contracts related to construction of the new municipal football stadium. The term is three years. The flat fee is $780,000."

The stadium deal has been held up for years by people with their hands out, reaching for a piece of a four-hundred-million-dollar pie. There were unions, contractors, architects, vendors, and of course lawyers. So this arrangement doesn't come as a surprise. But still, Peacemaker thinks, it's strange that there are no specifics, no responsibilities listed. Then again, he isn't surprised. It's par for the course—no information and no accountability.

"I'm the vigilante of the barristers," he told Darianna one night. "I'm all for enriching the firm, but I will never put cash in a brown paper bag. Never."

And privately, Esperanza has created a network of informants that has allowed him to crush the kickback gang.

"Law is a two-trick pony," Peacemaker lectured Byrne during one of their late-night phone meetings. "The candidate seeks big campaign bucks from lawyers. The damn candidate wins. The supporters are awarded lucrative contracts. Firms like Jeter, Brown become an extension of government. All legal all the time, but kosher? No frickin' way. Let's face it, Newsboy, politics is money, government is money, and law—L-A-W—stands for Liquid Assets Wanted. And then the ivory-tower barristers get involved in the worst kind of horseshit: They fund people who want to be judges. Payback time always comes, Newsboy. That's why so many rapists and killers are walking the streets of this city."

After watching the flames of the Roosevelt Boulevard fire, Angel waits in the Hideaway, his complex of offices and a bedroom in the Bellevue Hotel. He waits for the call from Byrne. At his side is Dr. Darianna Hoffman, health commissioner for Philadelphia, one of his two lovers. Darianna rests her head on Angel's chest and strokes his upper thigh with her left hand.

Slowly, he puts the reading glasses on the night stand. He picks up the portable phone and dials. Danny Caldwell answers.

"Hello, Caldwell speaking."

"Danny, this is Angel. Write this down. Tomorrow morning, the Jeter, Brown law firm will be formally under investigation for fraud and racketeering. The firm will be indicted on charges of paying off the city law office to get by the feds. This will cost them their lucrative football stadium contract. The corruption investigation is all out. Got it?"

Caldwell is thrilled. "You are never wrong, Esperanza. I'm going with it on the morning news. Thanks, man." He hangs up.

The doctor is getting tired. "Let's sleep, baby."

"Not yet, Darianna. I'm waiting for Keith."

Keith Byrne is a delicate project for Peacemaker. Watching him at a Chamber of Commerce media conference in 2006, Esperanza was impressed at Byrne's zeal to clean up the business. He is the likely successor when Marone retires. Angel knows Keith would never reveal his sources of information.

The phone rings.

"Hi, Newsboy. Still smell from the smoke?"

"It was nothing."

"I knew it was nothing before you knew it was nothing."

"What's up?"

"Tomorrow morning, Keith, Jeter, Brown, and Nathan will be indicted by a federal grand jury on charges of paying off the city law office to get that shitty contract on sewage removal. They will lose the stadium deal."

Peacemaker can hear the excitement in Byrne's voice when he says, "This is fucking incredible."

"Don't be sure," the leaker says.

"Why?" Byrne asks.

"Because I think Caldwell has it at Channel Seven. Get on it fast."

That is all Byrne needs. This is a solid gold source, and Byrne will break the story first. Or at least he thinks he will.

"There is one more thing, Newsboy."

"What's that?"

"That cocksucker of a law firm has other big-time clients, including Marone's famous backup anchor."

"Hopkins?" Byrne replies.

"Yes, things-go-better-with-coke Hopkins."

"Why would Hopkins need them?"

"Every man buys insurance. Check out your anchor buddy. Check out that firm."

Peacemaker pauses on the line. Byrne knows that a pause, dead air, always means that Peacemaker will have something important to say.

"Newsboy, in this town there is a direct connection between media, murder, law and government." He pauses again. "Just ask my friend the suffering cop."

"Who the hell is that?"

"He is a man who knows that . . ."

"Yeah?"

"He knows that in this town, Newsboy, there are those in your fucking business who can kill a person faster than you can say Danny Caldwell."

"What does that mean?"

"Be patient and watch for the killer in *your* newsroom."

Peacemaker has a triple play going. Both stations have the story; neither knows that they are being played by the city's most savvy player. The *Daily Philly* has the story, too. Overnight, the paper confirms the information with highly ranked sources in the local and federal criminal justice system and the top independent source in the city. The fury of the story is unleashed by 9 A.M. By 11 A.M., Lefler and Lefler, the high bidder on the stadium contract, will get the invitation to apply for it. The firm is the only remaining bidder.

LEFLER AND LEFLER LLC

The next morning, Peacemaker arrives at his day job. Lefler and Lefler, LLC is his employer of record, but he works for only God and self. As Peacemaker walks into the board room, his right hand holds a copy of the *Philadelphia Daily Philly*. He looks at the partners. He smiles. With both hands he grips the front page of the afternoon paper. The headline is huge, big red letters draped over a picture of the other law firm's headquarters at Seventeenth and Walnut Streets: "JETER, BROWN, AND NATHAN INDICTED IN SEWAGE REMOVAL CONTRACT SCHEME. FIRM LOSES STADIUM DEAL."

Peacemaker glances around the room. Surprise is always a grand option. The news about Jeter, Brown has been out for hours, but Peacemaker has gotten one of the first copies of the afternoon edition of the *Daily Philly* via messenger. He addresses the board members: "Ladies and Gentlemen, at two o'clock this afternoon, the city law department will award the contract and oversight work on the new stadium to Lefler and Lefler, LLC. We win. They lose. And the people shall prevail."

Board Vice Chair Bernard Fishkin stands up, embraces Peacemaker, and says, "You are blessed. You said this would happen. But Angel, how did you know?"

"I just had an instinct, a feeling," he answers confidently. Of course he is lying. He got the information from one of his friends in the underground world of crime and manipulation. Bobby Alvinato came through. The mafia kills, but it's also a strange bastion of truth. Peacemaker knows that information is power and that getting it, pure and simple, is more powerful than bullets. Although, on occasion, bullets properly aimed at the right people can perform economic miracles. Force can be fruitful. He learned that back in the day, in the beginning.

CHANNEL SEVEN NEWSROOM
5:59 P.M.–ONE MINUTE TO AIR

Floor Manager Billy Russell's job at Channel Seven is to point the anchors to the right cameras and keep them on time. Russell yells out, "One minute to air. One minute to live TV!"

Caldwell sits in the chair at the center of the long desk. His jet-black hair is swept back on both sides of his head. The molded earpiece in his left ear is hidden by a swath of hair. On his left is Sportscaster Marty Bester. On the right is Marina Potenza, chief meteorologist of Channel Seven.

Caldwell leans over and whispers to Marina, "I'd like to see your highs and lows after the show."

Marina smiles and whispers back, "Be at my place by seven. Danny, you're making me hot."

"Thirty seconds to air," Billy yells to the room.

In the control room, Director Yvonne Hurst screams, "Oh, shit, how did that sound get on the air?"

Eleven miles away, Sandy Caldwell is preparing the Christmas turkey and waiting for her husband to appear onscreen. She drops the bowl of stuffing on the floor. She folds her legs and drops into a crouching position, her rear resting against the dishwasher. She begins crying. Maybe it was in all in her mind, she thinks. But she knows she did hear the words, "Danny, you're making me hot."

The usual dramatic music launches the show. The announcer's voice says, "This is News Watch Seven at Six with Danny Caldwell, Marina Potenza, and Marty Bester. And now to Danny Caldwell."

"Good evening," says Danny, who still doesn't know what happened. "On this Christmas Eve 2007, millions of Christians around the world are preparing to celebrate the birth of Jesus Christ. Here in our community, services will be held at the Cathedral of Saints Peter and Paul, where News Watch reporter Sally Guvney is standing by. Sally?"

As the reporter begins to talk, the hotline phone lights up on the set. Danny answers it. News Director Eddie Bartel opens the conversation: "Danny."

"Yes."

"That little chit-chat with Marina was on the air. It came in strong over a fast-food commercial."

"You're shitting me."

"No, this is awful."

"I will kill the sound engineer."

"Danny."

"Yes."

"Fix it, and fix it fast."

"How?"

"Just fix it."

The anchorman has thirty seconds left in which to figure out how. Soon it will be fifteen, and then nothing.

He picks up the phone. The director answers.

"Listen, come to me on a super-tight shot."

The reporter ends her piece and says, "Now back to you."

Caldwell looks at the camera. "Before we continue with the news, an explanation. Sometimes in the midst of a hard day of news gathering, we in this hallowed business resort to moments of humor and sarcasm. We do a lot of jesting here in the News

Watch Seven broadcast center. You may have heard me jousting with Marina, and her suggesting that she might be joining me later tonight."

He is breathing heavily, so heavily that he can hear his heart beating. Thump. Thump. Thump. He continues: "That was our typical preshow unwinding routine, and it was in good fun. So I don't want anyone to get the wrong impression. Unfortunately, the microphone was open. I thought it would be important to clear that up before the demons of gossip news start posting this on You Tube, and before the sensitivities of my loving family and yours are compromised. Thank you. And now the wintry mix forecast from my weather friend, and just friend, Marina Potenza."

Marina is startled. But in a few seconds, she comes up for air with a momentous comment. "Danny, you *are* hot. Thanks for keeping my reputation intact."

Danny smiles, along with Marty Bester. Marina walks over to the weather set, gives a detailed Christmas forecast, and then a light burns in her brain.

"So that's our forecast. And Danny, have a great weekend, and don't forget, be at my place at seven."

"Yo, Marina," he says. "You are the top."

All three broadcasters and the studio crew, led by Billy Russell, crack up in an orgy of laughter.

"We'll be back after this."

The director fades to a live picture of the City Hall Christmas tree and then rolls the commercials.

Danny Caldwell, Emmy-awarding winning giant of Philadelphia TV News, reaches for the Kleenex on the desk behind him and wipes his sweaty brow. Once again, his career has teetered on the tightrope between success and the sewer. He has, mercifully, survived another near-fall.

THE HIDEAWAY

Esperanza is watching the six o'clock broadcast with Dr. Hoffman in the bedroom of his hideaway. "Broadcasters like Caldwell should know: Rule number one is you never know when a microphone is hot," he says. "Danny Caldwell is what's wrong with local TV news in this country. He is a sniveling, two-faced, egomaniacal bastard. Darianna, he's a disaster waiting to happen."

Darianna agrees. Privately, Peacemaker thinks that Caldwell will help make a disaster happen.

Christmas candles and Hanukkah lights burn brightly on the top counter of the bedroom fireplace.

"Honey," he says, "I have to make a few holiday calls."

"No problem, babe. I'll get dinner ready." Darianna leaves the bedroom and walks into the small kitchen and dining area.

Esperanza remains in the bedroom and settles down in the bed, his head supported by pillows. He reaches for the phone. It is time to call the working bees.

"Hello, Alvinato."

"Hello, boss. Merry Christmas."

"Back to you on that. How's the crew?"

"Boss, we have a lot to be thankful for, thanks to you. That concession deal at the new stadium will keep us in pasta for a long time."

"Bobby," he says. "Are you ready for the planning stages?"

"No question, Angel. I have surrounded myself with the best."

"Bobby, enjoy the weekend, and when the time comes, I'll tell you about the boys on the boat."

"Bye, Angel."

He hangs up and begins dialing again. "Hello, Garcia."

"The boss honors me on Christmas Eve."

"Garcia, my love to Maria, and my prayers as you remember Tony."

"Thank you, boss. Did you see Danny Boy on TV tonight?"

"Yes, Garcia. Once again, the masked marauder makes his ugly mark."

"What do you mean, masked?"

"I mean, my friend, that his life is a mask, hiding the evil and the dark mind of a man who needs more than success. He is so insecure and fragile that he needs power over others. He needs it so much that he will do anything to get it."

"Don't I know, boss. Don't I know," Perez says wearily.

"Garcia, don't forget to make contact with the dispatcher well before the target date."

"I will, boss. Merry Christmas."

"Good night."

Peacemaker has one more call to make, but he must be discreet. Darianna is in the next room.

"Hello," he says to his other lover. "Did you have to work tonight?"

"I work every night," she says. "But wherever I am, I think of you. And when I think of you, my body becomes a flowing temple of love."

"Good night, my love."

"Good night," she says.

Esperanza puts his head on the pillow and reminisces, as he always does during the holidays. He has been a lucky man, but he also believes that people make their own luck. He forged his relationship with Bobby Alvinato decades ago and has paid him handsomely over the years with hard cash, contracts for vending at city buildings, and the trash-removal deal at the performing arts center. Information is power. And how to use it? That is an art, pure and simple.

He calls his way of operating the "subtraction" of adversaries. The subtractions have given him the additions–the money and power–to do good deeds.

His favorite childhood movie was the re-release of the 1938 film *The Adventures of Robin Hood*. Young Angel did not look like Errol Flynn, but in his childhood dreams he fancied himself as a man who would do anything to give to those in need, even crossing over to the dark side to make it happen. At the age of twenty-two, he started his own Thanksgiving Day foundation for the hungry. The turkeys were stolen by punks from the mob out of South Philly. They hijacked a tractor trailer of frozen turkeys and delivered them to Peacemaker.

Just back from college, Angel Esperanza wanted to make his mark in the vast barrio on Fifth Street in Philadelphia. He met Bobby Alvinato at a funeral in Margate, New Jersey. Alvinato, a junior player in the Italian mob, was taken with the sheer presence of the man, his soaring height and his smile. The smile of an angel, the mind of a killer.

Over coffee at the Rose Café on Passyunk Avenue in South Philly, the young Angel made his first business deal, and his partner was Alvinato.

"I want you to understand two things, Bobby. I have no money, but I want to feed people on Thanksgiving. Therefore, I would like you to be at the Beet Warehouse on American Street at 10:30 A.M. tomorrow. A truckload of turkeys will be arriving. I want you to the steal the load and bring the turkeys to me. I will wrap them and give them to people who need them. Here is a promissory note."

Alvinato looked at the words on the lined yellow paper, written in graceful, flawless handwriting. It read, "For services rendered Thanksgiving 1983, I will someday pay you back for the work you have done for needy Philadelphians. A.E."

"No shit," he said. "I believe you will, man. I do."

The turkey feast was a success shared by hundreds. Thanksgiving 1983 was the day when a small legend began. Angel Esperanza got his first taste of using violence to serve humanity. He savored the power and delighted in the outcome.

Bobby Alvinato would never have believed that his petty theft of turkeys so many years ago would morph into a long friendship characterized by faith, love, and crime. Bobby and the rest of the small circle that understood Peacemaker's power knew that crimes committed on behalf of have-nots would occur without fanfare and without fingerprints.

Bobby kept the handwritten note from Esperanza as a souvenir of their beginning. Alvinato has a sacred bond with his invisible army of connivers, sociopaths, and psychopaths who do his bidding. One of them started out in November 1983 as a brash fourteen-year-old from the Port Richmond neighborhood of Philadelphia who joined Alvinato's gang. The kid was used as a lookout as Bobby's men tied up the driver and unloaded the turkeys. He was a student at Edison High School who loved action and wanted to grow up to be a cop. His name was Garcia Perez.

CHAPTER EIGHT: **DADDY'S GIRL**

*T**he world is timeless to me now. Can't keep track of the visitors. But I think I recognize the man at the door. Yeah. It's Police Commissioner Doug Underwood. Rebecca greets him warmly. He walks over to me. He says, "Mike, we need to talk." I shake my head. He says, "What the hell were you doing on the 422 bypass in the first place?" I can't believe it, but even Underwood has suspicions about me. It seems like everyone, from Washington to Philadelphia, is trying to cover their asses.*

REWIND
FATHER'S DAY 2007
CHICAGO

Lisette's body aches from the weightlifting. Keeping in shape is a priority, but like everything else in her life, overdoing it, reaching beyond her limits, is a problem. The phone rings.

"Hi Mom," she says into the speaker phone. "Having Sunday brunch at the Drake. I'll call you back."

Next, she performs her daring solo act in the car. Keeping an eye on the swerving cars in the rush-hour traffic of Chicago, she reaches one hand out to open the lid to her vanity mirror. Then she gets her lipstick case from her purse. She likes danger, the singular act of defying the odds of living on.

Glancing in the mirror, she keeps her left elbow on the wheel while carefully spreading the creamy, blood-red lipstick on her lips. Finally she surrenders to the simple reality that she can't drive the car with no hands and grips the wheel again. Fidgeting and nervous, she turns on the radio.

"This is WMMB All-News-All-The Time in Chicago Land," says the announcer. "Batten down the hatches. Wind gusts of 45 miles per hour will accompany thunder showers in the next three hours. Driving will be a little tricky. Happy Father's Day to dads everywhere."

"Dads everywhere," she thinks, envisioning little girls dressed in pink sitting on daddy's laps, looking up to them with admiring glances, each one nestling her head in her daddy's neck, the warmth of the hug so soothing and reassuring.

Lisette talks to herself, narrating the past. "Happy Daddy's Day. I had a Daddy once. And he loved me so much that he would do anything for me. He would bring me chocolates and flowers and buy me anything I wanted. The bastard."

Lisette glides her Prius into the right lane of the expressway. In her sights is the dramatic high-rise skyline of the city of Chicago, the Sears tower dwarfing the other structures.

"How does a human being live on?" she wonders. "How does a heart continue beating when the mind is paralyzed by the fear stalking the stairwell a few feet from my room, the pink room?"

At just twenty-eight, the woman with the deep blue eyes and the cropped blonde hair is the American stereotype of a model. In fact, she is a model. She is trim and curved in the contemporary way that some women would almost kill for. She's got a perfect complexion. Her lips, covered by the lipstick, are sensual and inviting. Her trim body and infectious smile stop people in their tracks. On a typical walk up Michigan Avenue, Lisette sparks more rubbernecking than a two-car collision.

Her full name is Lisette Zebronski, but she's known as Lisette Z. in the high-fashion world of Chicago's Miracle Mile, a wide boulevard of dreams in the east end of the glistening downtown section of the Loop.

As she glides the car into the exit ramp, the speaker phone rings again.

"Hello, whoever it is."

"Hey, baby. It's your silly from Philly. Where the hell are you?"

"I'll be at the Drake in five minutes."

"Bye, kid."

"Kid?" she says. Lisette smiles. She feels good all over, filled with confidence and inner strength. This man and this bond have become so important in her life. He is an instrument of comfort who shares a common crusade and a double life.

They love each other–not with the passionate, heated hunger for flesh and release that has eluded Lisette in her lifetime, but with the love of a mentor and his charge, with solidarity and compassion from shared suffering and shared goals. They meet on Father's Day every year, he without children, she without a father to speak of.

They met by chance in 2002 at the White House Summit on Drugs. The model from Chicago and the community leader from Philadelphia, both indirect victims of drug use. The support of these two public figures was invaluable, but few knew the secrets that had brought them there.

Esperanza spoke eloquently, providing graphic examples of the pace of drug trafficking in Philadelphia. He never talked of his mother's lifelong devotion to heroin, but inside, he knew that he would never cease looking for the dealers who destroyed her life. Lisette was invited for show, for she was a celebrity model who could sell the drug fight to young people. They shared a cab to

Georgetown. Angel asked her to dinner. With her usual prickliness about men, the model worried. But that fear had evaporated by the time the salad came.

"I like you, Angel," she told him that evening. "I wish I had a father like you. Something about you makes me want to trust you."

"Watch out, kid," he said. "I could be a damn serial rapist."

She looked down in shame.

"I'm sorry," he said.

"Please don't joke like that," she answered.

"I'm very sorry."

"Angel, let me tell you why I came to Washington," Lisette answered. She told him that she had grown up in DesPlaines, Illinois and that her childhood memories were stark.

"His name was Frank," she said. "He was about thirty-seven when he began to rape me. The guy was always high on drugs. Maybe the bastard would have touched me even if he wasn't high all the time, but he was. First it was grass; then he began sniffing. He walked up the stairs and got under the covers, and then, as my tears were flowing, he was uncontrollable. Let me just say that it was very painful, Angel. This happened for years. My God, I can't believe I'm talking. I mean, I'm still terrified. And I want to hurt bad men. I want to kill drug dealers. And sometimes, I just want to die, just end it." She took a deep breath, wiped her eyes, and looked straight at him across the table. "That's why I'm here."

"Oh, honey, that's so horrible." Angel was visibly shaken. "Who was this man?"

She opened her mouth. "He." She couldn't say it. But finally, the truth spilled out as her voice cracked and her hands began shaking. "Was my father. The pink room. That was my bedroom, and that's where he took my life and all the feeling in me. He just sucked it away."

"Where is he now?"

"I don't know. I don't care. But if I see him, I will kill him."

"Kill?"

"Yes, kill, as in murder." He could see from her fierce expression that she meant it.

"Well, my dear. We have a lot in common."

"Not you. You don't fit the part," she replied.

"Yes, honey, I do," he said. "When justice doesn't work, we have to do what God is telling us to do."

Five years later, as her car moves through the Loop, she remembers that evening and savors the comfort and understanding she knows she will find with Angel for the next few hours. The valet parking stand is in sight. Lisette sees him waiting beneath the façade. He waves and smiles. She beams.

Opening the driver's door, she grabs the ticket and runs into his arms. They embrace. She buries her head into his neck. Tension is gone, the anxiety-ridden tension that is part of every day and night and resumes again at the glow of first light.

"You look great, kid," he says.

"Of course I do. But if you keep calling me 'kid,' I'm going to bust your nuts."

PHILADELPHIA

Garcia hates Father's Day. His father is gone, having died just a year after Maria's. And their son is gone.

Quietly, he slips out of bed and tiptoes to the bathroom, hoping not to awaken his sleeping beauty. In the bathroom, he walks into the shower and begins letting the cold water massage his scalp with ripples of chill.

Father's Day. "It sucks," he whispers. He lathers down and lets the icy water wash the soap away as he turns his back toward the gushing stream. His spine tingles with shivers.

Draped in a towel, he sits down on the bed and reaches over to Maria. He whispers, "It's time to go, my sweetheart."

As they do every Sunday, Garcia and Maria Perez will drive through the northern suburbs and arrive at the northeast corner of St. Matthew's Church cemetery in Bensalem Township, a middle-class Bucks County suburb just north of the Philadelphia County line.

As the sun emerges brightly from the east on this late June day, the lovers walk hand in hand from the car to the small stone, now surrounded by tall grass and covered in morning dew.

The stone is simple, appropriate for a life that ended far too soon.

Anthony Alberto Perez
Born April 13, 1985
Died October 17, 2003

Maria clasps her left hand in Garcia's right as she sways to the music in her head. She does this every week. "It's so chilly for June," Maria whispers.

"Honey, here, take my coat." Garcia drapes his light leather jacket over his wife's shoulders.

Garcia gently drops the flowers on the stone. They stand together in silence. Their heartbeats sound so vivid, pounding like drumbeats while they look down at their baby's long sleep. Garcia turns to Maria and embraces her.

He whispers in her ear, "Sweetheart, I will do what I need to do. By the time I finish, they will be–"

"By the time you finish what? What are you talking about?" she interrupts.

"I will do what God wants me to do." Tears start flowing from his eyes.

She moves closer and takes a handkerchief from her purse. She wipes away the tears, clearly troubled by his mood. In addition to the usual grief, she feels his anger, and with it her own fear.

"Don't talk like that, Garci," she demands.

"Alright. Okay."

As they walk back to the car, he is filled with guilt. He has betrayed the love of his life. She can't find out that he is a liar and a killer and that, with the help of the boss, he will avenge his son's death. "Blood for blood," he thinks.

CHICAGO—THE DRAKE HOTEL

The boss is enthralled, as he always is when he visits with lovely Lisette. "How's Mom?" he asks her.

"Clueless about what I do. So fucking clueless."

"It's always been that way."

"Yes. Even back in the days of the pink room."

The pink room had brought Angel and Lisette together. Shrinks would call their shared trauma "shared blood," a union of dysfunction and dread. But no one in that army of pycho-babblers ever really understood. Esperanza does.

"If there's one thing I've learned in this business . . ." Lisette begins.

"Yes, sweetheart?"

"It's that food is overrated. But today my appetite is bigger than life." Lisette is on her third double deck of pancakes and fruit.

Angel stares into her eyes, realizing that this Father's Day, like every one he'd spent with Lisette, gives him the sensation of family more than his business-trip romances and rapturous dalliances ever did. With Lisette in Chicago, he feels contentment and security. They are their own little family, bonded by truth and always able to heal their scars by being together. Yet he is disturbed. A man with little guilt, Angel nevertheless wonders whether the dark part of their bond is appropriate for Lisette.

"Why don't we talk about the overtime," he suggests.

"Why should we? The overtime is what I want it to be. I could try to end it, but every time I think about it, I say screw it. This is what I have to do."

For a moment, the man of confidence feels a twinge of despair. He has allowed this gorgeous woman, a bright, engaging, and caring person, to enter his darkest world, and he knows, as she does, that it is immoral.

He sits back in the chair and folds his arms. "You shouldn't be doing it," he says. "You need to live normally and find the perfect man to share with, to protect, to comfort, to calm. After all, you know what they call me in Philadephia? They call me the Peace-maker."

Looking a bit hurt, her eyes moistening, she responds with force. "Look, I am who I am. I could walk away from the overtime, enjoy the luxury of fame, and still, believe me, still. . ." She puts her head in her hands. "Angel. I walk down any street and see a man, any man, and wonder if he'll be the next one to hurt me. Tell me Angel, aren't they all capable? Believe me, every day or night I go into overtime, my heart beats so fast, and when it's over, I know that I have, in my own way, dealt with my fear. And you do that, too. You use power and deception to erase the shit out there."

"But you deserve better, and I *feel* like a shit. Why did I allow you to get into this?" he says.

"Because you understand and I understand where it comes from." She nods. He smiles back at her, and they continue their lie, afraid to reverse the course they chose back in that first meeting in Washington.

CHAPTER NINE: **THE COMPETITION**

I keep sleeping and dreaming. I awaken now and see my brave wife's eyes connect with mine with that "it's going to be okay" look. Through all the years of love, it is that look that I long for. I drift off again into a deep sleep. I dream that Harvey is at the gate of hell, and Danny Caldwell is on the other side, waiting to open the door and welcome him in. When I awaken from the dream, Rebecca is there, still staring at me with those beautiful brown eyes. At least I know she believes in me.

DECEMBER 2007
CHESTNUT HILL

Saturday. Single and lonely is the rising star of Channel Five's news operation, existing emotionally between that liberating feeling of time away from work and the everpresent sense that he is missing some story, some development taking place out of sight. Not knowing is a reporter's nightmare. So it is on most Saturday mornings for Keith Robert Byrne.

Byrne is intrigued by the Cambria killings. Murder is bad enough. But the mutilation and the obvious attempt to make the victims anonymous make him wonder what's up.

He's also intrigued by the competition, Diana, but he has no guts. He's afraid to call, ask her out, and engage in some way, even though their brief encounter stirred feelings in him that he never imagined he could have. He knows that beauty is over-rated. But he can't get her face out of his mind. He taped her show a week ago and has been watching it ever since. He stops her in mid-sentence and looks at her eyes. Her eyes tell the story, glowing with intensity and sincerity. He wants to know more about her naturalness and the texture of her personality.

Byrne is an intense person. He always has been. Seventeen years out of college, he remains a mystery to himself. He fights harder and harder to become a great reporter and anchor. He succeeds, but his life has a hole in it, with no real reason for being, and he's taken some extraordinary steps to fill the nothingness—community service, renewed faith, and one very quiet act of selflessness.

Byrne was twenty-three and a street reporter at WISH TV in Indianapolis when he covered the story of Robert Darby, diagnosed with myelogenous leukemia. Darby was searching for a bone marrow donor. He couldn't find one in his family. He used his interview with Byrne to begin a public campaign to find an unrelated donor. Eventually, Darby was assigned a match and bought some time. In the process, thirty thousand people responded to the blood drive. After interviewing some of the blood donors, Byrne slipped in the side door of the donor center, offered a blood sample, and officially signed up. Would it lead to something?

Four years later, Byrne was working as the weekend anchor at WTAE in Pittsburgh when the phone call came. A sixteen-year-old somewhere in the West needed marrow to survive. The anchorman was a perfect match.

Doctors drilled into his pelvis and sucked out a pint of his marrow. He was left with puncture wounds and soreness. He told only his father.

"Dad, my ass is so sore, but I feel like I'm doing something good for a change, not just blabbing the news."

"Keith," his father replied. "You're an accomplished TV guy. Isn't that enough?"

"No."

"Why not?"

"Dad, I don't feel a purpose. I need more. I need to stand for something."

The ending to the story was not good. Because of the rules of confidentiality, it took Byrne six months to find the boy's name. At that time, he learned that Billy Morris had died just three weeks following the transplant. Ever since, Byrne has maintained a correspondence with Billy's parents and four sisters, one his twin. There are emails, photos in the mail, and calls a couple of times a year. Although the child is gone, Byrne feels a connection, and although it may be emotionally self-serving, the link to the Morris family remains a vibrant part of his life.

Socially, despite his notoriety, his life is a blank. Suzie Berman, the new reporter, wound up to be, in his eyes, a soulless woman interested in moving ahead. They had three dates, and all three ended in passionate sex, but philosophically, emotionally, there was nothing. Just a physical chemistry that had no afterlife. She knew it. He knew it. They passed in the newsroom often and nodded in a friendly way, but nothing more took place. They were two love buddies with no real destination.

So Byrne is, as usual, single and lonely on a Saturday morning. He decides to do something about it. Byrne dials the hotline number to the Channel Nine newsroom.

"Hello, this is Channel Nine. Dick speaking."

"Dick, this is Keith Byrne over at Channel Five. Trying to reach Diana about a fundraiser. I would like to invite her to make an appearance." He lies, but it's good cover. "Dick, can you call her and have her call me?"

"Sure, Mr. Byrne. What's the number? I'll try to get her to buzz you up."

Byrne gives his number to Dick. When he hangs up, he walks over to his sofa and sags into the corner, now feeling sad and worried and sick to his stomach. Did he really just make that call? He reaches for his I Phone. Quickly, he texts Dick at Channel Nine. "Yo Dick, if you did not make call to Diana…don't do it. Ok."

Byrne goes into a sweat. Did he catch him in time?

The phone buzzes on the glass of his night table. His fingers shaking, his heart racing, he grabs the phone. He looks at the screen.

"Sorry Mr. Byrne. Just made the call.

Keith is in a state of high anxiety. He feels his face. It's hot. He's burning up. He picks up a pencil, but there's no electric sharpener in sight.

LOGAN HOUSE APARTMENTS

Lost in the Saturday morning paper, Diana is still beneath the covers at 10:30 A.M. when the phone rings. She answers.

"Diana, this is Dick in the newsroom. Got a weird call."

"Who?"

"Guy says he is Keith Byrne and wants you to call him about showing up at a fundraiser. Here's his number. Just make sure, if you call the guy, that you block your caller ID."

"Dick, you're so sweet. Thanks. See you soon." She hangs up the phone. She grabs the covers and places them over her head, a protective gesture. From what is she protecting herself? Since the press conference, she has been absorbed by delicious daydreams. She knew it would come to this. Avoidance has been a major issue in her "civilian" life, away from the trauma of news and the pace of the deadline. She crawls deeper under the covers like a child trying to avoid being discovered. But it's not being discovered that bothers her, but the thought of what she might discover along the way. After all, even the most fastidious fact checker may miss the real story. So what is the real story on Keith Byrne, and is she ready to emerge from the blankets to find out?

CHESTNUT HILL

By 11 A.M. he is fraught with embarrassment and fear. He looks in the mirror as he strokes the razor down the sides of his face. What he sees, the way he would describe himself at that moment, is shit faced. He made the first move, rather awkwardly. There is no fundraiser, although Esperanza no doubt will be doing something for the kids just before Christmas. Not only is he a liar, but he is stupid. He finally meets someone he has a genuine interest in, and he acts like a doofus.

Being careful not to cut his face, Byrne finishes up the shaving job, rinses the lather away, and dries off. Naked, he walks by the full-length mirror in the corner of the bedroom, admires himself, and then sinks back to reality. He starts shaking. He's been so immersed in his Saturday morning adventure that he has forgotten to break his overnight fast. The combination of nerves and hunger is too much. He runs to the fridge and starts gulping orange juice from the carton. As soon as the first gulp heads into his system, the phone rings and he nearly chokes. He decides to let it ring a few times. The caller I.D. says "blocked." He grabs the phone, wraps a towel around his rear, and sits down at the small kitchen table.

"Hello?"

"Hi, Keith. This is Diana Hong. Hope I didn't interrupt anything like you so rudely interrupted me at the news conference. Did I?"

"Well . . ."

"Maybe I should call back. A guy like you must be awfully busy."

"Well . . ."

"We are competitors, Keith, so whatever is on your mind, I'm sure it can wait."

"Well . . ." He steeled himself.

"Yes, Keith?"

"Well, I have to tell you the truth. There is no fundraiser, although I'm sure we could find one. The truth is that I lied to try to connect with you."

"You lied? That's refreshing."

"What do you mean?"

"I mean, it's refreshing. Boy meets girl and lies to get her to call him. But you were honest enough not to complicate the first mistake by keeping your little lie alive. Now that says something about you–not a lot, mind you, but *something*."

"So how are you?" He changes the subject.

"I'm good. A little tired. I've got a confession to make," she says, her voice getting gentler.

"What's that?"

"When I got the message, I was going to throw the number in the trash, but I changed my mind."

"Why?"

"Because I've been waiting for this call, fearing it too, because I knew that you would reach out. I just knew it, and now that you have, I think we should meet and talk, and find out if this is love at first sight, or fright night."

He is silent. Finally, he speaks. "Are you for real?"

"Yes, I'm just like you, except I don't have to create a small lie to tell the truth."

"Maybe we can exchange notes on the Cambria murders," Keith says.

"Fat chance! I may be very interested in getting to know you, like you are to get to know me. We may really connect, but Keith, that's one thing I will never give away."

"Just kidding," he says.

"Why don't we meet at Steve Starr's new place at Thirteenth and Walnut?" Diana says. "Let's say one o'clock."

"Today?"

"Yes, today. And Keith, leave your pencil at home."

The heat builds in his head, like a fever is coming on. Does she know about his pencil-sharpening fetish, or is she referring to note-taking on the Cambria case?

"I'll see you at one," he replies. "No pencil. No pad. Just me."

"I'm looking forward to it," she says warmly. "I really am."

"Wait a minute," Keith says.

"What?"

"The restaurant is too public, don't you think?"

"I guess so," she says.

"Where do you live?"

"Logan House."

"I'll get us some fruit and sandwiches and we'll go to the park," says Keith. "Pick you up around one?"

"Sounds good. Looking forward to it."

He replies, "So am I. Goodbye." Then he heads back to the shower for a second time. He is sweating so much and his head aches so intensely that he thinks he's going to pass out.

ALONG THE WISSAHICKON CREEK

"And then just as one is about to sentimentalize on the beauty of nature and how it shames the crass work of man, one comes to what is perhaps the loveliest thing along the Wissahickon–the Walnut Lane Bridge. Leaping high in air from the very domes of the trees, curving in a sheer smooth superb span that catches the last western light on its concrete flank, it crashes along the darkened valley as nobly as an old Roman viaduct of Southern France. It is a thrilling thing."

In the heart of the Fairmount Park system, the largest city-park panorama in the world, is the winding road known as Wissahickon Drive, immortalized by the words of Christopher Morley, one of America's great twentieth- century authors, who captured the beauty of Philadelphia in his columns for the *Public Ledger* newspaper from 1918 to 1920. In Morley's day, only horses and riders traversed the drive, or Lincoln Drive, as it's called today, where drivers follow the dramatic curves, constantly distracted by the creek and its soaring landscape to the north and the rock and granite hugging the curves at the south.

Byrne is well aware of the area's beauty, and it is his destination of choice. But first, he has to get there.

He is running late, a victim of his quest for perfection. He drives quickly to a food market, where he orders sandwiches, fruit salad, and some bottled water. Before checkout, nervous to the point of distraction, Byrne returns to the take-out counter and asks for aluminum foil for the sandwiches.

At 1:15, he calls Diana from the Bluetooth car phone. "I'm on my way. Sorry," he says.

"No problem, Keith. I'll see you in the lobby."

"Good." He can't control the tension in his body, along with the sweat that envelops it on this cool, late autumn day. He whistles, as though whistling in the dark, as he steers the car through the winding curvature of Kelly Drive, glancing to his right at the rowers and coxswain of a racing shell that glisten in the sun as they speed along the Schuylkill River. As the car veers around the front of the art museum, Byrne tries again to calm himself. Now he travels down Benjamin Franklin Parkway, veers to Logan Circle, and steers the car into the circular driveway of Logan House.

The driveway is empty except for a solitary figure, hands tucked in the pockets of a black leather jacket, leaning against the wall on the side of the entrance. He pulls up, stops the engine, and walks out. "Hi. Sorry. It's so chilly out."

"I love the breeze," she says as he opens the passenger door for her. He closes the door, circles the rear of the car, and sits down, finally close to Diana, breathing the same air.

"I thought we'd go to Wissahickon Creek. That all right?" he asks.

"Sure, Keith. Let's go." She fastens her seat belt. He looks over. She removes her sunglasses and returns the glance. She takes off her right glove, reaches across the shifting console, and softly squeezes his right hand. "Keith, it's good to say hello in person."

"I know," he replies, breaking out in a wide smile, the tension in his face and body melting away.

WASHINGTON SQUARE

Saturday morning and early afternoon is their time. Veronica savors the moments, secret though they are, secret for reasons. The first reason is her notoriety, the second is Angel's. The third is unspeakable, unconscionable, though she accepts it as part of his public persona, and that is Darianna. Through it all, Veronica knows that she will ultimately prevail.

Freshly showered, Veronica sits in a lavender bathrobe on the love seat in her apartment, sipping coffee, and looking westward from Washington Square to the high rises in the west. He is in the shower.

The anchorwoman, so concerned about proving her competence, overwhelms her cohorts with her insecurity, her efforts to prove over and over again that she can do it and that her natural beauty will never get in the way. Here, in the comfort of her own apartment, are the few hours in the week when she relaxes. Just lying in his arms, just being in his presence overcomes the doubts.

He enters the room, towel around his waist. His hair, so shiningly black, is brushed back. Drops of water fall to the carpet as he sits down on the loveseat. He embraces her, his neck nestling in the comfort of her neck. He hugs her hard. She wraps her arms around him. The seconds tick away. They remain locked in a lovers' embrace, oblivious to the external world.

Still embracing her, he whispers, "I love you, sweetheart."

She squeezes harder, then presses her lips lightly against the deep of his neck. Softly, she whispers, "I'm so scared that we really have no future."

"Why?"

"Because there is your public love, and then, sadly, there is me."

He loosens his grip on her and, oddly, gets down on his knees, where he opens both arms and embraces her waist, his head now resting on her chest. She can hear his heart beating.

"I will love you forever," he says. "I will find a way. After all, it's not as if you're loving a married man, is it?"

She holds his head with both hands. "Sometimes I wish both of us were unknown," she says. "There is something to be said for anonymity, don't you think?"

"I agree, but then again, you wouldn't be the TV star, and I wouldn't have any power."

"Is power more seductive than me?"

"Nothing is more seductive than you."

"But?"

"Yes." He smiles. "Taking names and seeking justice is pretty close, honey."

She slowly takes his head and places it in her lap. "What I love about you, about us, is that we know everything," she says. "There are no secrets."

For when she thinks about what he does, the dark side, the plans, the brutal exercise of power, the quest for revenge and justice, it makes her love him even more. How many people would take those risks? But quietly, she worries.

And one question remains unanswered. Will he lose control? And if he does, will he be exposed, without mercy or a clear understanding of his motives?

He rises and blows her a kiss. "I'm going to get dressed and check my email, sweetie. Then I've got to call one of your cohorts. You can listen in."

ALONG THE WISSAHICKON CREEK

Two professional communicators are almost speechless on their trip on Lincoln Drive to the Wissahickon Creek. Halfway to the destination, unsure of the moment and of themselves, they just look at each other and smile graciously. Keith, steering the car, is naturally forced to bring his eyes back to the wandering roadway, but Diana keeps glancing at him. Each seems dreadfully shy to the other.

Then she starts laughing so hard that it startles Keith.

"Did I say something?" he asks.

"That's exactly it. You said nothing. I said nothing. I just think it's so funny that we are both so afraid to say anything for fear that we'll ruin the moment or whatever it is that's happening. I'll tell you this, Keith. I haven't laughed so hard in such a long time."

And then she touches him again. She takes her gloveless right hand and places it on his arm, this time as if to say how comfortable she is.

"Okay, so I'll talk," he says. He smiles as the words slip out of his mouth. "You *are* beautiful. And I'm happy to be here with you, but I have a confession. I've been watching you on TV, and what really gets me is that I know you are not 'phoning it in,' and that inside that beauty there might be something deeper. Maybe, who knows, a person with beautiful thoughts, and honor, and a sense of caring. Now, I could be wrong, but it's more than your breathtaking beauty that causes me to make an idiot of myself. I also want you to know that for me, basically a shy person, it was a true act of courage to call you, because I was scared to death that you would view me as some sort of ego-driven TV person who is totally self indulgent, which I am on occasion. So there it is. And I'd better shut up or I might really blow it."

She smiles and says, "Keep talking, Keith. I love it." She leans over and brings her face close to his right cheek. Without warning, she kisses him very softly. "I do have one question."

"What?" he says.

"Is it true that you have a love affair with an electronic pencil sharpener?"

"I smell a spy in the newsroom," he says, giggling and feeling instantly overheated. "How did you find out about that?"

"I have my sources, mostly camera people. But Keith, they all love you. Everybody does. I can understand how they feel. You're so honest–I think."

The car pulls up to the parking area across from the path that leads to the Walnut Lane Bridge a quarter of a mile away. Diana opens the door and Keith reaches into the back seat for his knapsack with the sandwiches. They begin walking on the path, which is strewn with autumn leaves. They walk in silence until Keith, now more self assured, asks her a question.

"So, tell me about you?"

"Not much to tell, really. Just grew up in a tough neighborhood, not far from Cambria. Got into Girls' High, attended Temple on scholarship, and became a writer. Writing was the key to getting into TV. Never thought of going in front of a camera."

"You're kidding."

"No, I hate my looks, and I can't see, so I wear glasses."

"So what happened?"

"Well, I've got a great boss, Phil. You know, Phil Hurley, who said that I was a terrific conversationalist. So he said, 'Try it.' I just talked into the camera. Then, Keith, they got really daring. They gave me the anchor job, solo. That would make me the least glamorous anchor in the nation."

"You know, you're right," he answers. "You are fascinating because it's just you talking to the viewer. But Diana, you look amazing, I mean, so striking."

"No, Keith. My eyes are small, my hair is black, and my skin is white as a ghost. I have a face for radio."

"You're funny and adorable. The fact that you have no clue that you're beautiful makes you all the more attractive. Did I say that right? God, the words are just pouring out of me. Maybe I should go back to the pencil sharpener."

She laughs. He looks up at the towering Walnut Lane Bridge. He holds his knapsack with his left hand and her hand with his right. He is shivering a bit from the cold.

"So, Keith, how did you get into our crazy business?"

"Well, it took me a couple of years to get here. I got *my* break in Memphis. The lead anchor walks up to me at 10:50 P.M. He says, 'It's yours, baby.' Thought he was joking. But he hands me the script and starts walking out, claiming that he ran out of glue for his hairpiece, which was, I noticed, slipping down his forehead. I went on air to replace him, read the thirty minutes of news, and then got very sick."

"So a sliding toupée gave you a chance at fame?"

"Yes, a sliding toupée and a bit of work and luck along the way. And now here I am, the luckiest guy in Philly, taking a walk with you."

"I think that would be a correct assessment," she answers. Suddenly she gives him a big hug, not the kind of hug you give a lover, but all things considered, he finds it pretty amazing.

They are under the fabled bridge when she begins to feel what she has never wanted to show, forcing her to turn around and walk away.

"Just wanted to see something," she calls back.

"What's wrong?" He slowly walks over to her and turns her around. Her face is down, and he lifts her chin up. Tears are trickling down both cheeks. Tenderly, he kisses them away and holds her close.

"What happened?" he asks.

"It's nothing. Well, that's not true. I cry sometimes when I'm very happy. I know it's strange. And Keith, I haven't cried like this in a long, long time."

He holds her head and moves his face closer. They kiss, very slowly and softly, and he caresses her neck with his right hand.

At that very moment, he hears the familiar sound of the Star Spangled Banner. They both laugh so hard that they almost can't stop. He walks away from Diana and picks up the phone.

"Hi, this is Keith."

WASHINGTON SQUARE

The speaker phone in Veronica's apartment is turned up.

"Hey, Newsboy. This is your secret leader. What's up, man?"

"Just taking a walk with a friend."

"Well, that's an improvement. Newsboy has a social life. Anyway, got stuff. Pay attention."

"Yeah?"

"Bastardo will be picked up Tuesday at two at the new beer joint in Fishtown. The Feds will have a warrant to search for his records. Organized crime division of Department of Justice is on the case. Tax-evasion charges. Got it?"

"You really hate the guy?"

"I want to chew him up and spit him out. Bastardo has poisoned thousands of Philadelphians, dishing out drugs to people who can least afford them. I will wait, patiently, for his end."

"You're not going to kill him?"

"His end is just a figure of speech."

"Thanks, Angel."

"One more thing. Veronica. She treating you well?"

"She's delightful. Why do you ask?"

"I just think she does great work, just like you, Newsboy."

"She does. Thanks for calling."

Peacemaker clicks off the speaker phone and looks at Veronica.

"You are so crazy," she says.

"Crazy? Crazy for you! I want you to know that people think you're great."

WISSAHICKON CREEK

"So, who was that?" Diana asks when Keith rejoins her near the bridge.

"None of your business."

"None of my business?"

"It was a tipster."

"Anything good?"

"Yeah, eat your heart out."

"Keith, you already have."

"Diana, we will fall deeply in love and have beautiful babies, and you will cry and I will laugh, and we will be happy, but I won't give my sources away."

"On that note, I have an idea," she says. "Let's make out."

"Are you kidding? Do you think I would just give myself that easily to someone I know less than a day?"

"Yes, I do, Keith." This time *she* moves. She wraps her arms around him and kisses him on the lips, and for a few minutes they stay close and loving. The late sun began its mid-afternoon descent to the west, shining glimmering rays on the rock-strewn creek. The two seem sheltered by each other, absorbed in their lips and skin, unaware that a cool breeze has whipped up the rust-hued leaves around them.

As they loosen their grip, they both look in wonder at each other's eyes. It is, as Diana will say later, a point of no return.

CHAPTER TEN: **WHAT'S THE WORST THING THAT CAN HAPPEN?**

*T*he people at this burn center are kind as they put salves and lotions all over my body. One of the nurses is sweet. Rebecca talks to her every day. The nurse says that soon I will have to get ready to travel. I ask Rebecca, "Where to?" She answers, "Washington."

CHANNEL FIVE NEWSROOM
FEBRUARY 13, 2008

"There are two things that scare the shit out of me," Barb tells members of her senior staff during the morning meeting on the day before Valentine's Day. "Drugs and bad press. So if you get a sniff of trouble, call me fast, or forget your next paycheck. Got it?" Everyone nods.

"So," she adds, "what's up for love day besides love, emails to soldiers, nursing-home flowers, and all that sentimental bullshit?"

Assignment Manager Bob Harris says, "How about the front page of the *Daily Philly*? That's what's up, Barb!"

"Your sense of humor will kill you someday," she replies. "And let me say something else to all of you. I used to say, 'What's the worst thing that can happen to you in this business?' I'll tell you: Herb Friebow is."

Barb picks up the *Daily Philly* and looks at the cover. The bold letters read, "HERB FRIEBOW EXCLUSIVE–WGET BACKUP ANCHOR HARVEY HOPKINS FACING DRUG REHAB."

"Let me tell you about Herb," Barb says. "Herb is more than a gossip writer. He makes a career out of chewing up and spitting out tidbits of crap about the mighty and powerful. Someday Herb will be out of a job, a victim of his own nightmare. I hope to take part in that. Because the fucker will be wrong and get nailed for it. All the assassins in print eventually wind up in the gutter. And Herb will be one of them. "

She looks at Bob and the crew. She lifts her right hand and points with her index finger. "One more thing. If I ever catch any one of you talking or leaking to Herb Friebow, you will never work again, here or anywhere."

I happen to know that before Friebow betrayed him, Hopkins was a modern-day "Deep Throat" to Herb for years, feeding him all the dirt he could on his colleagues. Barb's warning about leaks to Friebow was taken seriously by Hopkins. Harvey stopped his leaks, and refused to answer Friebow's phone calls. Eventually, Hopkins paid the price, People who give information to the devil usually do. Friebow released that story about Harvey's drug problem.

From the time, Harvey Hopkins dried up in his tips to Friebow, the writer began to hate Harvey for his lack of guts and started diminishing him in print whenever he got the goods. And on February 12, the eve of Valentine's Eve, Friebow got a phone call from operative Bernie the Weasel–Bernie Epstein, owner of the Parkside Rehab Centers.

"Hello, Herbie," Bernie said.

"What's up, Weasel Man?"

"Herbie, thanks for picking up the tab for me and the new chick at Forensic Grill. I owe you, man. Wanted you to know, that anchor drunk Harvey Hopkins just got cleaned up here after seven days. What a frickin' basket case. You got it?"

"I got it. Bernie, try the crabs at Frankie's. I got a chit there as long as Hopkins's dick. Thanks, man."

That is how Friebow wrecked Harvey's day. But much worse is coming. In the business of news, Herb Friebow is a man blessed by fortuitous encounters. Luck has it that Friebow is on Chancellor Street when Harvey Hopkins goes to the circus that very night.

Chancellor is a narrow alley-street in the heart of Philadelphia. On its west end is the Closure Bar and Grill. Inside the bar, Harvey Hopkins is well into a night of drinking, sulking from the story on his rehab, and falling off the wagon in a manner befitting one of the legends of Philadelphia local television.

A block away at Chez Poussaint, the classy French joint known for its escargot and Bourdeaux wine, Herb Friebow is enjoying dinner with his buddy Louie the Lip. Louie is a great source of information on all things dangerous: corruption, sex, drugs, and what Friebow calls "no-shit gossip." That's the news that inspires a person on the subway to say, "Did you hear about that?" The other passenger replies, "No shit? That really happened?" No-shit gossip has kept Friebow's career alive.

At the Closure Bar and Grill, Harvey sips his tenth Scotch and water. He is hot. He unbuttons the top buttons on his shirt. Not enough relief. The crowd doesn't see him take the shirt off, but they notice that his top is bare when Hopkins walks over to the antique jukebox and puts in a quarter. Soon, John Lennon begins the first strains of the autobiographical "I'm a Loser." The music is streaming through the bar. Harvey yells, "I'm Harvey Hopkins, and this is your News Pulse." On the word "pulse," he unzips his pants and tries to pull out his boner, but it won't come out. He pulls on the zipper, which catches his member in its icy metal grip.

Harvey screams, "Yikes. Little Harvey is stuck, folks. Yikes." The crowd looks over. Desperate, Harvey rips the trousers off his body, leaving only the zipper closed on his lovemaker. He kicks off his shoes. The bartender calls for an ambulance, but Harvey can't wait. He scurries out of the bar and onto Chancellor Street. Barefoot, his mouth dribbling Scotch-scented saliva, the anchorman hops down Chancellor. He is naked except for the zipper attached to his most cherished flesh. He takes a right on Seventeenth Street, passing the window of Chez Poussaint. An astonished Herb Friebow runs out the door, with Louie the Lip close behind.

Huffing and puffing, his oversized body strained to the limit, Friebow catches up to Harvey. "What's goin' on, Anchorman?" he says.

Harvey stops. He looks to the side. He says, "Yikes, it's you! Got hot, tried to take my pants off, and got caught in . . ." Harvey is breathing heavily. "Got caught in the zipper trap."

Herb is finding it hard to speak. The scribe is out of breath, and air is heating up his lungs. "Harvey, you been drinking?"

"Are you fucking crazy?" the naked man says. "Of course I have."

Louie the Lip, trailing behind Herb, stops long enough to dig into his pocket and comes out with his camera phone. Holds it up to his eye, clicks, and clicks again. He already snapped several photos from the picture window of the restaurant as Harvey was running for relief.

Herb's chest is still heaving. "Goodbye Harvey, and this time I mean goodbye," he says. Harvey resumes his trot west on Sixteenth Street, toward the bright lights of Market Street. It takes twenty-four foot-patrol cops to catch up with him. They get him into a car. And by 8:50 P.M., smiling nurses at Jefferson Hospital are delicately extricating the shrunken muscle from the zipper.

Harvey is kept overnight for observation. His first visitor is the weather-girlfriend. Then, at 5 A.M., Barb shows up. By that time, Harvey is sound asleep, his left hand clutching a pillow, his right hand cupped over his groin.

FEBRUARY 14, 2008, VALENTINE'S DAY

Barb Pierce is at the office at 6 A.M., an hour after visiting her damaged anchorman at Jefferson Hospital. She walks to her newsroom office, a comfort zone, she feels, a shelter from the incoming storm.

While waiting in anxiety and fear, Barb lets her mind wander in a melancholy trance to her roots. Most of all, she remembers Georgia. Barb grew up in Atlanta. First kid from her family to make college. Then she was the first twenty-five-year old to be a news director. Savannah was the town. Lots of history. Quaint. Lots of news. The minor leagues of news.

Barb was a genius from the start. She knew talent. By twenty-seven, she was in Raleigh-Durham, in the heart of tobacco country. Small market, but competitive. She had yet to become sordid, bitter and screwed up. The truth is, you spend enough time with egos, deception, liars, and greedy bosses, and you lose the dream, the dream that journalism counts. By the time she reached Philadelphia, she was a tainted thirty-five-year-old. Her tolerance for crap was nil. And now, her insecurities are growing like a hookworm inside her distorted body. Sitting in her office, she already feels anxious and sick, and the day hasn't even started.

Then she hears something heavy drop outside the station's swinging glass door. She walks out and picks up the paper. On its front page is a picture of Harvey. The anchorman is frozen in the air, his feet a few inches off the ground. His gray hair seems outbound, flying by his ears in waves. The color picture is ludicrous, something you would see on a comedy show. It looks like a parody, but it is real. Harvey's privates are covered by the zipper, but otherwise he wears nothing. The headline is appropriate: "NUDE ANCHOR TAKES FLIGHT ON CENTER CITY STREET." The credit line reads, "Exclusive Photo by Lou Potenza." It is Harvey's second cover story in as many days. Barb opens the paper and reads.

Veteran news anchor Harvey Hopkins of WGET TV is in good condition today after what he describes as a freak accident inside a Center City bar. Hopkins was treated at Jefferson Hospital for injuries to his penis after accidentally getting the private part stuck in a zipper.

"He had too much to drink," said Michael O'Brien, owner of the Closure Bar and Grill. "When the mishap happened, we offered to help. But Harvey ran down the street. He was hurtin'! He was looking for help."

This reporter was witness to the spectacle. I reached Hopkins at the hospital late last night and he said, "Look, I could'a hit someone, and I didn't. I never drive and drink. But yikes, I got my thing caught in a zipper. I couldn't stand still. Face it, man. I report news. I hate making it. I apologize to the bar patrons, the police, and anyone who saw me. I especially apologize to the children of Philadelphia, to whom I have dedicated my life. Oh yeah. I also apologize to my colleagues at Channel Five, always first when seconds count."

Barb takes a cigarette out of her pack. She lights up, her hand shaking in an uncontrollable tremor. She draws in the smoke. She watches out her office window as the sun emerges from the east. And in a remarkable moment, the iron lady of news begins sobbing. Is she sobbing for Harvey, or herself?

That afternoon, Harvey walks into the newsroom. He unlocks the special drawer in his desk and puts the cocaine in between the folders. He locks the drawer. At that moment, his eyes wander to a makeshift cardboard sign propped up against the computer on his desk. It reads, "Harvey, you dick! We love you."

Laughter fills the newsroom, as laughter does when news people, wary of the next disaster, go whistling in the dark.

TWENTY-FIRST AND JFK BOULEVARD
LATE AFTERNOON

The black limo moves west on JFK Boulevard, a four-lane thoroughfare and the flat point of a canyon created by dramatic high-rise structures. The boss is reading the *Daily Philly*.

He grins and stares again and again at the picture on the front page. He says to his man, "Hopkins. That's a man we can use. I wonder what he does for fun. Get everything you can on him. When the day comes, we'll be eating him for breakfast. He will serve us well."

The boss leans forward and says, "By the way, great pictures, Louie. You were in the right place at the right time. And to think it was a camera phone!"

VALENTINE'S NIGHT–THE HIDEAWAY

Darianna savors the moment. The roses are long stemmed, uncut. The message card reads, "Love, Angel." She is curious about the message, as curious as she is about his fast-changing moods.

Angel arrives home, but he is not alone. The door opens, and standing behind him is Louie the Lip.

"Hi, honey," she says. "Happy Valentine's Day." She pecks him on the cheek.

"You know Louie," he replies.

"Hello, Doc," Louie says.

"Hello, Louie. What brings you here?"

Before he can respond. Angel says, "Louie and I had some business in the limo. And I have to get something from the office for him." Angel heads to the corner office, while Louie and Darianna stand together in silence.

Louie says, "Doc, you see the *Daily Philly* today?"

"No."

"Check it out. My pictures of Harvey Hopkins are on the front page. The guy got his jackhammer caught in his fly."

"Really?" Darianna says. Every second is an eternity until Angel emerges from the office with a white envelope that he hands to Louie. As the door closes, Darianna embraces him. He returns her embrace with a soft kiss on the lips. She senses that he is in one of his cool moments. She steps back.

"Why do you hang out with people like Louie the Lip?"

"Because, my dear, for everyone there is a purpose in life, and Louie serves me well."

"But Lou Potenza?"

"Why not Lou?" he answers vigorously.

"Because, my dear," she says.

"Because what?"

"Because Louie the Lip is low class."

"What is class, anyway? We are all children of God, with our faults and the fruits of our upbringing. I mean, look at Lisette. She's got it all, but she's also got a mission."

"By the way, honey," she says.

"Yes, Madame Health Commissioner."

"When will I meet Lisette? I see her pictures everywhere. I'd like to get to know her."

"Maybe when she finishes her next job." He kisses her on the cheek, then holds her in his arms. Inside, he feels a brief adrenaline rush. He is worried sick about Lisette, and about what will happen next.

CHANNEL FIVE NEWSROOM

The bouquet arrives at Veronica's desk at 6:35 P.M. The smell of the roses greets her as she arrives from the studio. She opens the box. The roses are uncut, just like she loves them. The card reads, "With all my love, forever and ever. My love for you has no limits." She smiles. Her body heats up.

"Who's the guy?" asks Keith Byrne.

"I don't know," she says. "Just some lovesick guy with nothing to do."

CHAPTER ELEVEN: **TONY PEREZ**

*R*ebecca is up to her tricks again, since she can't talk with these government guys in the room. The note she just slipped into my hand is written on a tissue. It reads, "They suspect you of something. I don't know what, but I may hire a lawyer. Byrne says don't do anything till the two of you talk. P.S. You're going to be a grandfather."

Garcia and Maria Perez have thought of adopting another child to fill the hole left by the loss of their son, but in their late forties and unable to escape the grasp of depression, the cop and his wife decide to move on. The hole will always remain.

Garcia still loves the routine of police work, feels the lure of the street. Chasing the bad guys is a noble cause. Maria brings her talents to the operating room, where her knowledge of nursing's nuances reaches its apex in a life of worrying about other people.

The couple is involved in their church, in the Hispanic Council of Southwest Philadelphia, and in the Victims' Rights Association. The couple Perez believes in justice. Their life's work is dominated by one pursuit. They will, by whatever means necessary, make the man pay, although Garcia and Maria disagree on the method of payment.

Hospital of the University of Pennsylvania, 1985. Maria was in bed, and Garcia sat beside her, holding her hand. He kissed her hand, then rose from the chair and kissed her forehead. Then he put his head close to the blue cloth and kissed the forehead of the baby boy wrapped inside. The wonder of life, the joy of creation, overwhelmed every other feeling. The stirring of life and the creation of a family–these form the apex of a lifetime.

"There is nothing but you and him," Garcia said. He would say it over and over throughout the boy's life and has continued to do so for the five years since his death. Five years of waiting. Five years of pain. Five years of thinking of what could have been.

During Tony's last year in high school, on one warm April day, the family sat around the kitchen table, discussing Tony's future. Maria told Tony, "You can go to any college, anywhere in the country." Garcia added his own opinion: "Any college in the world, as long as you can walk to it or take a bus and pay your own tuition!"

Tony laughed. He knew that his grades, activities, and perseverance would get him into Temple. A few weeks later, he found out that he had received a full, four-year scholarship to the big university, which brought a thrill to Garcia and Maria.

"Garci," she said one night as they lay under the covers, "Tony is so lovable and good. We make beautiful music, and we hit the jackpot. I mean, he's everything. A good boy. A good student. A great laugh. Just being near him makes me so happy."

Tony was a package, all right, six feet two inches of pure muscle, a face of granite, a personality that had few traces of ego or selfishness. Without fail, whenever he was about to leave the house, he asked, "Momma, do you need anything?"

Tony was an avid talker when he was home, whether he was talking about school, girls, his beloved Phillies, or his ambition: to join the FBI. And whenever Tony would leave a room in which he had been talking with his parents, he would end the discussion with tender words: "I love you."

"I love you," he said to them as he walked out of the house on the morning of October 17, 2003, in the first semester of his second year at Temple. Not long after, as he climbed the steps to daylight at the subway station at Broad Street and Cecil B. Moore Avenue, he was surrounded by seven police officers. He was cuffed, pushed into the back of a police wagon, and taken to the roundhouse, the police headquarters at Eighth and Race Streets. The report of the arrest was broadcast on police radio.

"Broad and Cecil B. Moore. Hispanic male arrested as possible murder suspect on steps of subway. Suspect en route to Eighth and Race, police headquarters."

Dispatcher Buddy Lewis heard the report. Buddy reached quickly for his cell and dialed up Danny Caldwell.

"Yo. Mr. Caldwell."

"What's up, Buddy?

"Philly Police Radio reports a murder suspect in the gang killing taken in at Broad and Cecil B. Moore, and headed to the Roundhouse for questioning."

"Great, Buddy. We'll send a crew to headquarters. You did good."

"Yesiree, Mr. Caldwell.

Minutes later, Tony, cuffed and looking disturbed, walked into police headquarters. A waiting Channel Seven cameraman recorded a thirty-second sequence of video. The cameraman zoomed in on Tony's face.

By four o'clock that afternoon, Tony had been released with an apology from the police. There was no cameraman there when he quietly walked out of big round building and into freedom.

In a twist of fate, he had matched the description of a suspect in the gunshot murder of North Philly gang member Ronald Elite. Elite, just seventeen, had been shot in the head as he crossed the intersection of Second and Diamond. On the police radio, the dispatcher sent the word out.

"Wanted for murder. Hispanic male. Age eighteen or nineteen. One hundred seventy-five pounds. Dark brown eyes. Last seen wearing a cherry and gray Temple University sweatshirt."

Tony, reeling from the shock of an arrest based on mistaken identity, was being driven home by Garcia Perez at the same moment Danny Caldwell was writing the opening to the six o'clock News Watch Report. Caldwell was juiced by the story.

"This is classic Hispanic-on-black crime. They are combing every stinking alley in the Diamond Street corridor. I think we got some video of a suspect take-down," he told Channel Seven's news director, Ned Lemond.

Lemond, pumped up by the police radio report, replied, "Yeah, we got video."

"Where is it from?" Caldwell asked.

"I think it's from the Roundhouse."

"Let's look."

In the editing room, the digital video emerged on the screen. The suspect, surrounded by police, looked puzzled.

"They all look screwed up when they get their ass grabbed," Caldwell said. "Cut me about twenty seconds. I want to run it in slow motion, and let's circle the suspect's face, okay?"

At six o'clock, Channel Seven began its newscast with the news from North Philadelphia: "From the Jersey Shore to the Pocono Mountains and all points in between, this is Danny Caldwell, and this is Seven at Six with the News Watch Report."

Caldwell swiveled in his chair. He put his elbows on the desk. He continued. "As we hit air tonight, an area-wide search is on for a suspect in the murder of North Philadelphia gang leader Ronald Elite at Second and Diamond. Elite was murdered with a single shot fired from a building across the street."

The CK, the graphic behind him, read, "SUSPECT NABBED."

Caldwell continued. The director rolled the videotape of police fanning out across the city. The scene shifted from a series of police cars with sirens wailing to the big glass-door entrance to the Police Administration Building. A young, handsome man wearing a Temple sweatshirt was being escorted into the bulding. Caldwell continued.

"Suspects were captured all over the city, including one nabbed emerging from the Broad Street subway line at the Temple campus. Here, in this exclusive Channel Seven video, is the man arriving for questioning at the Roundhouse." The video ran in slow motion. A red circle formed over the man's face.

A horrified Maria Perez, watching at home, knew that her son had been released after questioning. She felt nausea beginning in her abdomen. She started shaking and picked up the phone. She dialed.

At the other end, the voice simply said, "Yes." Then Maria described what happened and the man on the other end of the phone assured Maria that he would level all legal weapons at Channel Seven for having shown Tony's face.

"Don't worry, sweetheart," he told his friend. "I will fry their asses."

Meanwhile, at Channel Five, I was in the studio with Veronica, delivering the news. Keith Byrne was at his desk, watching the TV monitors of all the stations. Most TV newsrooms have a bank of monitors, mostly so staffers can check on the competition, sometimes for them to eye soap operas and other programs during a slow news day.

Byrne's eyes wandered to the Channel Seven report. He gulped. He gulped again, his neck tightening as the hot coffee trickled down his throat. He ran into Barbara Pierce's office.

"They have done it again, those bastards," he said. "They put on video of a suspect. They laid this guy out, and they don't even know if he is charged. I can't fucking believe it."

"There's only one thing worse," Pierce answered. "It could have been us."

The Society of Professional Journalists had been warning for years that the broadcast of anyone's arrest for anything before they are charged is a violation of that individual's rights and a major breach of ethics. Garcia's friend, Peacemaker, knew this. After getting off the phone with Maria, he placed a call to a lawyer at the Federal Communications Commission. Then he instructed an attorney at his firm, Lefler and Lefler LLC, to prepare a statement about Channel Seven's egregious actions.

The next afternoon, Danny Caldwell issued an apology by emailing a written statement to every reporter in the state of Pennsylvania, including Herb Friebow at the *Daily Philly*. He sent it at 4:10 P.M., thirty-three minutes after the body of Anthony Perez was found behind the Temple University Administration building. Anthony, nineteen years old, had been killed by a single bullet fired directly at his heart. Detectives theorized that he had been jumped by two members of Ronald Elite's gang near the subway station, dragged a block away, tied up, and executed.

The killing created a storm of controversy. People condemned the use of the video of Tony, since it had led gang members with murder on their minds to the wrong guy, an innocent and loving person, an adored child and proud son of Philadelphia.

Caldwell apologized to the family and his viewing audience as well. On the eleven o'clock report, the sad man in Garcia Perez's dream looked into the camera and said, "There is no excuse for our mistake. But mistakes happen. I deeply . . ." He paused. He put the script down, reached for a handkerchief, and wiped his eyes. In a second, the anchorman resumed his mea culpa.

"I am so sorry for the pain I caused. Information is dangerous. This will never happen again. But we will not stop bringing you the fastest coverage of events in the tri-state area. Tomorrow at six, Newswatch will bring you an extensive report on the life of Anthony Perez. Thank you."

Danny Caldwell left the set, his head bowed as he walked past the technical crew, having completed the performance of a lifetime. He went directly to the private office of Ned Lemond, the troubled news director of Channel Seven. Lemond stood when

Caldwell entered and closed the door. Caldwell sat down on the couch and pretended to weep.

The real weeping had already started. Tony Perez's funeral was attended by hundreds of Philadelphians, including the mayor. A silent cortege made its way up Interstate 95 to the riverfront cemetery. One hundred police officers, some on motorcycles, escorted Tony to his final destination. Angel Esperanza was close by, sitting in the back seat of the family car with Garcia and Maria.

Esperanza saw the murder of Tony Perez as an act of violence perpetrated by a TV station with no morals and a creepy anchor who cared little about the city or its people. To the Peacemaker, the murder of his godson was inconceivable.

Maria's head was leaning on his shoulder as the hearse turned into the cemetery. She sobbed uncontrollably. Angel fought back his own tears and thought about the plan. He would, with all his power, erase the dark side—including not only molesters, killers, and addicts, but also the people who abused their power without firing a shot.

As the coffin of the child–he would always view Tony as a child–was lowered into the earth, he thought of the crucifixion, the resurrection, and the biblical interpretation of justice.

"Dust to dust, ashes to ashes," the Monsignor said, his voice elevated by the depth of the moment. Angel thought, "Murder for murder. Justice for the child."

After the burial, Angel sat in the hearse with Garcia and Maria as it headed back to Southwest Philadelphia. Climbing up the steps of their row house, he put his arms around the grieving parents. In the living room, family and friends gathered around in a circle, one by one embracing Garcia and Maria.

Garcia pulled his old friend aside. They embraced. Garcia said, "There must be justice."

Peacemaker said, "Don't worry, old partner. Justice will prevail. I promise."

"Muerte," Garcia whispered. "Muerte para Caldwell."

"Muerte, yes. But first we will use him to do our business. And then, only then, Garcia, will there be muerte para Caldwell." Angel kissed Garcia on the cheek. He slowly walked toward the staircase. As the crowd below murmured the soft whispers that follow death, he opened the door to Tony's room, looked around, discarded his jacket. He stared at the walls, the walls that told the story. Tony on the seventh-grade track squad. Tony at his high-school graduation in white cap and gown, his mom beaming proudly, his dad smiling in delight. Tony's Bible, stacked on top of the books scattered around the lamp. These were the pieces of his life. Angel kneeled at the bedside, tears flowing, burying his head in his hands. Shivers–ripples of cold fear–shook his body.

He looked at the picture of Tony, the little guy held gently by his parents on the day of his baptism. He clasped his hands. He said softly, "I will avenge your death, and the deaths of others. We love you, Tony. And as God is my witness, the devils will get their due. God bless you for eternity."

Angel got up slowly. He reached for the handkerchief in his pocket and wiped the tears from his face, preparing to join the mourners assembled in the living room. But first, he reached into the side pocket of his suit jacket, took the cell phone out, and placed a call to Chicago. He needed desperately to share this moment.

* * *

Caldwell arrived in Philadelphia six years after I did. He replaced the mustached Jimmy Bowser. Bowser was a legend at Channel Five. Thirty years he lasted, after arriving from Rochester in 1970. Bowser was great. Danny is good. I won't take this away from him: He is a good anchor. As a person? He is a soulless, sulking man who will do almost anything to get a story first. Lying is a part of his act. Desperation in the business of news-gathering can be hazardous to your health.

Danny and I have no relationship to speak of. I am respectful, but I know that he is, as Barb puts it, "the scum of the earth."

We met for the first time at a fundraiser, soon after he had arrived in town. It was a cocktail party. I don't remember the cause. I never forgot the conversation.

"Hi," he said as his hand reached across to mine.

"Hello," I responded. I shook his hand, and then he refused to release my hand, instead gripping it tighter and tighter.

"Tell me, Mike, do you rent or own your house?"

"We own a small home in Chestnut Hill."

"Too bad," he said. "You should be renting."

"Why?"

His hand was still gripping mine. "Because, buddy, by the time I get through with you and your gang, you'll be headed so fast out of this town that the best shot you'll have might be a TV market the size of Toledo, if you get my drift, Michael."

I got his drift, all right, and I knew I was dealing with a schmuck, pure and simple.

"You need help, Danny," I said. "Maybe a psychiatrist could fix what hurts you." I pulled my hand out of his, turned my back, and walked away.

The day after Tony Perez's funeral, Danny Caldwell was finishing the week with a flourish. A color picture of him that showcased his auburn hair, blue eyes, oval face, and pug nose appeared on the front page of the *Daily Philly*. It was a picture of a man in crisis, looking grim. The headline read in rich red letters, "CALDWELL COPS PLEA FOR PEREZ DEATH. 'I KILLED HIM!'"

Inside the Channel Seven newsroom in the old *Philadelphia Inquirer* building at Broad and Callowhill Streets, the mood was somber. Danny arrived after having spent twenty-four hours under "psychiatric evaluation," as the newspaper reported. Upon arrival, the anchorman walked into his office, which was separated from the main newsroom by a wall. He sat down and dialed the extension of the news director. He waited. He read the papers.

Ned Lemond walked into Danny's office. Danny's head was resting on his arms. When he looked up at Lemond, he also reached for a Kleenex from a box on the desk.

Danny said, "Ned, what the hell is going on? I don't know how much more I can take. Fuck. I am so depressed."

Tears started flowing from his eyes. He blew his nose. Showing the classic sign of depression, he took his hands and gripped them around the sides of his head. That was when Lemond saw a change come over Caldwell's face. Even as the tears nestled on the ridges of his lips, Caldwell's mouth opened and his cheeks widened, revealing his broad teeth. Then Caldwell's anguished face started beaming. Color came into his cheeks. Even as he grabbed another Kleenex to wipe away the tears, Danny Caldwell began laughing hysterically.

"Ned, it's unbelievable. We're just eight days away from the November ratings sweeps. Everybody is watching us now. Are we fucking lucky, or what? We fucked up, but we've hit the jackpot. Everybody will be watching me. Is this great shit, or what?"

Lemond was speechless. In three days, he would be jobless, a victim of the debacle, even though he was but one of its perpetrators. He stared at Caldwell. He said, "Wait a minute. We got a dead kid. We've been disgraced, and all you can think about is the ratings. Do you know how bad this is, Danny?"

"Sure," the anchorman retorted.

"Well, 'fess up, Danny, because we are walking a tightrope over oblivion, and we just fell off."

"No, Ned. You are wrong. *You* just fell off. I'm the goddamned franchise anchor. I will live on, because I'm the best damn TV personality in the East. Do you think anyone knows or cares about Ned Lemond, the man who insisted that we show the video? Ned, the buck stops right at your fucking desk."

"You are sick," Lemond declared.

"Yes, I am. Sick and very rich."

FAST FORWARD—FOUR YEARS LATER

Every October 17th, the Fraternal Order of Police holds a dinner to commemorate Tony Perez's murder. On the fourth anniversary, Diana Hong, making the rounds to introduce herself to people and organizations in the market, spoke at the annual dinner. Diana was greeted warmly by the cops and their families. She adjusted the microphone and began.

"I want to begin this address with a moment of silence for the family of Anthony Perez. He was not just a victim of mistaken identity, of a crime perpetrated by a gang of killers. He was also a victim of reckless journalists who wreak havoc with information. His death was a moment of great disgrace for our business. Not just for Channel Seven, but for all of us. Who knows what catastrophes we could create, with our lack of responsibility. I mourn for the Perez family. I pray for our business and for some of the people in it."

A hush filled the room, followed by polite and lasting applause. Diana left the podium and walked to her seat. She picked up the coffee cup. As she placed it close to her lips, her hand started shaking.

CHAPTER TWELVE: **THE DEEPEST CUTS**

Still at the burn center. God bless Rebecca: She tried to bring in a small radio. But big brother said no. Today I'm receiving pulmonary therapy, since breathing on my own is still a problem. And Keith just walked in with Diana. The woman is radiant. She holds his hand. I whisper, "What happened?" Little tears start erupting at the corners of his eyes. He says grimly, "Mike, they won't let me tell you. But I'll say this: It will never happen again." The shithead on the chair puts his index finger over his lips. It's a message to Keith. Then the guy puts his five fingers under his chin and sweeps them across his throat. That's also a message: Talk and you're dead, baby. Keith has guts. He puts his middle finger across his throat. The shithead grabs Keith by the arm and leads him through the door. Diana follows, but she glances back at me. Her eyes tell me everything will be okay.

FAST FORWARD
MEDICAL EXAMINER'S OFFICE, 1220 RACE STREET, PHILADELPHIA

It is now four months since the slaughter on Cambria. Diana Hong is relentless. She is also baffled. She sits in the office of Medical Examiner John Harvey and looks at the grim pictures on the wall behind his desk. There are photos of bodies, some riddled by bullets, others just lying in repose. Each photo is dated and has a caption. The pictures are a photographic biography of one of the greatest coroners in the nation.

Few cases have challenged Dr. John Harvey like this one. The bodies were autopsied, and the cause of death was fairly simple: gunshot wounds to the head and neck. The motive was a mystery, but the cuts that sliced off the fingers and toes were the work of a talented butcher who researched his challenge and brought along just the right tools. The doctor is desperate for information.

"Diana," he says, "all I have is a guess on the extrication equipment. What do you have?"

"They came here on a freighter out of Venezuela. The government there denies any knowledge of who they are. The vessel sailed before anyone could provide answers. My friends at the U.S. Attorney's office have been working the case round the clock. They've got nothing."

"This is what I know, Diana. You would need a damn surgeon to make the cuts necessary. And I think this killer did his cutting right after shooting them. So he only had a few minutes to get out before the cops came."

Diana is lucky to have such a great contact. She knows it. When you have off-the-record access to the medical examiner and you play by the rules of engagement, chances are good that you will expose the underbelly of a story.

"Diana," John continues, "it's not easy to shoot someone and do the grisly work that this perp did. I mean, can you imagine the speed involved?"

"John, was it more than one?"

"Don't think so. The blood path shows one person moving from body to body. Could be wrong, but it looks that way. This demon, and believe me, this killer is a demon, had this planned well. I think he used extractor forceps for the teeth. And I think he used disposable sterile scalpels, the stainless steel ones used in surgery, maybe number twenty's. Those were deep cuts. No way could you do that with a pocket knife. I've checked with some medical supply houses, but here's the tough part–you can get this surgical crap on the Internet. There are over two thousand websites that sell it, along with eBay. No way to trace eBay sales. So we've got two bodies, four gunshots, and mysterious and very deep cuts."

Diana feels sick to her stomach. She hands the medical examiner the report about the nineteenth-century murder that her coworker uncovered.

"This is good work, sweetie," he says.

"Sweetie? That's not your style."

"Diana, I'm old enough to be your grandfather."

"Okay, Pop. Just make sure you keep me in the loop. And I'll fill you in on anything new."

She was holding something back. Should she say it? Why not? "Hey Pop?"

"Yes?"

"Harvey Hopkins is telling the folks over at Channel Five that, on the videotape, it looks like the first officer on the murder scene, Garcia Perez, was wearing latex gloves. Hopkins says only detectives wear those gloves."

"Garcia Perez? Sweetie, Garcia Perez is the most dedicated cop in this town. I would trust him with my life."

NETWORK HEADQUARTERS, NEW YORK CITY

The search for suspects in what Barb Pierce still thinks is a two-bit murder never enters the world of Bernie O'Malley, who is a jerk in pinstripes. All you need to know about Bernie, titan of industry, darling of Wall Street, self-made mogul of the media, you can learn by how he fired his sales manager.

"Deep cuts?" he said. "I'll tell you about deep cuts. I asked you for 10 percent last year. You gave me five. Now I need deep cuts. So you're done. You're toast, lover girl. Contact Human Resources and get the hell out. Your ass is grass." Bernie was once again displaying his class. This isn't saying much, because Bernie never had much class.

The former whiz kid from Fordham sucked in his breath, loving the passion of his power.

"What do you mean?" Sarah Blaine quizzed, her face looking pale, her lips dry, and her eyes welling with tears. Bernie remained silent.

"What do you mean?" Sarah inquired again, voice quivering.

"You are toast, babe. Get the hell out."

Sarah, national sales manager of the network, had failed to meet her number, the monthly sales figure set by Bernie. Sarah met her number for nine years and eleven months, but this time she missed. In some businesses, you are only as good as your last act. Sarah had come to the curtain-call part of her career.

I'll tell you more about Bernie. He is fifty-seven, and he is fat. I don't like to use that term, but he is really fat, and he is surly. That is my attempt to be kind. He dresses like a slob. And he is difficult to eat with. Bernie is not a fine diner.

He took me once to the 21 Club on Fifty-second Street in the Apple.

"Hungry, Mike?" he asked.

"Sure, I'll have some soup."

With one hand he motioned the waiter to come over. With the other, he picked up the tablespoon, scooped a wad of creamy butter from the serving cup beside the bread, and shoved it into his mouth like it was vanilla ice cream.

What are you going to do? Tell the big boss with the medieval mannerisms to butter his bread instead of eating his butter for lunch? I sat there, queasy and pale. This eating act ruined my lunch.

Bernie also prides himself on being a sexual hyena, never realizing that his only genuine appeal is the size of his wallet. In that regard, size matters to the unlucky few who travel down to the river of ecstasy with my hero.

Bernie O'Malley loves no one woman as much he does the smell of paper, expense forms in particular. He learned at the feet of the ex-CEO who went on to Satellite Radio. But at least that guy had class. Bernie has none, which proves that in American business, you can rise to the top by dumping on people and being rude and crude.

I give him credit. He is good at what he does. His microscopic view of budgets is amazing. He has the authority to approve any purchase above two hundred dollars in the broadcast group. The chief executive officer of New Era Broadcasting and the NEB Network is like a pig in the mud as he sits at his huge, mahogany desk each night, redlining expenses from his executives. Why, he thinks one night, reaching across the desk for another chocolate-chip cookie and opening the next report with his solid gold letter-opener, would Channel Five in Philadelphia need a second security guard, or a goddamn coffee dispenser? When he gets to the monthly expense report from the Philly station, he fumes at the station's purchase of tickets to the Catholic Charities Fundraiser. Bernie is Catholic, but he does not believe in any fundraising but his own.

Bernie is looking over these expense reports with extra care, since he's getting ready for a meeting with Cynthia Cavanaugh, the boss of Channel Five.

When Cavanaugh arrives at his office the next day for the meeting, the assistant offers her coffee. She sits in the waiting area and thinks about Bernie. When members Congress deregulated TV, no restrictions, no guidelines, just a green light for a money tree, surely they hadn't imagined that a guy like Bernie would be in charge. After all, public service to him is when he checks off the box on his 1040 to contribute a dollar to the presidential campaign. O'Malley is both destructive and cheap.

"Good afternoon, Cavanaugh," he says as she steps into his office.

"Hi, Bernie."

"Let's get right to it. First of all, I keep getting expense reports for all that volunteer shit you do."

Cavanaugh replies, "Bernie, this is what we do here in local TV, and–"

O'Malley interrupts. "If you spent less time with that community crap and more time with clients, I'd have a bottom line from Philly. Right now, all I've got in my power is the future of your bottom. Who needs the charities? The hell with community service. I need bucks from your shit-hole station."

Since deregulation, Bernie has expanded his empire to twenty-one TV stations and 350 radio stations. And Bernie has lots of other fish to fry: the underwear business, foreign shipping, and the music business. But broadcasting, his first venture, is still where he enjoys counting the beans the most. Bernie O'Malley doesn't smoke, drink, or do drugs like some of his famous local anchors, but he inhales money like it is cocaine.

Bernie adds, just for emphasis, "You get with it or you might be facing the deepest cut of all."

"What do you mean?

"I mean you."

Cynthia is unprepared for Bernie. She always is. "You can fire my ass any time you want."

"Don't you think I know that?"

She is silent. She looks at Mogul Man. She hates him. But he is her boss. He gets up from the swivel chair, leans on his two hands on his desk, looks at her eyeball to eyeball, and says, "Before I fire you, I need you to break some knees."

Cynthia gets a queasy feeling. "Break some knees" is Bernie's classy expression for layoffs. Sensitivity is not his forté.

"Tell you what, babe. Clip the higher-paid producers. You know the biz is changing."

"Listen, Bernie. We already fired the second security guard. The heart of our newsroom is the old pros. Without them, we're fucked."

"Then you're fucked," Bernie replies. "Go home on the train, and do not go first class. Your T and E expenses are killing me."

"Goodbye, Bernie. We may never meet again."

"That would be good," Bernie answers, an impish grin appearing on his face. He seems to want to tell her that it's not personal—it's all about business. But with Bernie, every moment is about power. Every moment is about fear. The old pros, even before my day, called it mind fucking. Bernie was good at it.

Cynthia Cavanaugh takes the Amtrak train home. She travels regular coach. Watching the grim winter landscape of New Jersey, her face is scrunched into the window. That is the only way she can hide the tears.

CHANNEL FIVE NEWSROOM
NEXT AFTERNOON

I've been watching this game for years. Even number two or number three stations make big bucks in local TV, but the bastards in New York always want more.

By 5 P.M., an hour before air, Cavanaugh has arrived and taken shelter in Barb Pierce's office. The blinds on the windows that face the central office area are closed. The blinds on her office windows are never closed unless one of two things is happening: Someone is getting canned, or we are getting sued. The 6 P.M. program is uneventful that night, with the exception of the information fed to Keith Byrne from his anonymous source at the medical examiner's office.

"This is Keith Byrne at police headquarters. Sources report to Pulse Five News that detectives now believe that professional surgical and dental equipment was used to extract extremities from the bodies of two men found shot to death and maimed last week at Second and Cambria. The investigation continues."

The rest of the broadcast is filled with two-bit crime scenes, the closing of an X-rated video store in a small town, a three-minute report on Britney Spear's latest drug rehab, a traffic report, weather, sports, and only brief mention of Philadelphia Mayor Michael Miller's budget address, which called for a half-percent increase in the wage tax and a cutback in library hours. It is a typical newscast in the middle of the February rating book.

Back in the newsroom, I take off my coat. As usual, I begin my winding-down process. I stare into space. It always works. My deep trance is interrupted by a hand on my back. It's Barb.

"Come into my office," she says.

The blinds are still closed as I slump onto the couch. Cynthia Cavanaugh is sitting in the easy chair in the corner. She begins the conversation.

"Michael–Michael." She can't get the words out.

I say, "What's wrong?" My heart is beating faster.

"Michael, we didn't make our sales number. I have a list and, as a courtesy, I want you to see it. These are the layoffs."

I take the paper she holds out. Eleven people will, as Barb likes to say, "get the bullet" on March 1. Even I am stunned. They are canning Archer McDonald. God, his severance alone has to be a hundred grand. Quinn Michaels, twenty-five years on the writing desk, is a goner. The night assignment manager, Brandon Sylvester, whose wife is expecting twins, is on the list. But the real shocker is Wally Tracker. Wally breaks more stories in a day than most of our lazy non-self-starters have in a lifetime. His last day of work will be March 15. As usual, it comes down to eliminating higher-paid workers, sacrificing talent for people with questionable credentials. That's a nice way of saying that some of the remaining staff is clueless.

I look up at a tearful Cavanaugh. Barb has her head cradled in her hands.

"I guess you know that this is the beginning of the end of news as we know it around here," I say. "I feel shitty."

"So do I," Barb responds. "But what's the worst that can happen?"

I've heard *those* words before.

"I can tell you this," I answer. "These cuts are irresponsible, unfair, unwarranted, and all about leaving the people in the dark."

Cavanaugh doesn't say another word. Instead, she breaks down. Her face grimaces, contorted by her tears. She says nothing, but nothing has to be said. We all know that these deep cuts will hurt, on a personal level and in our professional pursuits.

The phone rings at Tony Avellino's Harvard office. I give him the news. My best buddy is not surprised; he's more concerned than anything.

"The inmates are running the asylum," he says. "It really pisses me off, Mike, because in the end you and that newsroom are left with a bunch of amateurs. Just pray that the big one doesn't happen in the next couple of months. That newsroom of yours is stark naked."

"Stark naked," I repeat.

"Yeah," he says. "It's like a 767 coming down, all the engines are out, and there's no foam on the runway."

CHAPTER THIRTEEN: **CRASHING WITH GIANTS**

I *make the transition again from wakefulness back into my morphine-induced sleep. I dream about the Cambria killings in November. And when I awaken, I remember these words: "a bloodstained map with arrows pointing to Valley Forge." Valley Forge, where Washington spent that fateful winter. Now I know why they have suspicions. Valley Forge is minutes away from the place where I found myself on the pavement, bleeding and halfway to hell.*

REWIND

Shared experiences. Let me tell you: In a newsroom, there's nothing like the time when something so damned big happens that it brings everyone together in a single tent of consciousness. It doesn't happen often. But when it does, we join as one in our joy or grief, desperation or defeat. And the audiences join us, too. Show me a shared experience and I'll show you a night when the audience for local news doubles and sometimes triples. The event could be a blinding snowstorm, a World Series victory, an election, or the tragedy of 9/11.

REWIND
CHANNEL SEVEN NEWSROOM
THREE MONTHS BEFORE THE CAMBRIA KILLINGS

"I've never seen anything like this. Not even close." Ned Lemond watches the computer screen on his desk.

Danny Caldwell, sipping coffee from a brown ceramic mug with his name on it, looks over at the news director, slumps back in the chair across from Lemond's desk, and says, "Life goes on. Just goddamn happy that I've got shit socked away."

The ticker that streams across the bottom of the screen tells a story in short bursts of words, a verbal last will and testament, it seems, to the dreams of millions: *"Dow down 972 points, all-time record loss. Nasdaq down 120. S and P loses 90 points. Panic engulfs Wall Street."*

"Fuck it," Danny says. "Ned, my boy, shit happens. Screw the market. Screw the little people. One person's loss is another schmuck's opportunity. And right now I'm buyin', baby. I'm the buyer who will clean up that mess."

Lemond, who has been with Danny and Channel Seven for five years, has a look of disbelief. Even in the middle of a national catastrophe, Danny the Terrible still pretends not to care. Is his lack of concern a mask to cover the insecurity that spawns his anxiety, which sparks more insecurity?

"Danny, you are a mean bastard."

"Yes, I am. I'm a mean ratings machine, baby, because the market is dropping faster than Channel Five's ratings. When those bastards go down, I perk up. I'm a self-adoring mean mother. And I love every minute of it. At least I'm a hetero, unlike you, Ned. If you weren't so good at killing the competition, I'd be afraid to bend down in front of you."

"You're a shit."

"What's it like being a fag?"

"You're a shit."

"You're full of it."

"At least I'm not full of *shit* like you are, Danny."

Ned smiles. He walks over to Danny and pats him on the back. Ned knows that humoring a demagogue is akin to feeding raw meat to a lion. The more you give, the more brazen the animal gets. Ned puts up with it because he has to. By industry standards, the ratings, Ned Lemond is a success, but in his mind, in his own necessary truth, he remains a huckster, a deceitful fraud. He knows from the Perez disaster that deeper trouble lies down the road as long as Caldwell and people like him help run the news. He just hopes he'll be gone when it happens.

HOME OF MICHAEL MARONE BUCKS COUNTY, PENNSYLVANIA

After thirty-seven years at the anchor desk, I treasure the quiet once I get home for the night. But on the night after Bernie ordered the layoffs, sitting at our small kitchen table with Rebecca, I am despondent.

"Rebecca, this is a mess. We're left with a ragtag bunch of producers. Can you imagine if something happened that required a voice of reason? I mean, this sucks."

"Maybe you're just an old timer who's resisting change," she says. "Like the dinosaurs you met when you were first coming up. They used to tell you the business was going to hell. Maybe these will be the good old days twenty years from now."

"That was 1969, when radio people and professional announcers were the first stars of local TV news. They weren't journalists, Rebecca, just very decent communicators. After that, the anchor-journalist came to local news."

"And you were lucky to be in the freshman class," Rebecca says, smiling.

"Right. And we put a heavy emphasis on getting the story, not just ripping wire stories. Those early, pre-newsmen days featured a lot of tabloid and gossip. Now we are returning to another tabloid era—blood, guts, and easy-to-cover crime. And with some of the big conglomerates, cash trumps credibility. I mean, Bernie doesn't give a damn about news."

"You're right," she says as she passes the vegetables. "It is pathetic."

"Listen, Rebecca. I'm scared. I mean, can you imagine what could happen with Rocket Socks or Julia at the helm? Rocket Socks alone could screw up a two-car funeral. Do you remember the night the verdict was announced in that doctor's trial?"

"Yes, I do. And do you remember the note I left on your pillow?"

"How could I forget?"

ROCKET SOCKS

"Agile. Fit. Ready for action." The caption was accurate, to a point. In *Philadelphia Magazine's* annual singles issue, Annie O'Brien's photograph was on the front page as one of the most eligible women in the community. One question remained: Eligible for what?

Annie was nicknamed Rocket Socks because she is always running after news. Her vigor is intoxicating and so are her reports, but she has one serious problem. She keeps forgetting that in a newscast you are supposed to try to be objective.

On the surface, Rocket Socks has it all: a degree from the University of Pennsylvania, a beautiful face, blue eyes, and dark hair falling over her shoulders. She can talk her way through a story with freezing rain at her feet and bullets flying around her. But the record speaks for itself.

It was July 4, 2006. Annie was sitting in her cubicle in the Channel Five newsroom, one ear on the police scanners at the assignment desk and her eyes on the latest edition of *Glamour*.

"We got some action," said Robby O'Toole, the weekend assignment manager. "Looks like a fireworks accident on the parkway near the art museum."

Annie closed the magazine, threw her paper coffee cup in the trash, and got up from her chair. Photographer Jimmy Manstein, working a rare weekend shift, was waiting at the assignment desk for her.

"Pop go the extremities," Annie screamed out to the newsroom, smiling with joy. She left her reporters' notebook behind, along with her pencil. Annie never lets writing the facts down get in the way of reporting a good story.

That night, she was "live at eleven" from Twenty-first and Ben Franklin Parkway, where an unexploded fireworks shell had landed in the crowd watching the annual July Fourth concert and exploded.

"This is Annie O'Brien," she said, "reporting from the scene of a fireworks accident on the Ben Franklin Parkway. So far, two very unlucky people have suffered minor injuries. Police say they don't know who's responsible."

"Annie, this is Mike. What are city officials saying?"

"Damned if I know, Mike. But they should start talking soon, because these people are frickin' pissed off, if you know what I mean."

"I—uh—know what you mean," I said. "Thanks, Annie."

Annie has another problem. She is a great verbal communicator, but she never bothers to learn about the times she lives in. Once, on her way out the door to a campaign rally, she said, "Mike, how long has George W. Bush been a Democrat?"

To say that she doesn't have a clue is more than an understatement. Every day brings more proof that Annie is an accident waiting to happen. Barbara Pierce, who hired her, is philosophical and honest. After the July Fourth incident, a reflective Pierce told a *Philadelphia Inquirer* reporter, "I would have preferred the hunchback of Notre Dame to the exquisite beauty and mindless imperfection of Rocket Socks."

One of Annie's idiotic moments became a legendary broadcasting joke. Its origin was a news conference that she covered with the D.A. of Philadelphia. The transcript was recovered from Annie's personnel files.

> *District Attorney:* We are still conducting a worldwide search for Einhorn, but until we get him back here, we have decided to try him in absentia.
> *Reporter Annie O'Brien:* Madam D.A., this is Annie O'Brien of Channel Five. I have a question.
> *District Attorney:* Yes, Miss O'Brien?
> *Reporter Annie O'Brien:* Exactly where is absentia?
> *District Attorney:* A few miles north of the city line in Bucks County.

Annie, one of the star "entertainers" on Channel Five, could track it and whack it with the best of the trackers and whackers. But she was, in a word, clueless.

One night Rocket Socks ran smack into a door while atttempting to pursue the news. Since we were standing right by the door, Veronica and I got clobbered by it, enduring more damage than the door did.

But the most notorious event of all so far occurred on February 7, 2005. The scene was the courthouse of Bucks County, Pennsylvania. Gynecologist Dimitrios Theorides was on trial in the suburban county courthouse on charges that he molested at least ten of his patients. The trial was supercharged with emotion. Tens of his clients testified to the generosity of a doctor who would stop at nothing to serve the medical needs of his clientele, adding complexity to the case.

At 10:55 P.M. on that winter evening, the jury had been out for three days. At 10:58, two minutes before Veronica and I would hit the air, Annie notified Assignment Manager Bob Harris and Nighttime Manager Janet Jablonski that the jury had reached a verdict. The show's producer, Kenny Abdul, chimed into our IFB earpieces, "Okay, guys. Got a verdict in the doctor sex trial. Heather, open the show with the headlines and throw to Michael. Michael, toss to Annie at the courthouse. Got it?"

I straightened my tie. Veronica applied some more hair spray to her golden locks. We both looked in hand mirrors, our final pre-show ritual, as if one more glance would make a difference.

Butterflies are something that disappeared a long time ago for me, but I was getting a bit jumpy. This was a major story. We had an exciting reporter at the scene, but both Veronica and I knew she was a loose cannon.

The opening music caused me to tense a bit. On cue, Veronica said, "Good evening, everyone. I'm Veronica Victor along with Michael Marone, and as we go on the air, the news is breaking at the Chester County Courthouse, at the trial of a well-known doctor charged with molesting his patients. Michael?"

"There has been a verdict. News Pulse Reporter Annie O'Brien is live at the courthouse."

Annie appeared on camera, positioned outside the door of Courtroom 278. Behind her, people started streaming out of the courtroom. Annie shouted into the microphone: "Dimitrios Theorides has been found *not* guilty on ten counts of sexual assault. Once again, he's *not* guilty. I repeat, *not* guilty."

Suddenly, Annie's expression changed. Her lips pursed. Her eyes glared at the camera. There is no way that you can stop something like this. Rocket Socks, her voice high-pitched and angry, reported to two hundred and seventy thousand viewers, "Frankly, I can't believe it. This guy is so frickin' guilty. I mean he *is* guilty, and a bunch of losers just found him innocent of fondling all these women."

I interrupted to try and change her direction. "Annie, where is the doctor now?"

"Michael, stand by, he's coming my way."

The doctor walked into the shot. Annie, along with the venerable veteran reporter Vernon Scott from Channel Seven, trailed after him. Kenny screamed into our IFB's, "Get her off. Please, get her off now, dammit!"

Before the director could fade to black, Annie stuck the microphone under the nose of the doctor and said, "Doctor Theorides, you are one free man."

The doctor replied, "I am thankful."

Annie shot back, "Will you ever molest innocent women again?"

He looked puzzled as he walked into a revolving door. The revolving door saved us. She walked in with him, but inside the narrow section of the door the two of them were trapped. The sound died. They were squashed together, acquitted molester and molester of information, visible but soundless, and mercifully, Director Bobby Bernstein cut to black.

When the crew put us onscreen again, Veronica started laughing uncontrollably. Cracking up on the air is a quick-spreading virus. Once you've started, it is hard to stop. I paused briefly and looked down at the next story, determined not to join her. Veronica continued to giggle.

The director focused the shot on me.

"In other news tonight," I said, "two people were killed . . ."

She kept giggling. Her face was now down on the anchor desk, with her hands holding her head. She was laughing so hard that tears were pouring out of her eyes, wetting her makeup. Her face was a portrait in liquid lines.

I said, "In other news tonight, two people were killed when a tractor trailer overturned . . ." I heard a squeal to the left of me. Veronica tried to contain her laughter by cupping her palms over her mouth. This stifling action resulted in a high-pitched squealing noise that was worse than the original belly laughs.

"On I-95 near the Girard Point Bridge." At that point, with a reporter who had lost it on the scene and a coanchor who had lost control of her own emotions on the set, I made one last attempt to save the situation. I looked into her eyes, hoping to convince her to get serious. But after looking in her eyes and watching her smile expand even more, I felt myself ready to break down in laughter. At that point, I decided to make a doomsday decision.

I said, "We'll be back after this."

Fade to black. Bring commercial up. End of segment.

As the commercial began, Victoria, still laughing, walked off the set. She never came back that night. I finished the newscast alone.

Veronica would later tell the newspapers that she'd had a coughing fit and couldn't continue. After that newscast, I never looked directly into her eyes during a serious news story.

That night when I arrived home, Rebecca was half asleep, but a handwritten note lay on my pillow. It said, "Michael. Retire already. And get Annie out of there, along with half the staff. Love, R."

As I drifted off to sleep, I started laughing quietly. It was a relief. I had waited since 11:05 to crack up.

Annie, who nevertheless won the Emmy that year for best breaking-news coverage, was reprimanded by the station and suspended with pay. Later that year, she graciously accepted a trophy as Woman of the Year from the WOAB, Women Organized against Abuse.

MARONE LIVING ROOM

After cleaning up dinner, Rebecca and I are sipping coffee and staring into the fireplace in the living room. I feel good, but I can't get the staff cuts out of my mind.

"You know, Rebecca, even if I did quit, I'd still wonder who was minding the store. I mean, let's face it. Bad information in the wrong hands is dangerous business. I worry about the writers and the producers. Some of them don't even read. But hey, honey, who can be as bad as Julia?"

"Julia Powers? Is she still there?" Rebecca asks.

"Yes. Lowest in pay, all-time leader of screw-ups. She's still there."

WHO IS MALCOLM THE TENTH?

As I've mentioned, newsrooms function with a certain "whistling in the dark" mentality. You tread lightly because, in news, you never know what's around the corner. I should add that you never know *who* is around the corner, waiting to totally screw you up.

Babs Carlito, once a young socialite and now married to the owner of South Philly's best bakery, was producing the Pulse Five Report at Six in fall 2004 when word came that the widow of a famed and controversial leader in the civil-rights struggle was holding a news conference in Washington to endorse John Kerry for president.

Not a big story, but it was certainly interesting. Babs assigned the story to Julia Powers. Julia had sold Barb with a good writing test and a resume featuring her last station, WGOD in Clovis, New Mexico. The fact that Barb always refers to Clovis as the pits is not lost on me. And as Julia's career unfolded in Philadelphia, Managing Editor Archer McDonald was once heard to say about her, "She can't write. She can't talk. But she gives great interview."

Archer McDonald is in his fifties, and he eats news like there's never enough of it. Archer, who never appears at work without a tie, even on the Fourth of July or during storm coverage, is a buttoned-down, hardass news guy who doesn't suffer fools and idiots lightly.

So one day I was sitting at the assignment desk, proofreading six o'clock copy. Archer was sitting across from me. He yelled out to Babs, "Your copy is way behind. Get your people moving."

Babs replied sheepishly, "Okay," knowing full well that Archer was referring to the sloppy work and slow pace of the pride of Clovis.

The time was 4:10. Julia, incompetent but with a pleasant personality, looked over at me, Archer, and Quinn. Her eyebrows were turned inward as lines formed on her forehead.

She asked, "Does anyone know who Malcolm the Tenth was?"

"Malcolm the Tenth," I thought.

"Malcolm the Tenth?" Archer McDonald replied.

Julia retorted, "Yeah, Malcolm the Tenth, some Negro guy who was shot."

Humanely, I answered, "You mean Malcolm . . ."

Before I could finish, Archer turned around in his swivel chair and knotted up his necktie even closer to his bulging Adam's apple. He would tell me later that at all costs he was trying to avoid causing a complaint to Human Resources, but he was a caretaker of the people's right to know.

Staring her down with eyes that expressed his frustration at how the news business was being ruined by these know-nothings who had infiltrated the sacred place of news gathering, Archer said, "I don't know where you are fucking from, but I presume, young lady, that they don't have books, *Negroes,* as you call them, or any plumbing in the fucking schools. Here's an almanac. You can look it up."

Julia's cheeks flushed. She wasn't angry or tearful, just determined. She thumbed through the almanac, found the spot, and looked genuinely enthusiastic. She began to write.

Archer looked over at me and we both shrugged. The time passed and her copy came through the computer. I will say this: Julia knew her roman numerals. The copy read, in part, "The wife of murdered civil-rights activist Malcolm the Tenth has endorsed John Kerry for president."

Hoping to spare her Archer's anger, I looked across the desk and whispered, "Julia. It's Malcolm X, as in X in the alphabet."

"No, Mr. Marone," she replied. "The almanac says Malcolm X, and X is the Roman numeral for ten."

I gave up. We would say it correctly on the air. That's all that counted. I would spare our new writer further shame. But that was a huge mistake, because the woman who gave us Malcolm the Tenth would soon label Bob Dole a "former Democratic leader" and call the Jewish High Holiday Yom Kippur "the festival of lights."

MARONE LIVING ROOM

"You know, Mike, maybe you're too obsessed with all of this," Rebecca says, taking my hand and squeezing it. "I mean, honey, you've done your thing. You are ethical. You'll never allow a disaster to happen."

Rebecca is always so good at calming me down. I lean back into the couch and let out a deep breath. But then I lean forward again, anxious once more.

"But what if I'm not there? The truth is that poorly paid lunatics with no common sense are steering the ship. Tony is right. We are stark naked. Giving incompetent people control over vital information is like leaving a glass of bourbon in the driver's side cup holder." I put my arm around Rebecca and say, "Bad information is not only dangerous. It could be fatal."

"You're such a drama queen sometimes," she replies.

"Honey, I know things are screwed up, but 'it could be fatal'? Isn't that a reach?"

CHAPTER FOURTEEN: "I WANT HER DEAD—I WANT *THEM DEAD*"

*A*t least I'm in rehab now, at the Moss Rehabilitation Center in Philadelphia. A nurse told me that the damaged highways have been fixed and opened. I hadn't known they were closed. Then that nurse was transferred to another floor. I am living in a police state. Even my best friends give me nothing. Tony finally arrives in the room, and he looks pale, which means that I look like shit. I am drugged up again. I say to Tony, "What came down?"

He says, "You, did buddy. From now on you'll be talking to one viewer—you." He laughs.

"Where's Caldwell?"

"I don't know," Tony replies, and he turns around to look out the window. Tony is the kind of guy who has problems lying, especially when he's looking at you.

THE HIDEAWAY

Angel is in his private office. It is now just weeks away. Why the middle of March? Just enough separation, he thinks, from the

Cambria "event," as he likes to call it. March 14. Everything will soon fall into place, but one detail remains, one nagging part of the strategic plan that is causing him to obsess, his apprehension grating on him as the calendar changes every day.

Enough, he thinks, as he reaches for the phone and dials the phone number in Chicago.

"Hi, baby, this is your silly from Philly."

"Oh, my goodness. It's so great to hear your voice. I'm all set for Father's Day again," she says. "You too?"

"Lisette, we can meet any day, any time. I'm always here for you." Angel smiles widely. Her voice always made him smile, but serious business is at hand. "Honey, we have to talk."

"You know I'm coming to Philly on March 14, Angel, whether you like it or not."

"Over my dead body," he replies. "I asked you to stop the overtime. Your life has so far to go."

"Look, Big Daddy," she says. "Have I ever called you Big Daddy before?"

"No," he sighs.

"Tony called me. I know how important this is to you."

"It's very important. I want this to happen, but I plead with you not to come here."

There is a pause.

"I have to come, but I'll make a promise. After this, I will work only my day job. I promise. I will get down on my hands and knees and promise."

He waits a few seconds.

"Are you still there?" she asks.

"The answer is still no!"

"I love you," she says.

"I love you too, Lisette, too much. You're the closest person to a daughter I've had. I want *them* gone, but I want *you* alive."

Another pause. She breaks the silence. "Why did you have Tony call me?"

"Trust," he replies. "But I've changed my mind. If anything should happen . . ."

"I'm a big girl." Her voice gets higher and begins to waver. "And nothing will happen." She is crying. Of all the decisions he has made in his life, he knows that his exploitation of a child's nightmares will be something he will regret for the rest of his life.

"Okay. But if anything goes wrong, get out, and get out fast."

"Thank you, Angel. I promise, after March 14, I will change. I will never do it again."

"Goodbye," he says.

"Love you, Big Daddy."

CHANNEL FIVE NEWSROOM

Veronica is standing at the door of my office.

"Come on in."

"Michael, I have something for you." She hands me a box of chocolates.

"Wow," I respond.

"And something else." She hands me a yellow legal pad with a page full of notes in her handwriting, which I can't read.

"Can you translate?"

"Sure." She takes back the pad. "D.A. Isaacs says victims of Cambria killings likely brought here illegally. One has scars from multiple bullet wounds. Second John Doe has scars from stab wounds. Military service? No. Stab wounds from an Archipa knife, manufactured in Venezuela. Two nights before killing, November 15, freighter *Caracas* docked at Juniata Yards. Owner of *Caracas*, Venezuelan government, will not cooperate. State Department seeking answers. Strange, D.A. says, for a foreign government to send illegals here. Isaacs confirms what commissioner won't: There was a map on the bodies, and on the map was an arrow pointing to Valley Forge."

My heart is pounding fast. I'm amazed at what Veronica has gotten her hands on. "Anything more?"

"Yes. The D.A. says the cops don't know. They are downplaying it, like it means nothing. The D.A. is suspicious. She wants to smoke this out. That's where the mighty five comes in." Veronica always calls the station the mighty five. "We'll break it and help her smoke out the rodent."

"Rodent?"

"She thinks there's a rat there. She's worried, Mike. Really worried."

"Why?"

"Because the first on the scene was Garcia Perez."

"That name is very familiar." I start thinking. Yes. It's him.

"His son was killed by gang members five years ago," Veronica continues, "after Danny showed his face on TV. Remember Danny's fake tears?"

"Yes, but wait a second . . ."

"I know what you're thinking," she says.

"Right," I answer. "That it's not a coincidence that Perez found these bodies." My adrenaline is surging. "That Perez may be the doer, not the finder."

"But what would motivate Perez? What do two men sliced to pieces on a Philadelphia street have to do with Caldwell?" she asked.

"You're right. He couldn't have known these men. But V, why did Isaacs give this to you?"

"She wants to float some of this on air to see if it draws flies."

"But why you?"

"Mike, don't you remember Billy Barron, that weekend anchor from the late '90s? He's the screwball who started stalking me at night, trying to find out what I was doing, who I was seeing. He's the guy who fed Friebow, the *Daily Philly* guy, with so much bullshit gossip about me that even Friebow didn't buy his act. He even tried to steal my mail. Eventually, the whacko got caught. Isaacs was the young prosecutor who convicted him. We became buddies, and she likes and trusts me. This is a great float, and the information is solid gold."

A float is an artful release of source reports to garner reaction. It may produce nothing, but it may provoke the strongest reaction you can ever illicit from a criminal: fear. Fear forces people to move, to react.

"Hey, V. Can't thank you enough. The writers? They have no idea what a newsman you are."

"First of all, wiseass, I'm a news*woman*. And don't ever tell them. Once they know I'm smart, they'll think I'm not beautiful." She winks. At least she can laugh about it now. In this ego-obsessed world of the newsroom, there is so little room for self-deprecating humor.

Veronica breaks the news on the air as a story from "reliable sources." The use of the term "reliable sources" is important; it's code for high-ranking officials. The subject of the blood-stained map has been referenced for months since the killing. Cameraman Jimmy Manstein of Channel Five reported seeing it. The police denied it. Diana Hong confronted the police commissioner, who flatly denied its existence. So Veronica has scored the first confirmation that the bloodstained map is for real. The report is a neat package of mutual motives: Channel Five gets the story, and the D.A. hopes the killers or plotters will be crazed by the fact that someone knows that the map is for real.

At 6:35, Barb holds the postmortem, the nightly review of our hits and misses in the six o'clock broadcast. She has assembled her staff in her office, where her desk is littered with the remains of the day–wrappers from Peanut Chews, napkins from the Dunkin Donuts shop on Market Street, and the big yellow pad with Barb's notes about the show.

"We'll make this short. Annie . . ." She looks at reporter Annie O'Brien. "The piece on the Freedom Award was fucking fantastic.

I mean, Angel Esperanza, kid from the streets, being honored by the movers and shakers. Now that's good shit."

She looks at me. "Michael, pick up the pace. What happened to VO Plenty? I know your face is not the same, but you still have some energy left. Own the pace, will you?"

"Veronica. What makes you so damn sure that the public gives a crap about the Cambria killings and this bloodstained map garbage? Diana Hong has been pushing that for months. Can someone tell me why we care about Cambria?"

Veronica has that crestfallen look. Tears start welling up in her eyes. Sometimes in the "mighty five" newsroom, no good deed goes unpunished. She slowly turns away from the assemblage and walks out of the office, takes a right at the assignment desk, and arrives at her corner office, which is ablaze in glorious color.

Her birthday is always an event in the newsroom, especially at Veronica's desk. Bouquets of roses are stacked on the desk, many of them from admirers she will never meet, others from real friends. She is an object of beauty and desire. Her life is filled with admiration and excitement, or so it would seem. But the glamour of the moment fails to brighten the soul of a beautiful person who would gladly trade in the artificial trappings of celebrity for a single moment of appreciation for her life's work.

For a moment, she sits and stares ahead, wondering why, at the age of thirty-nine, she has not yet become the only lover of her centerpiece, the nerve center of her happiness.

She gets up, closes the door of the office, and returns to the chair behind the desk. She picks up the phone, cradles the handset between her left ear and shoulder, and dials.

"Hello," she says. "This is V. Yes, 11:45. I'll be there. I can't wait to see you." In a sultry, affectionate voice, she says, "I love you."

"Oh, V?"

"Yes?"

"Where did you get that information?"

"About what?"

"About the Cambria killings."

"From Isaacs. Why do you ask, honey?"

"Just wanted to know. See you soon, love."

FBI HEADQUARTERS, PHILADELPHIA

The FBI and the Philadelphia Police Department, with the help of covert CIA agents in Venezuela, have identified the two victims of murder and mutilation. But that isn't enough.

"Barry, these guys were two thugs who did petty violence for the Hugo Chavez secret police," says FBI chief Marzano to Barry Brown, head of his Homeland Security section. "Horatio Santavera came from Caracas. His fellow traveler, Renaldo Gezzaro, was just released from the Caracas prison for some petty thefts. But this still makes me nuts," he says, shaking his head. "We don't know why they came here."

The two men are sitting on opposite sides of a small table adjoining Marzano's desk. Brown looks troubled. "I hear ya. But the map is what makes *me* crazy. Were they looking to pick off a 7-11 in the suburbs, or maybe attack Washington's headquarters at Valley Forge? I mean, two thugs with a history of violence. Who brought them in? My guess is that the killer had something to do with who brought them here and didn't want anybody to know who they were." His line of thinking is interrupted by a knock on the door.

"Come on in," Marzano shouts.

Special Agent Carley Romano walks in. She looks anxious. Romano is a veteran agent who defies the stereotype. She is elegant in her dress, wearing silver earrings, a silver charm bracelet, and a skirt and grey sweater that provides a look at her ample features. The charm bracelet jingles a bit when she holds a piece of paper in the air.

"Chief, I did a background check on Renaldo Gezzaro. The Chavez government recruited him from FARC, the terrorist organization that's been trying to overthrow the Colombian government. The CIA says he had a specialty."

"What was that?" Marzano asks.

"He was an expert in assembling and firing rocket-propelled grenades."

The three agents fall silent. Their instincts have told them all along that the Cambria murders were more than they seemed.

Their next moves must be decisive if they want to have any chance of solving this puzzle. Marzano lays out a plan.

"Carley, head down to Washington tomorrow. First, go to munitions at headquarters. I want to know exactly how far different rocket-propelled grenades can travel." He looks over at Brown. "Barry, talk to DOD about installations they protect around the Valley Forge area. I want to know manpower and their weapons of choice. Those Department of Defense people can be damned difficult, so if you have any problem getting this information, I will take this right to the director.

"And I want bureau silence on this. I don't want to panic city or suburban cops. I just want to know if the nuke plant near Valley Forge was a target. Or *is* a target. And are there backups for these dead guys? And finally, were they a part of a real plan, or just a decoy operation?"

Brown nods. His boss continues. "Also, call every punk in town, even Louie the Lip."

"The Mafia thug?" Brown says, lips curling up in disgust.

"Louie is a ruthless bastard, but believe it or not, he puts his country even before the mob. Louie knows everything. Pinch him hard. You have my permission to bust his balls."

"This ain't Guantanamo, chief." Brown looks at Romano, who rolls her eyes.

"Yeah, but I want information. And if he can't find it, I'll squeeze him till it hurts. Remember, Louie is a paper hanger. No paper, no money."

Brown looks quizzical. "Why would a guy like that do wallpaper?"

"Barry, in South Philly, 'paper hanger' has a different meaning. Louie writes numbers, as in illegal lottery numbers. You tell the paper hanger that if I get no information, we'll stop his operation."

"Isn't that a threat?"

"You bet your damn ass it is."

CHANNEL SEVEN HEADQUARTERS, BROAD STREET

The anchor at Channel Seven sits at a desk on a riser that overlooks the rectangular newsroom. The riser, set against the wall opposite the windows, resembles a small bandstand. It is fitting that the composer of the Channel Seven symphony of news sits above his cast of characters.

The general manager of Channel Seven, Robert Tompkins, has stepped onto the riser. With his hands folded over his chest, he listens to his franchise anchor.

"There is an old saying, Robert," says Danny Caldwell. "Take care of number one. That is simply my philosophy of life. To me it means that I take care of you and you take care of me, because I am number one."

Robert Tompkins does not savor this moment. He is operating the most successful TV station in the east. But although he is the boss, his multimillionaire anchor Danny Caldwell calls the shots. And now Danny wants a raise.

"Danny, your contract is not up for another year. I can't open it. What else can I do for you?"

"I'll tell you what you can do, boss-man: Get me a new car. That's just the beginning. I want veto power over new hires. And I want Bobby Travis out of here tomorrow."

"Wait a minute. Travis is your backup. I can't fire him."

"I say it with clarity, boss. The kid goes or I go. And while we are talking about the roster, how about getting a broad to replace that excuse for a co-anchor? She hates me and it shows. I expect my co-anchors to be respectful and deferential, and Dana is one callous bitch."

"Now Danny," Tompkins begins. "Dana stays. I axe her and she'll sue me and you. There is that little matter, my anchor star, of all those leaks you made to the papers about her boyfriends and her money trouble. Dana Bordaine is a lawsuit waiting to happen. And I tell you, Danny, that she will eat you for lunch in court."

"There is no proof of those leaks. Fuck her," Caldwell replies.

"You already have."

"Tompkins, you bastard, I'll kill you just like I killed all the other bosses. They don't call me the franchise anchor for nothing."

The general manager is unfazed. But he knows that life without Danny is life without ratings, life without revenue. He also knows that the local TV news business has been compromised by managers like him who allow immoral star talent to run the joints. Someday Danny will witness his own day of judgment. But until then, business is business. Until then, Tompkins will have to kiss Caldwell's ass.

Caldwell, who was once described by sportscaster Jim Calvetto as "the most insecure human being on the planet," has been obsessed with what has developed into a major crisis, at least to his damaged and dangerous mind. The co-anchor has been getting much too much attention. She won the coveted Emmy Award for best anchor. Then, much to Danny's disgust, Dana won the Philadelphia Medal for community service. But what really made Caldwell go over the edge was her bold frontal attack three months earlier. In this case, the co-anchor went straight for his most sensitive part–the ego that lingers like a sickness in his demented brain cells. Caldwell would refer to this attack as "the leak."

Dana became Danny's co-anchor in 2006. Dana is thirty-five. Her looks are, as some people would say, to die for. The co-anchor is nearly six feet and curvy in a sensuous way, and her voice is deep and sultry. Dana was born of a mother from Nebraska and a father from the largely Hispanic neighborhood of the South Bronx. She is known in the tabloid newspaper world as the bronze beauty.

In the early days of her tenure, Dana needed a proper briefing on the ways of the Philadelphia region. So instead of doing her own research, she opted for a doubleheader. She decided to sleep with Danny. Hampered all her life by an insatiable need for sex, Dana was hungry for action and information. Danny provided both.

Eventually they stopped sleeping together. And by December 2007, Danny was tired of sharing the anchor duties with Dana, who had been waging a quiet war against him. In late November, a few weeks after the Cambria killings, she'd scored an interview with Officer Garcia Perez. Perez said little, but the "get" was disturbing to Danny Caldwell, whose history with Perez was always a sore point.

Also disturbing was the news war raging between them. Retaliating for leaks about her dating life, Dana made a series of phone calls to gossip reporters, including the feared Herb Friebow at the *Daily Philly*. The last one was "the leak." It resulted in the following column on December 1, 2007.

ANCHOR KING DEMANDS A THRONE

by Herb Friebow

Here in Tattle, we have learned that Channel Seven Franchise Anchor Danny Caldwell has demanded a new clause in his contract requiring that he sit at least "three inches taller" than any other person on set. Our sources report that Caldwell is deeply upset by appearing to be dwarfed by his co-anchor, Dana Bordaine. We've always said that Captain Ego would go to any heights to declare his absolute superiority over all other broadcasters.

Caldwell was furious. There was no such clause in his contract. The evening after the item appeared, he confronted the co-anchor as she arrived for work.

"Why the hell did you feed Herb that shit?"

"Because, my dear, I think you deserve it. You do everything possible to hurt me. Consider it a small volley in a bigger plan, Danny Boy–to get you where it hurts, that inflated ego that makes you such a dangerous bastard. I have more up my sleeve, Danny Boy, so don't fuck with me."

"You are sick, Dana."

"But it feels so good."

The anchor was stunned at her honesty. She was screwing with his mind. But one deviant knows how to screw another. In a matter of minutes, Danny had traveled to the bathroom, where he combed his hair and prepped for a special moment.

"What do you want, Danny?" General Manager Tompkins said as the anchor arrived, without notice, and sat down in the leather armchair facing Tompkins's desk.

"You now have the power to get rid of Dana Bordaine." Danny stretched out his hands and cracked his knuckles.

"Why?"

"Because the bitch just admitted that she leaked that crap about the height clause to Friebow."

"That is serious shit. Anybody who leaks an item without proper authorization is violating the moral turpitude clause of a contract. Proving it is damn near impossible, but she admitted it? I'm calling legal right now."

"Thanks, Robert." Caldwell turned around and exited the office. He would go home sick. He didn't want to be there when Human Resources confronted Dana. He believed that she would be out soon. That's all that counted. On the way home, Danny thought how flying solo was his strongest suit. The bronze beauty would soon be gone. He would be alone for a while, no competition for attention.

But Tompkins didn't do the deed after all. Despite the confession of the leak, Dana is still Danny's co-anchor, and he is still trying to get Tompkins to fire her. Danny is desperate, and desperation in the land of ego can lead to erratic behavior.

THE HIDEAWAY

Esperanza sits in his private office and thinks about his problem. He loves the health commissioner and loves Veronica, and soon, he knows, the triangle of passion will lead to a personal and perhaps public disaster. Veronica knows about Darianna, but Darianna is an innocent in this, unaware that he has fallen in love with Mike Marone's sidekick. More unpredictable than his big plan, and deeper than his absolute need for power, this problem is like a stick of dynamite with the timer fuse about to run out.

What an irony, he thinks. The new woman in his life is at the heart of the business he wants to destroy. And for the first time in his organized, methodical existence, Peacemaker doesn't know what to do.

As he ponders his dilemma, a phone call comes. He answers on the second ring.

"Hello, this is Angel."

"Angel, this is Danny Caldwell. What's hangin', man?"

"Just the ordinary challenges of leadership and community service, Danny."

"Angel, I need a favor, a big one."

"What's it about, anchorman?"

"Well." Caldwell pauses. The normally composed Caldwell sounds halting, tentative in his speech pattern. "I have a problem named Dana Bordaine."

"What's the problem, Danny Boy?"

"Well, she does everything she can to make me crazy. She's a nasty bitch. Wins all the awards, brags about it, leaks stories to newspapers. I, I have to tell you that I think about this broad every day. I think of putting stuff in her coffee that would make her puke. I think of slicing and dicing her and feeding the pieces to the poor street dogs of Philadelphia. I hate her. I fucking hate her. She leaks like a ruptured, shit-filled toilet."

"And you don't leak, Danny Boy?"

"Well, sometimes. But this is different. This broad wants to destroy me. She's the only living thing in my way of total control. Yeah, I'm number one, but I want it to stay that way. I need a young beauty with no ambition, just a great face and a great body, to sit there and look and sound deferential, and make me look bigger than life, which, Angel, I am. I can't take this any more. I'm obsessed with Dana, if you know what I mean."

"Are you in love with her?"

"No, Angel. I just want her out of here, and management won't move on it. I hate it. They surrender all power to talent."

"Like you, Danny."

"Yeah, but I put out, man. Without me, there are no ratings. I'm the king."

"Isn't that enough? Does the king have to be alone on the throne?"

"Yes, I need it all."

"What is *all*, Danny?"

"All is no one around to try and challenge me. All is being the only number one. I don't even need a fucking co-anchor. I want her out."

"What do you want me to do? Do you want pictures, like porn photos? I don't think Dana is into that. Do you want me to get Friebow to plant some shit? I mean, what can I do?"

"Angel, it is simpler than that." The anchor's voice grows guttural as his throat clogs up with stress, creating the blockage of the vocal cords that makes a person sound forced. His voice, usually calm and soothing, has gotten higher and higher, conveying his desperation.

"What do you want from me, Danny Boy?"

"Isn't there a bus, a car, a motorcycle that can accidentally find her on the street, or maybe a rape and strangulation, or even a stray bullet? Angel, I want her dead."

Esperanza laughs into the phone. "Danny, you need a shrink. What the hell are you talking about? Do you think I have the power to kill?"

"Yes." Caldwell is emphatic. "Yes, Angel. I know all about you. You're just like me, you sonofabitch. You are a cold-blooded exterminator. And I want you to make Dana Bordaine disappear."

"Danny, you are mad. And if I could, what would you pay me with?"

"Words, baby. There is nothing more powerful than words. Nothing."

Angel has to admit it; Danny's got a point. "Danny, you are crazy. But soon we might have a barter arrangement. I might need payment very soon. And if you don't pay, you don't play."

"Thank you, Angel. What's it all about? When will it happen?"

"If it happens, it will happen when God says it happens."

"Angel, you really believe there is a God?"

"Yes, Danny. Yes. In fact, right now I'm staring at him in the mirror. And he says that the second week of March will really define your career, Danny. Don't take off on March 14. March 14, Danny, is a Friday. Be ready, News Stud. You're about to take a wild ride."

LE PALM CAFÉ, SOUTH STREET

Lou Potenza, aka Louie the Lip, is fastidious. He waits in a back booth of the café, his Coach briefcase by his side. Louie is wearing a dark, pinstriped suit with a blue shirt and a slick Brioni tie.

FBI operative Barry Brown walks in and sits down across from Louie. "Nice tie," he says.

"Saw it on the Sopranos."

"Good taste." Brown gets right to the point. "Louie, I've been instructed at the highest level to tell you that your writing career in South Philadelphia will end if you don't deliver information on why the two departed characters from the freighter Caracas were brought to America. I want to make it clear that, if your information is bad, there will be legal consequences."

"Hold on, man. Hold on. I will not be threatened, especially when I don't know every goddamned fact of life. I know a lot, but not everything. Kapeesh?"

"What *do* you know?"

"They came here from Caracas to do some dirty work. Maybe a few robberies. They screwed up. But we don't know who took 'em down. That's it. What do *you* know?"

"What I know is none of your fucking business. Who brought them here?"

"Beats me," Louie said. "Good luck, lawman. You'se happy now?"

Brown got up and left, thinking that at least Louie hadn't concocted some weird story. He presumed that Louie really didn't know a lot. He was correct.

Five minutes passes before Louie dialed Peacemaker's cell phone. "Hi, boss. Feds are poking around about the Cambria guys. Isn't it time you tell Bobby and me what's goin' on?"

CHAPTER FIFTEEN: "YIKES, I'M IN DEEP SHIT"

They say I could be getting ready to head home on Rebecca's birthday, which she tells me is in three days. We'll see. Right now I might as well be in Siberia, I am so cut off. A newsman without information is like a man without food. Everyone says, "I'm so sorry, Mr. Marone." Sorry for what? Sorry for me? I'm sorry for the people on the highway. Sorry for Philadelphia.

I overhear an orderly saying the president is in town. Why would POTUS be in the area? Was the accident that big? And do they have a clue about what caused it?

COLLEGEVILLE, PENNSYLVANIA
MARCH 12, 2008

The dispatcher is in heat. The yard sale at their house that day was a success. They sold a lot of their possessions, since they won't be needing them any more. Now Buddy sits in the hot tub on the small wooden deck with Judy, pondering his Bud Light and getting all turned on by dreams of green.

It is 26 degrees, but Buddy is just warming up to his girlfriend. "Baby, in a few weeks we'll be sitting pretty. No more dollar stores for us, baby."

"Oh, sweetie," she replies. "I am damn happy. This hot water is frickin' paradise, honey. Frickin' paradise."

"Yes siree, mama. We are pure gold. The cash will be in my hands by tomorrow. Then it's off to Caracas with all that green."

"Honey, rub my frickin' back. Then move down lower."

"Yes siree, mama."

"Got a call yesterday from Keith Byrne," Buddy boasts.

"What a hunk. Just thinking about that guy makes me hot," she whispers in his ear. She kisses him, her tongue slipping into his mouth. As they pick up the pace of their lovemaking, Buddy becomes distracted. He pulls away.

"Let me tell how I got my instructions," he says. Buddy rarely goes to Philadelphia, but three days ago he met Garcia Perez at the Red Crow Tavern on Sansom Street.

"Hey, Buddy," Perez said, wrapping his arms around the big man. "Are you happy, man?"

"I'm okay. Yes siree, sir."

"Buddy, if you could go to a fucking sundrenched country and live like Donald Trump for the rest of your life with Judy, would you do it, man? Would you do it? Just the sun and Judy and the food and the beach and all that good shit?"

"Yes siree, sir."

"Let me tell you about the job."

Ninety minutes later, after five Bud Lights, the dispatcher headed to the commuter train that would land him in Lansdale. For the whole forty-five-minute ride, Buddy daydreamed about sun, sand, Judy, a plane ride, and four hundred thousand dollars in cash.

He memorized the instructions. And he asked not what the outcome would be.

Once he got home, Buddy had to plan quickly. First, in three days, he and Judy would hold the yard sale: That would be on

March 12. Then they would pack up their duffel bags and send their landlord enough cash to cover till the end of their lease. On March 14, Buddy would make one phone call. He would wait for the others to come pouring in, and he would answer them. Then he would get out. Yes, siree.

SUNSET

Peacemaker is pacing at the Hideaway. He is nervous. It is Wednesday, two days away from Friday, March 14, the big day. Where is Perez? Eight feet forward. He turns around. Eight feet back. Unaccustomed to nerves, Angel Esperanza is nervous. He hears the door open to the outer foyer of the office.

The windows are panoramic. He can see the last remnants of the sun peek in over the dramatic peaks and pillars of the Philadelphia Museum of Art. The bright yellow rays signal the longer days ahead. He turns away from the view and walks to the foyer.

There is no receptionist out front. Garcia Perez sits in the leather armchair, relaxed.

"Buddy is ready," he assures Peacemaker. Peacemaker sits down in the receptionist's chair. There are no notes. No records. The only memories of this conversation will be lodged in their brains.

"Commandante," he begins.

Perez has never understood why Angel calls him commandante, but it sounds good.

"Here is the plan for March 14," continues the boss. "Yuri Zopaloff will be in the basement of Moscovia Lounge at the Red Lion. He will be there from 2 to 4 P.M., collecting receipts."

Perez listens intently.

"Barbara Faisonette. She will be in the rear office of the Feldstein Recreation Center. Two-thirty P.M., Haldeman and Bustleton." He pauses. "The bastardo, Luis Vallarta. He will be meeting with his staff at the new beer joint, Second and Girard. Hours will be 1 to 3 P.M. And Richie. That sucker will be in the whorehouse at Nineteenth and Packer. He gets laid at 2:45 P.M. Never misses. This is how the bloodthirsty killers of kids will go down. They killed my mother. They infect the innocent. They are the masters of the drug trade. There will be more after them, and Garcia, one by one, we will find them and kill them. Do you approve?"

"I got it. I got it, Angel."

"One more thing."

"What?"

"Deliver the cash to Buddy at 10 A.M. tomorrow. We'll get it to him in advance so he owes us something. The visas will be in the same envelope. Tell Buddy to get out quickly and head for the Marple Middle School. The chopper will be waiting on the second soccer field. JFK is just forty-five minutes away." He hands over the envelope.

"What about Caldwell?"

"Wait for my call."

"Why?"

"Just wait for the damn call."

"Muerte?"

"Muerte," Peacemaker responds. "And one more thing."

"What's that?"

"Back up the woman!"

"Who do you want there?"

"You, my man. Nothing can happen to the Chicago woman."

The two embrace. The meeting is over.

CHANNEL FIVE NEWSROOM

Harvey Hopkins just delivered his story on the contract for the new convention center. He unknots his tie as he walks back to his desk. He is tired. Drugs will make you tired.

The backup anchor looks over at me and V. "Good job, Mike. Good job, Veronica. Be at peace, kids."

Hopkins opens the drawer in his desk with his key and puts his earpiece and hairbrush away. The fingers of his right hand slide between two file folders. He is looking for the tobacco pouch with the cocaine. His fingers move up and down. Nothing. He makes the rare move of taking the folders and placing them on the desk as his pulse rate elevates and the adrenaline surge makes him emotionally paralyzed. His career flashes before him. He knows that someone has the coke. How the hell could it have happened? The second security guard's layoff meant that someone could get in here, he thinks. He whispers to himself, "Damn it. Yikes. I'm in deep shit."

He needs to get his mind on something else. He reaches into the drawer and gathers a stack of black and white photos that he will begin to autograph for admiring fans. Harvey has his problems. But viewers have a deep affection for his down-home style and his interminable clichés. He reaches people, makes them feel good. If only they knew, he often thinks. Despite his excesses of drugs and sex, Harvey escapes the narcissistic trance that envelops him in order to feel real guilt. But the guilt soon evaporates as the drugs and booze hide his truth.

Harvey signs glossy after glossy. He stares at the wall. He notices the message light on the phone. He dials up to get the message.

"Hopkins, this is your caretaker. We have the cocaine. We have your prints on your little black pouch. Listen. Listen carefully. And don't even think about fucking with this. On Friday, March 14, at approximately 2:30 P.M., your phone will ring. Pick it up. Don't say a word. Just listen and write down what you hear. When the phone clicks, you drunken drug-infested bastard, this is what you will do. Go to the assignment desk and tell them what you have learned. Be emotional. Be loud. Then suggest that someone call this number.

Buddy will answer. He will give confirmation. Marone will be at a special appearance. Once the information is confirmed, you will go on TV and with a great sense of urgency warn the people of the tristate area. You will do this with great gusto, man. The shit will just happen. Erase this message. Listen, fucker. If you tell anyone about this, the pouch and your fat fingerprints will be sent to the feds. If you talk about the tip, two things will happen. The pouch will go to Drug Enforcement, along with the name of your supply guy. Second, and don't for a minute think I'm bluffing you bastard, you will be tortured and murdered in such a way that there will no trace of you, not even dust. Do I make myself clear, Captain Druggie? Don't fuck with us. Understand." A click on the phone.

Hopkins feels dead. The breath is not being sucked out of him, but he is unable to move. He picks up the phone and dials Ann Marie Hartz. "Hi," she says.

"Hello there, cupcake."

"What's up, double H?"

"You got stuff?"

"Sure. Good stuff."

"Great. I'll be over. I'm callin' in sick tomorrow. Can I stay till Friday?"

"You can stay forever."

Hopkins feels cold. He looks down. Liquid is seeping through the crotch of his trousers.

Awkwardly, he hangs up the phone and stands up. He puts his overcoat on and walks toward the elevator bank. He feels terror. He feels moist and sticky. A foul odor emerges from his trousers. And only one thought comes to his mind: "Thank God I'm wearing black."

MIDNIGHT

Diana walks the dog alongside the Logan Circle Fountain. The water is illuminated by sparkling lights. The scene is quite European looking, as is much of Philadelphia. The wind blows from the west. Diana slowly walks to the apartment house. She glances down the parkway toward the museum and feels the chill of late winter. She is breathless once again. She has often been breathless these past six weeks, since him.

"Hello and goodbye," she says to Keith as she unlocks the door to her apartment and finds him there.

"Hello," he says. "Your cheeks are all red."

"Hello and goodbye. I've got a long day tomorrow."

"Tomorrow can wait." He walks closer. His face is inches away. He raises his hands and gently holds the base of her neck. It is the same daring and sensual move that he made on the first date, that beautiful love language. Very gently, he tips her head forward, and his lips touch hers. He backs off. And he moves his lips over hers again. This time she thrusts her mouth into his. Her arms embrace him. They are joined at the lips. There is no sense of time passing, only the oneness of two.

Letting go, he looks at her. Beyond the skin and the eyes and the hair and the mouth is that other beauty, the inner joy of a good human being. The combination of the outer and the inner confounds him. He knows the truth: There will never be another love like this.

Keith lets his arms fall away. She holds his hand and they walk to the picture window.

"It's so beautiful outside," she says as her eyes glisten and stare into the night sky.

"Like you," he says.

It is a beautiful night. A beautiful city for a couple deep in the glow of love. Beneath them, westward, in the direction of the river that glow silver from the moon and toward the ridges of the suburban hills, a storm is brewing.

CHAPTER SIXTEEN: **IT STARTED OUT LIKE ANY NORMAL FRIDAY**

APRIL 2008
RESIDENCE OF MICHAEL MARONE

At least I'm home. But the Feds keep interviewing me again and again. And Congress is all over this. Most of the time Congress is brain dead, but now they've got a chance to bleed us. Did I see it coming? That's what they'll ask when I testify next month.

They keep pressing me. D.A. Isaacs came to visit. She said, "C'mon, Mike, what happened?" All I can say is, "It started out like any normal Friday."

FRIDAY, MARCH 14, 2008
MORNING
STUDIO B, CHANNEL FIVE

Marty McCann, the weatherman, is smiling. His grin stretches from ear to ear as he waits for the red light to illuminate above the camera. McCann is Channel Five's morning weather guy. He has been since almost the beginning of TV. Dressed in a green sport coat with a brighter green tie and his trademark dark glasses, McCann is in a state of glorious anxiety. Snow may be on the way, and he tells Barb Pierce that he is happier than a pig in shit.

Now McCann is broadcasting a weather update.

"Hey, folks, it may be March, but we're in for a blast of white. First snow arrives in town around 2:15 P.M. And by the time it's over, folks, we *will* have one to three. You might want to leave work early, very early."

Marty puts his pointer down. The doors of the studio open. Barb Pierce walks over and offers her arm in a rare hug. Marty embraces her.

"To what do I owe this honor?"

"Marty, you scared the shit out of them. I love it. This, my handsome weather nerd, is how we put food on our tables."

CHANNEL NINE

Over at Channel Nine, it's a different story. "Hi, this is Cathy O'Brien," says their weather woman. "And I've got the weather update. A storm is forming along the Gulf Coast, and I expect it to barrel up the eastern seaboard by early afternoon. Snow? The amount will be determined by the exact track of the storm. Track one brings the storm close enough to give us 2 to 4 inches. Track two would put the storm far enough east to keep the heaviest precipitation offshore. So the story is, be cautious, but this could amount to zero trouble."

Cathy O'Brien's forecast covers all the options. She says nothing about the need for an early exit from work. Unfortunately, more people will pay attention to McCann.

PASSYUNK AVENUE, PHILADELPHIA

Lisette is in the cab, her eyes perusing the high-rise skyline of Philadelphia. This is her first job in Philadelphia–her first job since her takeout assignment in Detroit. Detroit was preceded by the nighttime attack on the predator in Indianapolis. On this Friday morning, Lisette is edgy. She has promised that this will be her final overtime. She will savor it. And perhaps she'll find other outlets for her rage when she returns to Chicago.

When she walks into the Bistro on Passyunk Avenue, the menagerie of desperate characters faces her with curiosity. Louie the Lip opens the door. He says nothing but leads her to a back room. Inside, the two temps are seated in folding chairs, sipping coffee, looking around curiously and trying to relax. They are tense. The guy from Providence is sweating, and his tongue runs over his lips to catch the saliva dripping to his chin. Providence man thinks that Lisette appears to be a bad fit. She is blonde, and that will stick out, he thinks, but then again, he feels that it may help with Bastardo, who will have one last boner. The other two are regulars, Bobby Alvinato's brother Nick and Nick's driver, Little Stevie Palazo. Stevie is having a miserable morning. His front tooth is abscessed. His deep pain accompanies the usual nerves.

Bobby has been briefed by the boss on the suburban plan of attack. He will not share it with his cohorts. Best to keep them focused on their jobs.

Each team member is equipped with a semiautomatic pistol. There is a steak knife in each briefcase. A spare cell phone lies in a pouch inside. The mini-bombs filled with C-4 are distributed. And each person has a laminated card listing emergency phone numbers.

Alvinato knows the score. This will be a day the founding fathers would have cherished: freedom to all to ply their trade without the obstruction of the animals. Bobby is true to the cause of common criminality. It is, after all, a tax-free enterprise.

Bobby speaks, his throat hoarse from the morning smokes and the cold. "Providence man, you okay? No room for fucking error here. You miss, you go home in an urn. Got it?"

"No problem," Providence man replies. "I never miss. But I got one question. You sure the cops are gonna be elsewhere? Because I ain't killin' no cops."

"I'm sure," says Alvinato. "Lisette," he says, turning to her. "Bastardo is big. Fire fast. Use the knife straight at his zipper. I want to leave a message."

She answers, "I'll cut fast."

"And," he replies, "run fast." She nods.

"Brother Nick," Bobby says, "the rec center will seem empty, but Faisonette will be in the basement. Faisonette may look innocent, but she's one dangerous chick. Take her down before she has a chance to get you back."

"Okay, Bobby. I'm ready."

Bobby looks at Stevie. "Stevie, you gonna make it with that tooth of yours?"

"Sure, Bobby."

"Just remember, the whorehouse will be empty except for Richie. He owns it. He opens it. He gets laid mid-afternoon, and then 4 to 5 P.M. is his private time. But if you have to, do it whenever you can. Trust your instincts, man."

"Okay, Bobby."

Sitting and watching from the corner of the bistro is the cop.

"Garcia," Alvinato says. "You will move after midnight." He hands the cop a sheet of paper. "This is the disposal location."

Garcia listens. For now, he will return home to be with his beloved Maria. By mid-afternoon, he will be trailing the Chicago woman. His official street shift will end at 11:15. Then he will *really* go to work.

CHANNEL FIVE NEWSROOM

The scent of coffee always brings comfort on a chilly morning. The jelly donuts are waiting at the center of the conference-room desk. The picture windows look out to a deep shade of gray.

"But who gives a shit?" Reporter Wally Tracker insists. "I mean, in March the stuff melts, just like you do, Marty, when the forecast is wrong, which at last report was what–40 percent of the time?"

"You are incredible, Wally," the weather man replies. "Talk about batting averages. When was the last time you broke a major crime story? You have a nerve, you bastard. Even Hopkins gets more stuff than you."

"True," says Tracker. "But he also gets more ass than a toilet seat. And he drinks vodka like it's water. So don't put the resident druggie on a pedestal!"

"Are you infantile assholes finished?" asks Barb Pierce.

"Yeah," they reply in unison. Barb sits down in the big chair.

"Okay," Barb says. "Go wipe yourselves. Enough of the fear and loathing. What's up today?"

Bob Harris looks down at his pad. "City Hall, 10 A.M., mayor's budget advisory. Look for cuts in the restaurant tax."

"That's enough to put you to sleep. Next."

"Kenny Gilroy, decorated Marine from Iraq, rings the Liberty Bell to honor soldiers."

"Shoot it," Barbara says. "Any good visuals?"

"Not really, unless you consider that he's a double amputee," Bob responds with a wise-guy face.

"You're a prick," Barbara replies.

Bob says, "Gay pride parade. Know you'll love that, Barb."

"Don't play with me, Bob. I'm working at WPMS today, if you know what I mean, you sackful of shit."

Rocket Socks arrives late. She yawns as she takes a seat. "Got a story," she says.

"That's a development," Barb answers.

"There's a guy in King of Prussia Mall. His name is Joseph Bennett. Runs a magazine stand. After work every day, he rounds up stray animals and brings them to shelters. They call him Animal Bob."

"Okay, Annie. Do it. So that's vets and pets. We still need tits and tots. Always told you, the secret to success is tits, tots, pets, and vets. Content is king, like I say."

Bob Harris blurts out, "You don't think a cut in the restaurant tax is big news?"

"Like I say." She ignores him. "Let's find some real news. Send Wally Tracker over to the D.A.'s office to see if there's anything new on the Cambria killings. One of my worst calls, to ignore that story. Even I screw up sometimes. It's been four months already. Also, how the hell did Harvey get that story on the law firm? This is the second law-firm scandal in a couple of months."

"He says he has sources," exclaims Babs, the managing editor.

"And Bob?" Barb continues.

"Yes?"

"Ask Harvey why he's wearing dark glasses."

"And what about the weatherman?" asks Harris, the assignment manager.

Barb looks at Marty. "He doesn't count. He's an idiot. But Marty will remain on, just his case his damned forecast is actually correct."

Marty looks down at his hands, offended.

"Roll call," Barb says. She glances at the assistant news director. "Susan, anybody sick?"

"No," Susan Orlinksy says. "But Mike Marone called to say he'll be in late. He's got a lunchtime speaking appearance in Pottstown. He'll head back after the speech to make the six o'clock broadcast."

"Make damn sure that he gets back on the road early. We got the snow, and who the hell knows what will happen after that?"

LOGAN HOUSE

"Rise and shine, beautiful."

Back from a morning run, Keith holds out a cup of coffee to Diana, who emerges from the pink covers of the bed. When she turns over, she sees his eyes first. Their eyes lock in an embrace of love.

"I honestly think that I can't be without you," she tells him.

"That is a not a problem, beautiful, because I feel the same way. There is one difference, though. I don't think I could *live* without you. If you ever decide to walk away, I would probably disappear."

"Sometimes you're so silly. We will be together until the end of time." She stands up, kisses him softly on the neck, and races to the bathroom to get to the shower first.

COLLEGEVILLE, PENNSYLVANIA

"Yes siree, babe. We're all packed. Your stuff and my stuff, all loaded in the trunk of your car."

Judy is pumped with anticipation. "So I drive to the chopper site and just wait."

"Yes siree, my little pussycat. Just wait for Daddy. By tomorrow morning, we'll be at the destination." Buddy reaches over to stroke her cheek. "Don't forget, sweetie," he continues. "Make sure you hold on to your passport. And don't make any calls today. None, okay? Also, shred all the bills and any phone records. They can still find it online, but the cop friend says no paper trail."

"Okay, baby. I'll get there nice and early, before the shit happens."

He pecks her on the cheek. "I'm going to the dispatch center. I've got the money in my pocket. The Venezuelans love greenbacks. See you soon."

The dispatcher walks out the front door. He turns around to take one final glance at their home. He feels a bit sad, but the adrenaline is flowing and the blood is surging toward his groin. And to think, this will all happen on his forty-second birthday.

THE HIDEAWAY

Angel has spent a rare weekday night with V at the Hideaway.

"What a gorgeous day." Veronica sips her coffee nervously. She is about to confront him. Without him, she has no real life, just a series of accomplishments followed by loneliness. Veronica senses that Angel is a bit nervous, too. "Angel, are you okay?"

"Sure, just a full plate today."

"Is there anything I can do?"

"No, just tell me that you will always be there."

Here is her opening. She takes a deep breath and begins. "Angel, that's hard. I can't commit my love to a man who is involved with two women at once. Why is Darianna still in the picture? And why is our love hidden in the dark?"

He pauses. The man of power and decisiveness is suddenly paralyzed. What he says next, he knows, will forever affect the life they have.

"Veronica, Darianna is an old friend. We go way back. It is a different relationship. We are bound by respect and time. If I walked away, it would devastate her."

"If you don't walk away, it will devastate *me.*"

He looks at her, clearly troubled. The secrets of his life are about to collide in a storm of emotion on the same day. "You don't know the real me," he says.

"I know enough. I know that you are ruthless and cunning and that secrets fill your life, but I'm willing to accept that. Why? Because no one has ever loved me like you do. Whatever, whoever you are, there is one thing I know—that your respect for me is the deepest that anyone has ever felt for me. You respect my feelings, my shortcomings, and my success."

"I do," he says. "I do, and tomorrow I will begin the process of disconnecting my life from Darianna. It will take time. Today will be a very busy day."

She moves closer. She wraps her arms around him tightly and cradles his head on her shoulder. They sit in silence for a few minutes.

"I'm going in early today," she says quietly. "Mike has a lunch in Pottstown. Harvey will cover till three, and then I'll stand by in case anything big happens."

"Good," Angel says. "The station is a good place for you to be today." And then he tells her what will happen, and how to react, and to make sure that she stays inside the station. "Do not leave the building. And please Veronica, use this to show that not all newspeople are demented."

They embrace. Now she understands the depths of his involvement in the mystery of the last several months. The bodies. The cover-up. The plan of attack. Soon, she realizes, a cluster bomb will be dropped on her business. She will remain calm and allow the unfolding events to help shape her future. But she is nervous and afraid, for all the people but mostly for Angel.

DILWORTH ARMS APARTMENTS

Harvey Hopkins needed the days off. The missing cocaine and the phone call with the instructions have shattered him. But he does remember where he left the stash in Ann Marie's apartment, and she's been there to share it with him, since she works weekends and is off on Thursdays and Fridays.

So their Thursday rendezvous was a nonstop menu of cocaine, sex, and cigarettes. By Friday morning, the weather woman pleads for a rest.

"Harv, I am beat. I can't move."

"Yikes, little girl, this big man just can't get enough. Got a big day today, big phone call coming in, and I have to be relaxed. You are just one little honey. Yikes, I think I might even love you."

Ann Marie, sitting on the edge of the double bed wearing a strapless bra and nothing else, begins crying.

"Yikes," Harvey says. "Do you love *me*?"

She says nothing but shakes her head up and down. He walks over, picks her up, and carries her across the room to the red sofa. He places her down softly and kneels in front of her. She shakes her head up and down. He says very softly, almost in a whisper, "Yikes, honey. No one has ever said yes to that question."

His confidence grows quickly. He is loved. He will make this a drug-free day so he will be prepared for the phone call and the directions he will need to follow.

FBI, PHILADELPHIA HEADQUARTERS

It is a summit meeting of sorts. Regional FBI Director Marvin Marzano has asked the medical examiner's team to join him for a discussion on the new findings in the Cambria case.

"Thanks to all of you for coming here this morning," says Marzano. "Let's get started."

Medical Examiner John Harvey is sitting at the opposite end of Marzano's rectangular conference room table. He speaks first.

"We have DNA results on all the blood, and they show no DNA except for the victims'. The bloodstained map produces the same results. I have to admit that we are at a dead end."

District Attorney Diana Isaacs is sipping black coffee, but the coffee cup is shaking as she puts it to her mouth.

"What's wrong, Diane?" asks Marzano.

"Well, it's bad. My first assistant, Roger McBride, has just returned on the red-eye from Miami, where he had to stop on a flight back from Caracas. Roger visited the central prison in Caracas. He found the last known address of Ronald Gezzaro, one of our murder victims. I'll let him tell the rest."

McBride is a career prosecutor who has never lost a case. His guile in finding facts is uncanny, and to do so, he often steps over the line. McBride has dark circles under his eyes. His hair is disheveled. He looks like a mad scientist as he holds up a piece of paper.

"I have here a sheet of a Google map. The starting point is the Penn's Landing waterfront in Philadelphia. The end point is 547 Goodline Road in Limerick Township, Pennsylvania."

"Where the hell is that?" quizzed Marzano.

"The end point," McBride says as he holds up the paper, his right hand shaking. "The end point is the entrance to . . ." Suddenly, the first assistant district attorney of Philadelphia is unable to speak.

"Get yourself together, Roger," says the D. A.

Finally he speaks. "The entrance to the River Edge Nuclear Power Plant."

CHANNEL FIVE STUDIOS

"Hello again, everyone. This is Marty McCann the weatherman with a Channel Five weather update. Three inches of snow will move into the greater Philadelphia region, west to east, beginning at about 1 P.M. The temperature will range from twenty-eight to thirty-two degrees during the early afternoon, providing a wintry mix on the ground. Driving could be dangerous. We'll update you throughout the morning."

As McCann is about to leave the Storm Center set, a surprise visitor appears.

"Way to rock it, doofus," says Barb.

"Can you stop calling me that?"

"Sure, knucklehead." Suddenly she looks serious. "By the way, Marty, how much do you think we'll get?"

"To be honest, Barb, this sucker might miss us altogether."

"So it might be a big 'oops'?"

"Yeah, boss."

"Who gives a shit," she says, shrugging. "I'd rather scare the shit out of people than let them die on snow-covered highways. Wouldn't you?"

STUDIOS OF NEWSRADIO 1070

"And now with the Accurate Weather Cast, exclusively for News Radio 1070, here is fearless forecaster Clarke Macungie."

Radio News Anchor Brandon Bartnikoff takes his one-minute break from his half hour of the twenty-four-hour news cycle to listen to Clarke.

"Thanks, Brandon. And first of all, let's be accurate. Some of my TV friends are forecasting up to three inches. I'll eat my Penn State Nittany Lions hat if we get even one inch. Look for a cold afternoon, temps in the low thirties, and a chance of flurries. A great getaway afternoon. Back to you, Brandon."

Listening in his office, News Director of Programming Warren Warren is proud of his station's restraint.

RIVER EDGE NUCLEAR POWER PLANT

"Get the place ready," Neil Gerber tells his senior staff. "We've got visitors headed here by 11 A.M. I'm talking FBI, Homeland Security, Pennsylvania National Guard Chief, and Governor Shapiro. Make sure the pad is ready. We'll have helicopters, cars, and for all I know fucking tanks. Put the place in lockdown till I find out what the hell is going on."

Neil Gerber has been supervisor of the twin-towered power plant since 1992, and he has never seen anything like this. Since 10 A.M., he has been getting specific instructions from a variety of sources: Go into lockdown mode, don't let anyone leave until an all-clear, patrol the perimeter until the all-clear, open up the emergency food supplies, and the most ominous of all–prepare emergency radiation protection, including medication stored on the premises.

Gerber, his face flushed with anticipation, his head feeling like it will explode, grimly addresses the senior staff. "When I know what's going on, I'll tell you. Until then, be calm. If anyone breaks the secrecy code on this situation, I can promise you, and I mean this, you will never work again."

They all nod and walk away, aware that there is enough radiation surrounding them to kill twenty five million people in the northeastern United States.

LOGAN HOUSE

Keith Byrne is edgy. No story ideas for today. To Byrne, no news is a form of mental starvation.

Diana left a little while ago for a noontime appearance at the Philadelphia Garden Club. He is alone, sitting at the computer, searching for new stories or ideas. His eyes wander from the screen to the view of the Ben Franklin Parkway, and he thinks of how much has changed lately in his life.

The March 10 death of Dana Bordaine has been haunting him. When life is extinguished quickly, you start reassessing the value of it. When Dana's car veered off Kelly Drive and into the Schuylkill River, she drowned. In one instant, her life was gone.

The death makes him more grateful for Diana and how much she has changed his life. He now understands real, unqualified love. Beyond infatuation, beyond the physical needs, there is an unspoken bond–that no matter what happens, they will be here for each other. No news story and not all the public success in the world could ever surpass what they now have together.

He moves the arrow of the computer mouse over his calendar. March 14, 2008. There are two notations: "Update information on Cambria killings" and "Reminder: Send contribution to Dana Bordaine Memorial Scholarship Fund." Did Dana live her years well? Was she haunted by the vagaries of the business? Was she happy?

Heady questions as the heir-apparent to Mike Marone's broadcast empire turns off the computer and walks into the bedroom, inhaling the scent of the woman he loves, getting ready to enter the shower and begin another day in the pursuit of local news.

MONTGOMERY COUNTY POLICE RADIO ROOM, SKIPPACK, PENNSYLVANIA

"Roger that. Accident on State Road 529, intersection of Route 202. Ambulance dispatched. This is Montco Radio."

Buddy puts the microphone down and reaches for the third drawer of the filing cabinet to his right. He hopes it will be a quiet morning so he can save his energy up for the job in mid-afternoon and spend his morning with the magazine he keeps hidden.

The dispatcher is a regular subscriber. He never reads the articles. He carefully opens the magazine to the centerfold and looks nervously at the nakedness, thinking about Judy. Sometimes he shares the magazine with Judy. "Yes siree, baby," he says. "This baby can't even get close to what you look like." Judy knows he is lying, but she loves the reasons.

In addition to analyzing the centerfold spread, Buddy is thinking about the coming hours and the moment of truth. He will handle the calls he makes as he would handle any other tip call, except that he might, considering the situation, put some tension in his voice. He might even say that he is "scared shitless," or he might offer his trademark: "Yes siree, sir, we have a situation." And he has brought a tape recorder with a tape given to him by Perez to add some background noise during the calls.

The dispatcher puts the magazine down and opens up a package of beef jerky. He needs a jolt of energy. The afternoon will be dangerous, maybe even thrilling.

RIVER EDGE NUCLEAR POWER PLANT

Neil Gerber is at the end of the conference room table. To his right sit the FBI's Marzano and Homeland Security Regional Chief Barry Freeman. To his left sit Governor Myles Shapiro, Philadelphia Mayor Michael Miller, and Montgomery County Civil Defense Director Connie Cantangelo. Behind each principal stands a cadre of aides and note-takers.

Gerber begins. "I want to thank everyone for coming, especially Marvin Marzano. Before the agent-in-charge speaks, I want to advise everyone here of the need for total, top-level confidentiality. Like you, I'm ready to find out what this is all about. And I assure you that the staff of River Edge is ready to cooperate in its usual professional manner. Agent Marzano."

"Thank you, Neil. Before we begin, I draw your attention to the screen at the far left of the room. Here is FBI Director Louis Hastings."

All eyes turn to the teleconferencing screen. A tall man with a moustache and slick-backed hair looks into the lens. He speaks.

"Ladies and gentlemen, I speak now for the attorney general and the president. We have received word of a possible, I say *possible* attempt to attack the River Edge plant. The information is based on background checks relating to a double murder that occurred in Philadelphia in November. The information is sketchy but realistic enough to suggest that someone may have been plotting to use rocket-propelled grenades to attack the plant. We are not sure if the plan is still viable or if it is imminent. Nor do we know who might be behind this. Nevertheless, as a precautionary move, Agent Marzano has been appointed to lead a combined task force to shore up security in and around the installation. Once again, I want to make it clear that the threat level is questionable, but we are not in the business of choosing inaction when it involves the potential for trouble at a nuclear power plant. Agent Marzano has come up with a preliminary plan that we will put in place almost immediately. The most important thing is to keep this quiet. We don't want the general public to be put in a state of panic. Rather, we want to take secret actions as a precautionary move. Thank you. Agent Marzano will now brief you on the plan."

The people look at each other in silence. The governor, just thirty-nine years old and in his second year in office, looks pale. Marzano stands up from his chair. "First off, if anyone asks about any unusual activity, our answer will be that we are shoring up homeland security measures at power generating plants all around the nation."

The governor interrupts. "My press office will not be briefed on this. But I will advise the press secretary to call me immediately if there are any questions about security. Agent Marzano?"

"Thank you, Governor. First off, the Twenty-Fourth Division of the Pennsylvania National Guard, based in Pottstown, will be on standby, meaning that unit members will remain on a call list." He pauses. "As of 2 P.M., Navy Seal teams from throughout the northeast will be manning security locations on the perimeter. They will be used for advance surveillance. The Seals will be the first line of defense." He looks at the plant director. "Neil, we will explain to plant employees that the current lockdown will end at 3 P.M. today but that security measures will continue to be stepped up. That means, DO NOT LEAVE YOUR I.D. BADGES AT HOME! You won't be able to get in without them. Make sure the employees understand that this increase in security is happening all over the nation."

An interruption. "Why am I here?" asks Mayor Miller of Philadelphia.

"Mayor, we need to ask you for help. In case there is an attack, can you send us about a thousand officers to reinforce the perimeter?"

"That will leave us pretty vulnerable, Marvin, but we'll do what we have to. I will brief the police commissioner within the hour."

"Thank you, Mayor."

"I have something to say," says the governor of Pennsylvania.

"You've got it, Governor."

"You know, Marv, that the current federal administration plays into people's fears on purpose."

Marzano replies, "Governor, I can assure you that there is no politics in this."

"Dammit, Marv, you didn't let me finish. What I was about to say was that whatever the reason for these measures, this state will be prepared to act with rapid response. We will do whatever it takes to quell any attempt to hold this Commonwealth under a state of nuclear blackmail. In addition to your directions, I will be convening a small group of advisers to establish a command post at State Police Barracks Fourteen in Valley Forge."

"Thank you, Governor. This state will be protected."

"It had better be, Marv. Or I will hold you and the Feds personally responsible. This is not Katrina, Marv. This is Pennsylvania." He looks at Marzano with a menacing stare. "Marvin."

"Yes."

"Don't screw it up."

CHAPTER SEVENTEEN: **MARCH 14, AFTERNOON**

*I*t's good to be home, but it is painful to watch the story unfolding. I mean, if only I hadn't taken that speaking gig in Pottstown. I guess life is full of "if only's." What stuns me is the cascade, the frenzy, the race that went on. All of the officials finally figured out I wasn't a part of it. But I'm still guilty, because I stood by for all those years and didn't have the spine to change how newsrooms function. I wish I had spent the afternoon of March 14 in the newsroom, not on my ass on a heat-scorched highway.

CHANNEL FIVE NEWSROOM

It is a shock to the midday staff of Channel Five when Harvey Hopkins arrives for work at high noon, the earliest he has ever been spotted in the newsroom.

"Harvey, what's up, man?" says Bob Harris, the always-cheerful but ever-insecure assignment manager.

"Yikes," Harvey replies. "It's so early that my eyes are blinded by the sunlight, but y'know, Mike's doin' a speech, so I got to cover just in case the frickin' lid blows off."

"You're a good man, Harvey Hopkins, even if you can't keep your pants on."

"Thanks, Bobby, I needed that."

Harvey is taking no chances. He wants to be at the station for the phone call from the folks who stole the cocaine. He will follow their instructions to the letter, and that will be that. But, he keeps wondering, how the hell did they get in, and what do they want? He can't report the theft from his drawer. And if he doesn't play along, he knows he will be sniffing glue in the repair shop of a federal prison. So Hopkins sits at his desk, combing his hair as he looks into a hand mirror and listens to the sound of the Pulse Five News at noon.

"Hi, again. This Marty McCann the weatherman with our storm update. Still lookin' at two to three in mid-afternoon. Might be a good day to leave work a little early."

HOME OF GARCIA AND MARIA PEREZ

Garcia Perez is supposed to work the night shift, four to midnight. But when the trouble begins, of course he will go into work early. That's what he would normally have done in a bad time, and if he were to wait till 4 P.M., people would notice.

Maria and Garcia are sitting at their small kitchen table, eating a light lunch. Garcia looks at his wife. "Honey, what are you doing this afternoon?"

"Just some shopping. Garci, thanks so much."

"For what?"

"For convincing me to take a day off. I really needed the time."

"So what exactly are your plans, baby?"

"I was thinking of driving up to the King of Prussia Mall in Valley Forge. Some good sales on today."

Garcia has to keep her from going there. The mall is only twenty minutes from River Edge.

"Maria, I wouldn't go up there. They're forecasting some snow, and you know how messy traffic can get."

"But I really want to get out."

"I would feel better if you went into Center City. Really, I'm worried about you driving up there."

"You are so protective."

"You're all I've got."

She gets up from her chair, walks behind him, and kisses him on the head. "I love you," she says. "I'll stay in town."

He gets up, embraces her, and then walks to the bedroom for a nap, happy that the love of his life will be in a safe zone. His nerves are rattled, but he'll need a nap to deal with what's to come.

THE HIDEAWAY

"Garcia, it's good to hear from you," says Peacemaker. The voice on the other end of the phone is halting.

"Boss, the feds have mobilized a National Guard unit not far from River Edge. The dispatcher also tells me that perimeter defense units are on their way to the plant."

"That is ironic," Esperanza says. "All that manpower for nada."

"What do you mean?"

"My friend, by seven tonight, you'll see what I mean. The two quasi-terrorists you killed on Cambria were never even necessary. We have a stronger force. Happy hunting tonight, Garcia, and love to Maria." He hangs up the phone.

Peacemaker watches the sky. It is gray, and bad weather seems to lurk in the clouds. If the forecasters are correct, snow will add to the chaos. Hopefully, only a few will be affected.

By early afternoon, head buried in a soft pillow, he is reflective. Although his public life has the dimensions of influence and service, few understand the real motives of a man possessed. The death of Tony Perez, his godson, and the years of gross excesses by the media have convinced him that retribution is necessary. The two Che Guevara wannabes from Venezuela were stupid and careless–freelance highwaymen looking for a quick buck–so they had to go. But thank God, he thinks, the first part of the plan–to screw with the media–can be conducted without them. The second part of the plan is the elimination of the dirty competitors. He has no problem with gangsters, but he detests the drug trade.

Two enemies of the American way, the news whores and the drug monsters, will get their day in hell. And Tony, poor Tony, will be avenged.

RIVER EDGE NUCLEAR POWER PLANT

The small Seal teams begin to arrive at River Edge shortly after 1:30 P.M. Satellite surveillance shows no suspicious activity in the perimeter area.

Navy Lieutenant Harry Lovell, born in Philadelphia, is glad to be near home again. His platoon begins to install the high-powered rifles and super scopes.

Lovell, a Seal for two years, is familiar with perimeter defense. His last assignment was the U.S. Embassy in Baghdad.

CHANNEL FIVE NEWSROOM

Harvey is pensive as he waits for the phone to ring. He wants desperately to write an email to Bernie O'Malley. After all, it was Bernie who ordered the firing of the second security guard. He blames Bernie for the breach in security that allowed a blackmailer to enter his private space and rip off his cocaine. But how can he complain to Bernie without reporting the theft?

On schedule, the phone rings.

"Hopkins here, hello."

The voice on the line is muffled, hard to understand.

"These are your instructions. After I give you the information, go to your news director and advise her that you have received this from a *very reliable* source. If she doubts you, suggest that she call the dispatcher. We want this on the air by 3 P.M. If we do not see it, the cocaine package, with your prints on it, will be dropped off at police headquarters. Do you understand?"

"Yes, I do."

"Listen, you fuckin' junkie, do you type or write?"

"I type."

"Don't type. Write it down on a piece of paper. Here's what you need to say . . ."

CHANNEL SEVEN NEWSROOM

"Hello, Caldwell here."

"Danny, this is Esperanza."

"Angel, how are you, buddy?"

"Great, Danny. I have the biggest tip I ever gave you."

"Bigger than the law scandal?"

"Bigger than big."

"What's up, Mr. Peacemaker?"

"Danny, as I speak, several Latin American terrorists are preparing to fire rocket-propelled grenades at the River Edge Nuclear Power Plant. There is imminent danger. Imminent."

"Do you have anything more?"

"No, just move on it."

Caldwell is apprehensive. "Are you sure?"

"Are you the greatest local anchor in America?"

"But Angel, this is huge."

"Check it out, Danny."

"Right away." Click.

Caldwell phones the dispatcher. Buddy is waiting. "Montco Police Radio."

The sound of screaming coming from several scanners is in the background. People are yelling in tones of angst and desperation. Caldwell hears someone say, "We are overwhelmed, dammit. Get us some help."

Buddy says, "Hold on, Danny. All hell is breaking loose." Buddy lowers the volume on his small Sony recorder.

"Buddy, what the fuck is going on?"

"Danny. It is frickin' chaos. Yes siree. What do you guys call it, bedlam?"

"So what is it?"

"Danny, some guys with grenades are firing them into the River Edge Nuke Plant. We got the world on the way. I mean, the shit is coming down."

"How many attackers?"

"Could be three or three hundred. We don't know, but let me tell you, I'm so frightened. Yes siree Danny, I could piss in my pants."

"Buddy, you sure?"

"Well, I've dispatched hundreds of cops to the scene. This ain't no fire alarm."

"Thanks, Buddy."

"Yes siree."

The dispatcher has to talk with one more newsperson, and then, before the rush, he will get out and meet Judy at the helicopter.

CHANNEL FIVE NEWSROOM

"Yikes, Barb, it is a tip. But it sounds legit."

"Harvey, you been drinking?"

"No, sweetheart."

"Where is Byrne?"

"He's in the newsroom."

"Byrne," Barb yells. "Get your ass in here."

Keith runs in. "What's up?"

"A man says he's got a tip that River Edge is under attack. You still tight with that dweeby dispatcher?"

"Funny you should ask. I've got a message on the line."

"Call him back now! I'll listen in."

Barb turns on the speaker phone. Harvey sits down to listen in. Keith dials.

"Montco Police Radio."

"Buddy, this is Keith Byrne. What's going on?"

The dispatcher turns up the volume of the tape recorder. Byrne, Barb, and Harvey can hear the screaming. "Keith, it's all hands on deck. Can't talk long. Gotta get more cops in. The Feds are on it. Don't know how many, but some terrorists are firing grenades at the twin towers of River Edge."

He turns the volume even higher.

"I need confirmation," says Keith.

"You got it. Right here. But call the plant. I have to go. Yes siree, Keith, I've got to go. We all could be melted any minute." Click.

Keith dials a number on his cell phone: Neil Gerber's private line.

"Hello, Gerber here."

"Neil, Keith Byrne."

"What do you want?"

"Is your place under attack?"

Gerber pauses. The bastards have gotten the drift of the security buildup. "I will have no comment." Click.

It is the second call to Gerber. A few minutes before, Danny Caldwell asked him the same question. Gerber is determined not to let the bastards find out about the potential threat. All they'll get is "No comment."

To the world of aggressive news gatherers, "No comment" means you've got something to hide. "No comment" can set the wheels in motion for an information disaster.

THE HIDEAWAY

Esperanza knows that there is no turning back.

He picks up the priority cell phone and dials Keith Byrne.

"Hello, Byrne here."

"Hey, Newsboy, this is Daddy."

"I am so glad you called. Something is going on at River Edge."

"Yeah, that's why I called. Some lunatics are attacking the plant with rocket-propelled grenades. I can't believe it. But Danny Boy just called for confirmation. You can beat him to the punch. Also, I understand that local police are forcing everyone to stay on duty. Can't be sure of that, but I can confirm the attack. And Keith?"

"Yes?"

"Be careful, Newsboy." Click.

Peacemaker picks up his second cell phone and dials.

"This is V."

"Veronica?"

"Yes, darling?

"Promise me something."

"Anything."

"Do not leave that station. Stay there. Just in case something has misfired. And one other thing: Refuse to go on the air with the story."

"You sure?"

"I am as sure as I am of my love for you."

CHANNEL FIVE NEWSROOM

Julia Powers arrives for her shift at 2:30 P.M. The novice is now a newsroom veteran because of Bernie's budget cuts and has lately served as the "breaking news" writer. Barb knows it is dangerous, but the woman can write.

"Julia," Barb calls out, "can you join Harvey and me in my office?"

"Sure, boss. Right away."

BROWN ARCHITECTS, SEVENTEENTH AND WALNUT, PHILADELPHIA

Harriet Alterman is working on the plans for the new First Prime Bank Center. It is a monstrous job, and she supervises a permanent staff of seventeen fellow architects. Every afternoon, the First Prime team gathers to relax for a few minutes in the company lounge and kitchen. They sip coffee, munch on snacks, chew the fat, and watch some TV.

Harriet, a rabid hockey fan, is debating the future of the Philadelphia Flyers when she notices the face of Danny Caldwell on the big plasma set.

"Wait a second, everyone. I think something is up." She grabs the remote and turns up the sound. Behind Caldwell's head is a graphic showing two towers. They look like the towers at River Edge.

"Good afternoon. This is Danny Caldwell with a Channel Seven exclusive report on breaking news. Reliable sources report to us that the River Edge Nuclear Power Plant may be under attack by terrorists using rocket-propelled grenades. An official at the plant, responding to our request for confirmation, simply said, 'No comment.' Our combined sources report that federal forces have been called to the scene. Stand by for further updates as they become available."

Harriet is agitated and anxious. She says, "Okay everybody head home. Just leave as fast as you can." Members of the team quickly deposit their cups of coffee and soda in the trash cans and leave the lounge.

Harriet grabs the cell phone from her purse and dials.

"Hi, baby," she says to her sixteen-year-old daughter, Ashley. "Where are you?"

"Mom, I'm in school."

"Ashley, go home and stay there. Don't ask questions, just go home."

Harriet has two concerns: her daughter's safety and whether the plans will need to be altered. The First Prime Center is located off the 422 Bypass near River Edge. Harriet's team planned to buttress the building with special steel girders. They are more expensive but could handle a large explosion. She wonders if they would withstand a nuclear blast.

CHANNEL FIVE NEWSROOM

"I am going to puke. Channel Seven beat us." Barb is furious. "Julia, do you have the copy ready?"

"Sure, boss. Wanna see it?"

"No, give it to Harvey. Harvey?" She looks at the dazed anchor. "Head down to the studio."

"Yikes, you're going to let *me* do it?"

"Yes."

Within two minutes, Hopkins is on set. Julia Powers's breaking-news copy is in the teleprompter.

"Good afternoon, everyone. This is Harvey Hopkins. This just in to the Channel Five newsroom: River Edge Nuclear Power Plant, according to reliable sources, is under attack by terrorists with grenades. The grenades could be rocket-propelled. The director of the plant, Neil Gerber, responded by saying, 'No comment.' Considering the situation . . ." Hopkins pauses.

"Considering what is happening, civil defense officials suggest that everyone leave work early. Combined with the expected snow, a staggered drive home is recommended. Leave work safely, everyone, and by all means, be careful. This is Harvey Hopkins."

Cynthia Cavanaugh jumps up from her desk chair in the management suite one floor above. She runs so fast to the elevator that she trips on the way. In deep pain, with both knees bleeding, Cavanaugh takes the steps instead, barrels through the doors to the newsroom, and screams, "Have we lost our minds?"

Barb grabs Cynthia by the arms and walks her into her office. "Julia, get your ass in here," Barb calls.

"What's wrong, boss?"

"What's wrong is why you put that shit in about everyone going home right away. There have been no recommendations by civil-defense officials, so you made the station broadcast a lie. And you could be creating a huge traffic problem in the city. Why did you do this?"

"Well, Harvey asked me to tell everyone to get out fast and go home. I thought it was worthwhile advice. I mean, let's face it. We could all be toast in a matter of minutes."

Harvey enters the newsroom from the studio. Barb calls him in. "Harvey, go home. Drink two quarts of vodka and get out of my life."

"Yikes, that's a great offer. See you." Harvey takes the molded earpiece out of his left ear, removes his tie, sits down, and reaches into the desk for his personal papers, including his passport. He has followed instructions to the word. Now it's his time, as those in the crime world would say, to "go missing."

STUDIOS OF NEWSRADIO 1070

Warren Warren, the director of programming at Newsradio 1070, has suffered all of his life. His first name is his last and vice versa. Warren also stands out in other ways. He is a guardian of ethics, a keeper of the flame, a practitioner of getting the facts. When he watches the two television reports, he is flabbergasted, incredulous.

His top reporter, Ariel Simone, watches the reports with him. She knows very well that Warren is a devotee of strict ethics and upholds a policy that keeps his twenty-four-hour news station from going off half-cocked on any story.

"Ariel, have you made any calls?" Warren asks.

"Yes, and Gerber gave me the same answer. He also said I shouldn't bother to call him again. Something is up, but something is missing. I mean, the White House, the Feds, where are they? I don't like the feel of the TV reports. But there might be an even bigger story for us to cover."

"What's that?"

"Traffic is reporting a massive exodus from Center City and from suburban business parks. The traffic team hasn't seen anything like it before."

ROUTE 422 BYPASS NEAR OAKS, PENNSYLVANIA
3:02 P.M.

Mike Marone is cruising south on the bypass, listening to some Beatles music from his MP3 player, which is connected to his sound system. He has always loved the Beatles–the range of their music, their ability to reflect the times. He is also an avid Newsradio fan. News is also music to his ears.

Close to the Oaks exit, Mike notices a line of traffic ahead of him, a rare mid-afternoon traffic jam. What's happening, he thinks. He turns on the radio to AM 1070. As he clicks the switch, he looks to his left, where a sleek-looking tanker, its body resembling a silver missile, is leaking a small amount of smoke. An SUV suddenly crashes into the rear of the tanker, and as the tanker hits the guardrail, a plume of black smoke erupts from the rear of the silver container, which explodes in a ball of bright orange flames. Just before Mike is hurled out of the car, he hears the word "nightmare scenario" on the radio.

RIVER EDGE NUCLEAR POWER PLANT

"Miss Cavanaugh, this is Gerber, director of River Edge. I have never seen such crap in my life. We are not under attack. I will say it again, we are not under attack."

The general manager retorts, "Mr. Gerber, first you say, 'No comment.' Now you say, 'We are not under attack.'"

"I will only say that we are not under attack. I will not comment any further."

Cavanaugh is confused. Although a general manager for three years, her background is in sales. She has never read anything about ethics in news coverage. But she knows that getting beaten on a story like this would be death to the station. And so would being wrong on a story like this.

She dials Barb. "Barb, I know you're comfortable with your sources, but who got the original report?"

"Harvey."

"Where is he now?"

"I sent him home."

"Thanks."

Cavanaugh dials Harvey's home number. The phone rings and rings. There is no voice mail. She then dials his cell.

"Hi, this is Harvey."

"Harvey, this is Cynthia. Where are you?"

"Right now, Cynthia, I'm in the first-class section of a jetliner en route to runway nine. Really sorry about the incident with the zipper and all that, but yikes. It really hurt. Bye, and say hello to all my proud compatriots. Cheers."

Cavanaugh sees all at once the hopelessness of her current situation. She is caught between a rock and an avalanche. And she knows that what comes down next will be the beginning of her end.

CHANNEL FIVE STUDIOS

"Hello, I'm Keith Byrne," he says to the cameras.

"And I'm Veronica Victor."

"The director of the River Edge Nuclear Power Plant tells Channel Five that the power plant is not under attack by terrorists, even though Pulse has had two key sources confirm this report. Meanwhile, another story is quickly developing. A massive gridlock is occurring on area highways. The traffic is so bad that the New Jersey and Pennsylvania police are urging people not to drive. We will be back shortly."

A few minutes later, back in the newsroom, Barb explodes. "Channel Seven says it's firm. I'm going on the air!"

"*You're* going on?"

"You bet your ass."

THE HIDEAWAY

Esperanza knows that Caldwell checks his Blackberry while on the set, during breaks in the news broadcasts. He sends him a terse text message: "Continue story on attack till 5:30. Do not fail, unless you want the truth out about Dana. Do not fail."

Caldwell has such a rush of adrenaline that he feels like throwing up. He wishes Dana was here so he could leave for a bit. But then again, the bitch deserved what she got, he thinks.

The commercial break is over.

"Good afternoon," he says. "This is Danny Caldwell. Despite official denials, Channel Seven is continuing to report that an attack of some sort was made on the River Edge Nuclear Power Plant."

CHANNEL FIVE STUDIOS

"Good afternoon, everyone. This is a special report and I am Barbara Pierce, the director of news here at Channel Five. Once again, the River Edge Nuclear plant supervisor Neil Gerber denies there is an attack on the plant, but I want to make it clear that we are still unsure if he is telling the truth. So we cannot responsibly tell you that there is no danger. Please stay with Channel Five for further updates."

Barb returns to the newsroom. Veronica, angry, runs up to her. "That was so damn irresponsible."

Barb replies, "Go put on some more makeup, blondie. You don't know shit."

"I know this," Victoria says. "I will not go on the air with bad info. I'm done until we are more careful with our information."

"How about you?" Barb roars at Keith. "Do you want Caldwell to beat us?"

"I'm with V. Barb, you'll have to do it all!"

A voice carries from the far end of the room. "No she won't." It is Cynthia Cavanaugh. "Barb, get a load off. I am now in charge of this newsroom!"

STUDIOS OF NEWSRADIO 1070

"You know what I can't figure out? Why would Caldwell stay with the attack report when Gerber now denies it? Either he has impeccable sources or he's smoking dope." Warren looks at Ariel Simone.

She answers, "I think he's smoking dope. The guy is a moronic adventurer who doesn't care about the truth."

"We're sticking to the denial and keeping a very close watch on the traffic panic. Ariel, I want you out there. I want the story from the drivers' view. Take a train to Norristown and meet Randy Segal. Head out together in his car. And Ariel?"

"Yes?"

"Brace for the worst. Here's some change. Get some junk from the vending machine, and some water. You may need it. This could be the mother of all traffic jams."

CHANNEL NINE NEWSROOM

Phil Hurley, the news director of Channel Nine, always feels that, when in doubt, one should not take chances, especially when public safety is at stake.

Diana, his anchor, is getting ready for the station's first break-in on the River Edge story. But in her mind and her gut, something seems terribly wrong. She asks Charlie Bergman to call every source he has. While Bergman works the phone furiously, she steps into Phil's office to have a conversation.

"Phil, I called Buddy the dispatcher. There was no answer, no answer at all at the police radio room. I called Limerick Police, and they hung up on me. I called Gerber's office at the plant; he didn't return my call. I called Dynamo Traffic Service. The director says an exodus is taking place from city to suburb and the other way around, because these reports are making people crazy. Then, Phil, I called Philadelphia Civil Defense Headquarters. My source there, Lieutenant Milt Mallowe, says he can't figure out what's going on."

"What do you mean?" Phil says.

"If there is an attack going on, the White House would be issuing statements. So he thinks something is very fishy here. But then again, we are in uncharted territory." She takes a deep breath. "Phil, I think we should play it straight."

Bergman walks through the door. He looks alarmed. "I think that this is what I would call a coicle joik," he says.

"Can you translate?" Phil says to Diana.

"He means it's a circle jerk."

"Yeah," Bergman says. "The infamation moves in a coicle with everybody runnin' around it, tryin' to cover their aahses. Truth is, no one knows weah it came frahm."

"I think restraint is critical," Diana says.

"Absolutely," the news boss replies. "Let them all claim they were first. I would rather be right. Get on the air as soon as you can. Keep pushing the fact that there is no confirmation. Also, let's go to traffic to see what's happening."

At least Phil and I are in sync, Diana thinks as she heads to the studio. She wonders if the original story has incited the developing chaos. She wonders if the attack was not on the plant, but on the unsuspecting and panicked people of Philadelphia.

MARPLE NEWTOWN MIDDLE SCHOOL

Buddy arrives at the school parking lot at 3:30 P.M., avoiding the mad rush by using his GPS to locate and travel on small country roads. Judy greets him with a sensual hug.

"Honey," she says quickly, "I am so pumped up about getting out of here. And I'm so scared to fly. What is this helicopter going to be like?"

"Hell if I know. I've never been flyin' on anything, either."

They linger in the parking lot for twenty minutes, holding hands and walking in circles, like two teenagers discovering themselves. Just before four o'clock, they hear the roar of an engine.

"The whirlybird has arrived," Buddy says. "Yes siree, babe."

The pilot of the private commercial chopper has a manifest listing his passengers as Mr. and Mrs. Charles Harper of Columbus, Ohio. They will be flown to a private landing pad near Kennedy Airport, where a car will transport them to Air Venezuela. The flight from Delaware County, Pennsylvania, to JFK was prepaid by the Venezuelan government. The bureaucrats involved are the same thugs who sold the services of the murdered men to the mob in Philly. Buddy and his woman will be protected for life, and they know it. Afer all, Venezuela has no extradition treaty with the United States.

With the whizzing sound of the rotors frightening them, Buddy and Judy climb into the chopper, dragging two huge duffel bags.

"Welcome aboard to the Harpers," calls the pilot.

Strapped in and sweating bullets, Buddy and Judy look at each other with fear. Then, as they fly north and west, curiosity and shock wipe away the fear. Below, on the roadways and expressways of suburban Philadelphia, they see thousands of cars stopped. Every few miles they see a puff of smoke, some of it dark, and a mosaic of red emergency lights. The smoke causes a haze in the air.

They stare without speaking. Buddy breaks the eerie silence. "Yes siree. Happy to say goodbye. I'll miss the old city, but it looks like it's a good day to leave."

Judy starts crying. Buddy doesn't know whether she is already homesick or is grieving for the victims of the disaster unfolding below. Buddy decides not to ask.

CHANNEL NINE STUDIO

"We interrupt this program to bring you this special report. I'm Diana Hong, reporting to you on a most unusual sequence of developments. Panicked by unconfirmed reports of an attack on the River Edge Nuclear Power Plant, hundreds of thousands of drivers are caught in what appears to be a traffic nightmare. We will switch to live coverage from Dynamo Traffic Headquarters. Here's Patricia Porillo."

"Thanks, Diana. Given what we're seeing on our fifty-two traffic cams in the area, we can only describe this as a complex of the worst traffic jams in the history of our region. Let's take a look at Route 422, not far from the power plant."

The traffic cam shows a line of southbound traffic standing still. "As you can see, Diana, the traffic is stopped, but there also appears to be a large fire burning near the Oaks exit, causing thick black smoke to fill the air. From having covered so many accidents, I can say that this appears to be flames and smoke from an explosion caused by propane gas. Going in a bit tighter, I can see . . ." Patricia stops speaking, waves to the camera, and pulls her right hand across her throat, a signal to cut. Before the cameraman moves off the scene, however, viewers and the anchor see bodies laid out on the pavement.

The traffic reporter continues. "There appear to be injuries. Back to you, Diana."

"Thanks, Patricia. Once again, a top official's denial and no confirmation of broadcast reports of an attack on River Edge. But the top story is the total hammerlock that a panic traffic jam is causing in our region, including the main north-south corridor in the United States, the New Jersey Turnpike. We'll be back with more updates."

PERIMETER, RIVER EDGE PLANT

Lieutenant Lovell is dug in. So are his men, two of whom are walking in a continuous circle around the entire two-mile perimeter of the plant. The reconnaissance team is trying to answer the important question of the day: Is there an attack on River Edge?

This is the third time the recon team has made the full-perimeter hike, assisted by National Security Agency Satellites, special sound-detection equipment, and fly-bys from Dover Air Force in Delaware. Thus far, the Navy Seals perimeter team has seen not one single shred of evidence that there is an attack and no sign of one planned.

THE HIDEAWAY

Cell phone number one rings.

"Esperanza," he answers. He listens to his caller and replies firmly. "Yes, Bobby, it *is* a go. Call all four of them now."

RED LION CATERERS, NORTHEAST PHILADELPHIA

Yuri Zopaloff is oblivious to the news happening fourteen miles away. He is cloistered in his place of work, holding a small calculator in his right hand.

"Robby, pass me the book."

Robby, the trusted bodyguard, is sitting on a barstool of the Moscovia Lounge, reading the penciled entries in the big ledger book. He closes the book and passes it across the bar to Zopaloff, who is sipping beer from a bottle. Zopaloff opens the ledger to the section marked "C." "C" has changed Zopaloff's life, allowing him to live a lavish suburban lifestyle under the cover of his legitimate business, the Red Lion Caterers.

Robby hears a noise from the right and his neck turns in that direction. The dark double doors of the service entrance open. In a matter of seconds, Providence man, adorned in a black mask and wearing a bizarre child's bonnet, takes aim and fires. Once he has disabled Robby with a bullet to the right arm, he fires four shots into Zopaloff's white Polo sweater. The sweater turns crimson as Zopaloff falls backwards to the hardwood floor behind the front of the semicircle bar.

Providence man runs off. Robby screams in pain as Zopaloff bleeds out. It has all taken place in less than sixty seconds.

TWENTY-SECOND AND PACKER, SOUTH PHILADELPHIA

Alvinato's brother Nick walks from the Broad Street subway to a red brick duplex in South Philadelphia. Two neighborhood kids are racing their bikes down the street. Light flurries are falling. The usual heavy police presence near the stadium complex has disappeared, with so many of the district police officers assigned to control the bedlam unfolding on the suburban highways.

Reaching the top step at the front of the house, Nick, an accomplished burglar, presses a slim piece of metal into the lock and quietly opens the storm door. The house, a façade for a hooker joint, is adorned with scarlet red wallpaper. Nick knows that, at this time of day, it is mostly empty.

As Nick climbs the stairs, he places the Eagles ski mask over his face. If Nick is loyal to anything, it's the hometown team. At the top of the stairs, on a giant bed in the center of a large room, Richie squirms on top of a deeply tanned woman. He needs Richie to exit the woman before he fires. "So Richie, you fucker, stand up," he calls. "Now."

Startled, Richie Antiglaro, Philadelphia's premier heroin distributor, disentangles himself and stands up. Nick fires four shots, two to the heart, two to the head. The woman, though shrieking in horror, is not touched by the squirting blood.

Nick leaves the house, removes the ski mask, and returns within two minutes to the subway. He manages to catch the northbound express.

CHANNEL NINE NEWSROOM

Diana is under pressure. Channel Seven is sticking by the story of the attack. Keith and the Channel Five people are backing off and concentrating on the calamity of the exodus. She knows it's risky to deny the attack, but safety is more important. Right now she trusts her own instincts. Right now the story is on the highways.

As the Channel Nine chopper flies over the battered Blue Route, the big east-west suburban expressway, Diana can see the footage of smoke pouring from burning cars, and ambulances and rescue trucks trying to use the outside lanes to get through to those in need.

When the weather person starts her update, Diana hears, along with the viewers, that the threat of snow is over. She wonders how the erroneous forecasts earlier in the day contributed to the current mess. Diana has about a minute left. She picks up the red phone on the set and calls Phil Hurley.

"Phil, I'm going to stay with the fact that there has been no confirmed attack on River Edge."

"Stay with it," Hurley answers. "We have to be right. This whole catastrophe may have been fueled by bogus reporting. Right now, only Newsradio and our gang are doing the right thing. I'll bet my ass, my job, that Seven and Five have screwed this up, and they've done it so badly that people are dying."

"Phil, I've got thirty seconds left. Where is Keith?"

"He's back co-anchoring with Veronica. Harvey vanished from the station earlier."

"What do you mean, 'back' at the anchor desk?"

"Well, Barb went on air herself to try and validate the original story."

"Are you kidding?"

"No."

"Well, at least Keith is okay," she answers.

"No one has heard from Mike."

"Oh my God. Where is he?"

"I don't know."

The cue comes seconds later. There are now two chopper shots. "This is Diana Hong, and we are back with live coverage of the chaos on this Friday afternoon. We are looking at sections of the Blue Route, where fumes and seven accidents have caused what Delaware County officials are now calling a medical emergency. Three hospitals, Bryn Mawr, Paoli, and Montgomery, are reporting an overflow, with perhaps as many as seven hundred patients."

The picture changes. The photographer in the chopper zooms in on a rear-end collision involving at least fifteen cars and trucks on a six-lane expressway.

Diana continues: "We move now to our second chopper over I-95 near the Bucks County border. State police now confirm three hundred fifty injuries from smoke and fuel inhalation, six separate accidents, and fights that have broken out among motorists. Most of the injuries are being treated on the scene because area hospitals have no further capacity. Civil-defense officials report that accidents on the Schuylkill Expressway in the city have filled city hospital emergency facilities and trauma centers."

The director tells the cameraman to take a tight shot of Diana. The anchor's eyes are welling with tears of fear. She tries to continue but can't speak. This is the nightmare of all anchors: rigidity, a brain lockdown, emotions overtaking you. Some can fake this and will do so for effect, but Diana Hong has truly reached a moment of no return. She is sweating profusely. She feels nausea overcoming her. But she has to keep talking.

"I want to say something," she says at last. She clears her throat. Then she speaks to the cameraman. "Charley, can you come a bit closer?"

The screen is now filled with her face. Her eyes are wide open. She talks slowly. She talks to one person. She always does.

"I want you to understand that there is no evidence or confirmation that there was ever any attack on the River Edge Nuclear Power Plant. Whatever the real story, the original story reported by two other TV stations set off a panic that is unprecedented in the history of this community. While we pass judgment on the cause, we remind you of the more pressing issue: that over seven hundred people are now being treated for injuries at area hospitals, and many more are suffering."

She pauses. This is no longer an anchorperson delivering urgent news; it is a person in distress, sharing her own grief during a grave situation. On the side of the screen, a hand appears, holding a yellow piece of paper. Diana grabs it and looks. The words are written in black ink.

"Oh my God." Diana's voice gets higher. "We have just confirmed that the rush by hundreds of thousands to leave the area has resulted in at least . . ." She falters. "In at least ninety-five deaths, most of them from major accidents and some, according to the Pennsylvania state police, from heart attacks and the inhalation of fumes, along with the failure of rescue crews to get through. The president has declared a federal emergency in the tri-state area. And National Guardsmen from the Valley Forge barracks are now being dispersed to keep order. We've also learned that over a thousand Philadelphia police officers, originally sent in to ward off an attack on the power plant, are now being redirected and are fanning out across the suburbs to help rescue injured drivers.

"I repeat," says Diana, regaining control of her voice. "No confirmation of a terrorist attack. But we have confirmed multiple fatalities as a result of the panic."

FELDSTEIN RECREATION CENTER

Little Stevie is the first to use his emergency fanny pack. He gets out the cell phone and calls Bobby.

"I'm in the rec center, Bobby," he whispers. "I don't see her. In fact, the place is a ghost town."

Alvinato responds. "Stevie, the goddamned place is closed. That's why you're there. Go into the billiards room. At the far end, near the picture of the mayor, is a trap door. It leads to a basement room. Knock on the door and say 'delivery' or some shit like that."

"Okay, boss."

Stevie, still in pain from his troubled tooth, walks through the rooms of the rec center and winds up in a ping pong room. He sees a small billiards room to the right.

"Bingo!" he whispers to himself. He walks to the trap door and bangs on it with his right foot.

A woman's voice rises from below. "Who's there?"

"Delivery. I've got an invoice for you."

"Come back tomorrow."

"Can't."

"Shit," she says. The trap door opens. Barbara Faisonette, director of the center, emerges from the steps. "So whattayah have?" she says.

He reaches into a bag and pulls out the Glock. "You are a looker, babe, but orders are orders. Bye." Three rapid-fire pops and Faisonette's body falls back down the steps to the basement.

Stevie walks down. He adds a final shot. Insurance. Then he looks around. He sees packages, small and large. Joints, plants, packages of cocaine. He pauses and thinks about taking some. But he's been told to touch nothing. Orders are orders.

CNN CENTER, ATLANTA

"This is Harry Lemonick with breaking news from CNN. The Philadelphia area, encompassing eastern Pennsylvania, New Jersey, and Delaware, is in the middle of what Homeland Security officials are calling a human catastrophe. Incited by unconfirmed reports of an attack on a nuclear power plant, hundreds of thousands of motorists took to the roads at mid-afternoon, creating a total gridlock. No traffic is moving on the region's highways, but there are reports of accidents and sickening air that have caused hundreds of injuries. Initial reports indicate a sizeable number of fatalities. Rescue squads are attempting to reach the victims with little success. I'm told that we have a statement from Governor Myles Shapiro in the state capitol of Harrisburg coming up in a few minutes. Stay with CNN for more on this breaking news as the nation's fourth largest metropolis is locked down and choking from an unprecedented crisis caused by panic."

SECOND AND GIRARD, BEER BELLY NIGHTCLUB

Lisette is smooth, velvety smooth. Her skin has always been so soft and white. Lisette's magic lies in her sensuality; there is no assassin like her. The German-American beauty always wears white gloves. People are startled by the gloves, and few understand that they are worn not for fashion but for avoiding the hazard of leaving fingerprints. Her shoes have an almost invisible cover of ultra-thin plastic on their soles, not noticeable but so important for covering her tracks. On this day, she wears the fanny pack she was given and plans to take advantage of looking like a tourist.

When she shows up in the late afternoon at Luis Vallarta's new nightclub at Second and Girard, she saunters over to the bar.

"Can I have a Bud, please?" she says in a voice that sounds so young and innocent.

"Sure," says Buddy, the bartender. He fills up the mug with the beer on tap and places it in front of her.

"Great town you guys have. Love it. So much history."

Luis, "Bastardo" to his friends and enemies, walks over from his corner table and sits down next to her.

"Hey, sweetheart, is there anything you need?"

"Sure. What's your name?"

"Luis."

"Can you get me to Valley Forge? I love history."

"Not today, baby. They got a frickin' mess. People are getting hurt and sick on the highways. The action is right here in Phillytown."

"Then there is something else I would love. Do you have a pen?"

"Sure."

She takes the pen and writes slowly on a napkin. She moves it toward him on the bar.

He picks it up. His jaw drops. The note reads, "Do me. Do me now."

He grabs her hand and walks her behind the bar, not noticing that she has put the pen and the napkin in her pocket.

He walks her down the corridor near the kitchen to his small office. After he locks the door behind them, he drops his pants.

She says, "My goodness, Bastardo. You are so big."

Suddenly he goes pale. How does she know his name? With lightning speed she opens the fanny pack, takes out the switchblade, presses it against the swell of his organ, and puts her finger on the button. As he collapses to the floor, she grabs the pistol from her pack with her other hand and shoots him once in the head. She is a bit disappointed. She missed the spot in between the eyebrows. Practice makes perfect, she thinks.

After returning all the equipment to the fanny pack, she pulls out the black wig, places it over her head, and walks out the rear door at the back of his office. She crosses the street, hoping to board an El train that will take her to Center City and then the airport. But as she walks up the steps toward the train, a cop stops her. Grabbing her arm softly, the officer walks her back down the stairs to street level. He hails a cab.

As the cab speeds away, Officer Garcia Perez picks up his cell and calls the Hideaway, with the word that Lisette is on her way to the airport. In an hour, her plane will be wheels up on its way to Chicago.

Perez, who was waiting outside of the bar for an hour, is almost done with this part of his assignment. Now he prepares himself mentally for more chaos, and then, the mission of God.

THE HIDEAWAY

Peacemaker is surprised by the level of the chaos that has resulted from his plan. One of his cell phones rings. The voice on the other end is familiar.

"Angel, this is Danny again. The other guys say there is no attack on River Edge. I could be in deep shit."

"You already are, Caldwell. Remember Dana Bordaine. Remember what I told you. Stay with the story for one more report, then back off. Remember, Danny, what I did to Dana was a gift to you. Today was just a great tip. The plant was under attack."

"Yeah, but the government is saying nothing."

"Hold it a minute, Danny. What did the dispatcher say?"

"He said it was a real attack, that he was scared and getting the hell out. He said he didn't want to die of radiation poisoning."

"Let me ask you a question."

"Sure."

"Do you want to live, Danny?"

"Yes, but I feel screwed."

"Now listen, Danny. Forget we talked, or–"

Danny interrupts. "Gotta get on the air. The governor is about to speak."

Esperanza hangs up the phone. He waits for Bobby to call with the results of the visits to the drug lords.

INTERSECTION OF I-476 AND THE PENNSYLVANIA TURNPIKE

TV reporters travel in herds. Three of them are reporting live from the entrance to the Pennsylvania Turnpike. The intersection of the Schuylkill Expressway and the turnpike is a safe haven. Traffic is stalled, but a crafty reporter can find her way to the roof of the turnpike building, which gives a clear view of the mayhem, east and west.

Suzie Berman of Channel Five is team-reporting with Annie O'Brien, a.k.a. Rocket Socks. Suzie realizes they are in the middle of perhaps the biggest story she has ever covered. To accentuate the intensity of the situation and give them greater credibility, Suzie and Annie are wearing radiation masks, which have always been a part of the station's emergency closet. To the drivers in the cars, stranded, hungry, and scared to death, the two look like clowns. But for the viewers at home, the masks convey a sense of the crisis.

Suzie is moderate in her tone. "Keith and Veronica, we are isolated here and can't get to the 422 bypass where a propane truck exploded. So, although we have a picture of the seriousness of this traffic deadlock, we have no exact figures on casualties."

Annie, characteristically, is hysterical. "Keith, I have to tell you, I can't breathe through this horrible mask. But I'm scared. I mean, how many times in your life do you get a few miles from a power plant that's under attack, and in the middle of absolute, unmitigated bedlam? I can guarantee one thing, Momma. Poppa's gonna be late for dinner tonight. So hold the frickin' chicken and pray, baby, pray."

Suzie looks away. Back at the station, Veronica doesn't know whether to cry or laugh. Keith looks at the camera, plainly disgusted. He says softly and grimly, "We will be back after this."

The screen fills with a list of emergency numbers. Keith Byrne looks at Veronica and says, "We are in the midst of a regional emergency, and we've got a child reporting from the scene. Hold the chicken?"

Keith picks up the phone to Barb's office. "Has anyone heard from Mike?"

"No, not a word." Barb's voice is heavy and sad, as though she is already in a state of mourning. She thinks about Rocket Socks's final words to the viewers. "Pray, baby, pray."

GOVERNOR'S OFFICE, HARRISBURG

The governor is back in Harrisburg. In his outer office sits a wooden podium, flanked by the flag of Pennsylvania and Old Glory. Governor Myles Shapiro approaches the podium, head hanging low. He is surrounded by state police security, several cabinet members, and regional officials from the Central Pennsylvania Office of Homeland Security.

"Ladies and gentlemen," he begins as he addresses those in the room and television and radio audiences across the country. "I have just finished speaking with Governor Prescott in Delaware and Governor Alldale in New Jersey. They have been briefed. The president was kind enough to call all of us with the federal assessment.

"Since rumors and misinformation are dangerous, we are now setting the record straight. First, there has not been an attack on the River Edge Nuclear Power Plant, nor we do have information that an attack will be made. I repeat, there was never an attack on River Edge. The news reports based on so-called reliable sources were fake. It appears that after the first fake report on Channel Seven in Philadelphia, a second station, Channel Five, followed the stampede, further creating the environment for a whole-sale panic. That panic, that hysteria, has created a frightening scenario–a stampede that has created an emergency situation in eastern Pennsylvania, southern New Jersey, and the state of

Delaware. We will deal with this deadly hoax later, but first, our plan of action. The Pennsylvania National Guard, Fifteenth Brigade, is trying to penetrate the menacing gridlock. I have given a right-of-way order to the National Guard to use tanks and heavy equipment, if necessary, to destroy vehicles to get through. At least a thousand Philadelphia police officers have been diverted to the suburbs, where the problem seems most severe. The death toll, although this is just an estimate, could run into the hundreds. Priority number one is to get the sick and injured to immediate care. Finally, because of the traffic nightmare and the redeployment of police, there are some evidences of looting in eastern Pennsylvania. Although civil libertarians will no doubt challenge this later–and this is the most difficult decision I have ever made–I am ordering that looters be given one warning. If they do not cease their actions, under emergency powers granted to me, I have authorized that looters who do not cooperate be shot and stopped. Once again, there is no attack on the nuclear power plant. Please be calm. If you are listening on a car radio, be patient. Deal with the sick and injured. We will get to you as soon as we can. I will take no questions. Thank you."

The governor steps away from the podium, stumbles, and drops his notes. As he leans down to pick the papers up, he takes a moment to wipe the moisture from his eyes.

CHANNEL SEVEN NEWS STUDIO

"So there you have it," says Caldwell. Then he pauses. This is a rarity: The super anchor is speechless. The governor's talk has unmasked the terror in his mind. Finally, he resumes: "Governor Shapiro denies that the Channel Seven exclusive of an attack on River Edge is accurate. As early as twenty minutes ago, our reliable sources reported to us that the attack was real. So obviously there is a conflict here. We will return after this break."

Danny Caldwell looks around the studio. No one will make eye contact with him. Eddie Bartel, the news director who replaced Ned Lemond, walks through the heavy double doors of the studio.

"Danny, what should we do?"

"You're asking me? You're the fucking news director."

"Danny, you have a microphone on, be careful."

"You be careful, Eddie. We've either got the biggest exclusive in America or we are stupid, idiotic, and insane mass murderers, and we did it without a shot. Can you get somebody in here to fill in? I gotta make a call."

Caldwell rips his microphone off, opens the studio doors, and runs to the bathroom.

Inside the men's room, Caldwell pulls his cell out of his pocket and dials the Hideaway.

"Hello, Angel, what the fuck is going on?"

"It was a reported attack on a nuke plant. I can't help it if you guys, as usual, did your 'let's freak out the viewers' act."

"Angel, was it wrong? Maybe you set this fucking thing up."

"Maybe, Danny, I have a tape of you asking, or insisting, that Dana Bordaine be taken out. Maybe, Danny, you are fucked."

"You bastard. You used me."

"So it is, Danny Boy."

"I'm going to finish my work here tonight. And then, Angel, I will think about exposing you."

"No you won't, Danny. You won't because, frankly, no one will believe you. I mean Danny, your record of irresponsible journalism is well known. Remember Tony Perez, you bastard?"

When he hangs up the phone, Caldwell gets a cold, horrible feeling in the pit of his stomach. He wants to get away, and fast.

WHITPAIN SHOPPING MALL, SUMNEYTOWN PIKE

The mini-mart is almost empty. The owner, Simeon Barry, is disturbed. From watching the TV coverage, he knows that the suburban community is in distress. Barry wants to close up and bring some food down to one of the ramps leading to the Blue Route. He starts packing some cartons right when plainclothes Whitpain detective Logan Chase walks in.

"What a mess, Barry, what a mess," he says. "Can you fill my Thermos with black coffee? It's going to be a long night."

Chase and the store owner turn around when they hear strange sounds from the rear aisle. Two young men are stuffing plastic shopping bags with drinks and snacks. The men appear to be in their teens and are wearing hooded sweatshirts and dark glasses.

"Pay up front," says the owner.

"Fuck you," says the one in the blue sweatshirt.

"Pay up front."

"Hey man, this is an emergency." They walk quickly down the aisle and make for the exit.

Detective Chase says, "Halt, or I will shoot you."

"You gotta be shitting me."

"Halt."

"No way."

The bullet hits the kid with the blue sweatshirt in his left arm. He falls. His buddy stops in his tracks.

The detective stands over the injured looter and picks up his two-way.

"This is Officer Chase. I'm at Whitpain Mall in the mini-mart. Got one looter down. Need an ambulance ASAP."

On the other end of the two-way, the dispatcher says, "Are you kidding? There are no ambulances, no available emergency rooms, no doctors, nothing."

"Shit. I'll be right back." Chase runs to his car, pops the trunk, and runs back with his kit. He cuts the sweatshirt and wraps a tourniquet around the right arm of the punk as the young man moans in pain. The storeowner watches.

"Anything I can do?" he asks.

"No, this should hold it for a while. Keep calling till they get here, and if time runs out, cover him with something, okay?"

The owner sits down next to the wounded looter. A few feet away, the punk's friend is sobbing.

CHAPTER EIGHTEEN: **NIGHT**

I'm walking outside every day now. It feels good to breathe the clean air. All the network shows are calling for interviews. For now, I just want to heal, enjoy the family, and wait until after I testify in Washington to grant any interviews. And frankly, I might pass on all of them. I'm so ashamed. I can't tell you how ashamed I am.

THE BLUE ROUTE, PLYMOUTH TOWNSHIP

Newsradio 1070 reporter Ariel Simone has managed to make her way from the Norristown train station to the county courthouse, where she joins up with Randy Segal, the station's suburban reporter. With all roads stopped by clogged traffic, the two take a forty-five minute walk south and west to the place where the Pennsylvania Turnpike and the Blue Route merge. Ariel sends a text to Newsradio's Warren Warren. "Get ready to break in. Nasty out here." Warren's return text arrives quickly: "Use your cell phone. Call the hotline.

Simone goes on air at 5:57 P.M. She is walking on the highway in the westbound lanes, trying not to cough.

"I am just past the toll booths on the Blue Route," she says. "I must tell our listeners, please, do not panic. Panic has already become the enemy of the people."

She covers the microphone to cough, but listeners, many of them in their cars, can hear the muffled sound.

"My advice is to shut your cars off, try to stay inside, and avoid the fumes. The fumes are burning my lungs and causing me to cough. Randy, your turn to try to describe the scene."

Randy Segal takes the phone. "This is sheer pandemonium. It looks like a parking lot on both sides. Most people are coughing, and some are lying on the road and throwing up, too sick to move. Down the road, it seems there have been a series of rear-end collisions. So the smoke from those collisions is combining with the pollution of the other cars and trucks. As we walk through the line of cars, we see people sprawled on the pavement, some gasping for air. The big rig truck drivers are taking their first-aid kits and traveling from car to car. But there's too much to handle. Ariel?"

"There is no way for medical techs and police to penetrate the barriers created by this much traffic. It may take hours to clear this up. Many cars are out of gasoline, so some people are trying to walk off the highway and into surrounding communities. I know that many of you must be wondering whether there are any serious injuries. Serious? It's a word that we don't use casually. I can tell our listeners that there are many injuries; how serious they are will be determined by how quickly and efficiently the victims can be evacuated. For now, this is Ariel Simone reporting with Randy Segal on the Blue Route."

Inside the radio station's newsroom at Front and Market, Warren Warren is typing with one hand on the computer while controlling the volume on the radio with the other. He has just made a decision. He sends this email message to every member of the Newsradio 1070 staff:

To: staff@1070.com
From: Warren@1070.com
Re: Emergency
All employees, on-air, production, sales and marketing: Please report to work immediately. Take public transit. Forget buses. Take trains. Bring as much food as you can carry. Bring a sleeping bag. All hands on deck.

Warren knows that this story will be a nonstop flow of information for days. He wants the entire staff on board. The situation out there is bad and getting worse. He will not be a follower. He thanks God that his staffers didn't buy the story in the first place. He knows that the fakers have finally gone too far and his radio station will go into emergency mode to get those stranded drivers and victims the help they need. After all, the stranded drivers, most of them, will be getting their information from Newsradio.

His phone rings. He hears the voice of Marc Rafer, the general manager. "Warren, how did Caldwell and the others get it so wrong?"

"Marc, I do know one thing. That damn weather scare, the forecast for snow, caused a panic, too. But right now we're the only link to those drivers. I'm calling everyone in. That okay?"

"Are you kidding? Of course it's okay."

"Thanks."

"We've got to get those people safely off the highways. And one more thing."

"Yes?"

"Warren, kill all the commercials. This is an emergency, and the sponsors can wait, for god's sake."

BROADCAST TOWER, NEW YORK

Bernie looks into the distance, staring across the Hudson River at New Jersey. Alone with his power, separated from his minions, all of a sudden Bernie O'Malley, the darling of Wall Street, feels very much alone.

Bernie has been following the calamity on CNN, MSNBC, and Fox. For the first time since deregulation gave him awesome powers to shake the money tree, the boss of all media feels a sense of guilt. How did this happen? He thinks of all the scenarios, and, strangely, his concern is less about money now and more about how the industry and his buddies on Wall Street will view his legacy. Will he be seen as a financial visionary, or as the man who let it all fall down?

He dials Cavanaugh's number. "Hi, Cynthia, it's Bernie. What's the latest?"

"Well, we think that there have been twenty-three collisions. There are at least a thousand people needing treatment or seeking treatment. The roads are emptying out, but the National Guard estimates that this will take another six hours. And there was no attack on the power plant."

"What happened?" Bernie asks.

"I'll tell you what happened. Somebody screwed Channel Seven with bad info. We followed like animals. We got screwed by sources. Before you knew it, we who got screwed then screwed the public, big time."

Bernie pauses, then speaks. "But how could this happen?"

In a matter of seconds, the usually careful and guarded Cynthia Cavanaugh changes her tone. "I'll tell you, you bloodsucking sonafabitch. You took away my best people. We were left with amateurs. No, that's no excuse, but you should be hanged for murder, you cocksucker misfit maladjusted prick. Yeah, we got snookered, but so did you. You're finished, O'Malley. You deserve a lot of the blame." She hangs up, leaving him listening to a dial tone.

Bernie stares again at the far off clouds. For a brief moment, he stops breathing. And then, quite unexpectedly, he passes out.

CHANNEL FIVE

Keith needs a break. Veronica continues to anchor the live coverage. When Keith returns to the assignment desk, Barb is violating company rules by sucking in the smoke from a cigarette.

"How are you?" he says.

"Done. Done at last," she answers. Barb is talking about the possible end of her career. "But there's one piece of good news, if you can call it that. Mike is alive but in critical condition at Abington Memorial Hospital. He was blown from his car by a propane tanker that exploded in one of those god-awful rear-end collisions. I just talked to Rebecca. She says to pray."

"I'm not much into that, but for Mike I'll do anything."

"Got a question for you."

"Sure, boss."

"Where's the dispatcher?"

"Don't know."

"And who confirmed the attack, the other source?"

"Can't say just yet."

"Why?" Barb turns to give Keith a hard stare.

Keith says, "Barb, walk with me to the assignment desk."

"Why?" Barb turns to him. "Why can't you reveal the source?"

Keith puts a pencil in the sharpener and seems to feel relief as the whizzing blades carve the pencil. He puts another pencil in and presses it harder.

"Because, Barb," he says, "I want to nail him first."

But he knows this is a lie. Protection of a source, even a bad one, is the holy grail of American journalism.

THE HIDEAWAY

"Hi, this is Angel." He answers his phone knowing that Keith is calling. He has been expecting this.

"It's Keith. What happened?"

"I don't know. I got a call from inside the plant, and the dispatcher was positive. I also got a Pentagon tip," he lies.

"Angel, you didn't set us up?"

"Of course not. Would I set off a community catastrophe?"

"I don't think so."

"Keith, I know you will never reveal your sources."

"You're right, Angel, but I would like some answers."

"In time, my man, in time."

"Goodbye, Angel."

"Goodnight, Newsboy."

Esperanza knows that Byrne will never reveal his name. But he is confident that Danny Caldwell will, if he has a chance. He thinks over the day. The druggies are gone, and their murders will be buried in the chaos and aftermath of the human crisis. There has been only one surprise. Angel had underestimated the destructive power of hundreds of thousands of people paralyzed by panic.

BROAD AND WALNUT

Danny Caldwell is sick. His stomach is a mess. He can't think. Of course he will apologize tomorrow, as he always does, but with so many people affected by the stampede, the apology will not work. So, he thinks, I'll go back to Lansing, where I started. Or maybe I'll retire.

He walks into the underground lot and goes directly to spot number one. When he sits in the cushy leather driver's seat, he has a sense that someone is behind him. The blow to his head leaves him unconscious.

DELAWARE RIVER WATERFRONT

The kit is going to be useful once again. The extractor forceps will get rid of the teeth. The sterile scalpels will eliminate the fingers. The instruments used at Second and Cambria will be utilized in the destruction of Danny Caldwell. But first, the murderer wants to see Caldwell's eyes.

When Caldwell awakens from his stupor, he sees Garcia Perez in uniform, pointing a pistol at him.

He says, "What happened, Officer?"

"What happened was that I knocked you out and drove your car to the river, and in a few seconds I'm going to blow your brains out, cut you up in pieces, extract your teeth, and cut off your fingers. You, Danny, the news thief, the information executioner, will never be heard from again."

"Why?"

"For Tony. For my son, Tony."

Caldwell begins to whimper. Resolutely, Garcia fires the first shot.

TWO DAYS LATER
MONTEGO BAY, JAMAICA

He will miss the action, the excitement. He will miss the adoration. But he is clear now, away from the storm and headed for a life of sun, rum, and carefree nothingness. Eventually, he will write a letter and tell everyone that he is so ashamed to have been a part of the fraud that all of them perpetrated. Maybe in a year or two. But for now, he will relax and watch his money grow. No makeup, no rules, lots of fun.

Harvey Hopkins lounges on the terrace of his room. In one hand, he holds a pina colada. He leans over his other hand and sniffs a line of cocaine.

The hooker stayed overnight, and as far as Harvey is concerned, she can stay forever. She is tan all over. Her name is Eva. In addition to her work ethic, Harvey is impressed by her smile and her cheerful disposition.

"Eva, honey, come and stroke my neck."

"Sure."

Before walking out to the terrace, Eva walks into the kitchen, where she opens the top drawer of the cabinet adjacent to the sink. She pulls out a steak knife with a black handle. She slips the knife into her bikini panties.

Eva slowly walks in front of Harvey. She unbuttons the push-up bra and blows a kiss to Harvey, who doesn't notice the knife, but in his situation, why would he.

"Surprise me, baby," he says.

Eva circles behind Harvey. She begins kneading the muscles below his neck with her left hand. With her right, she takes the knife and brings it near his carotid artery. Gracefully she leans over, sweetly kisses his left ear, and starts moving the knife closer.

She lunges the knife. The sharp, rigid dig goes deep, deep into the pineapple in the fruit bowl on the small table in front of them. She cuts off a slice and drops it into Harvey's drink.

"I know you like the sweet taste of pineapple in your colada," Eva says as she places the knife on the table and sits on his lap, kissing his face.

"Yikes," he says, taking a sip of his drink before putting it down. He looks at the ocean, at Eva, and at the stirrings beneath him and says, "Is this fucking great, or what?"

SIX MONTHS LATER
POST MORTEM

What can I say? I may have been luckier to have been stuck in the worst traffic jam ever than to have been stuck in the studio to face the damage done. Then again, I wouldn't wish physical pain on anyone.

I still keep the *Philadelphia Inquirer* from March 15. This headline gives you the overview:

"BOGUS LOCAL TV NEWS REPORTS INFLAME MASS EXODUS AND HISTORIC PHILADELPHIA AREA CATASTROPHE–110 DEAD, 500 INJURED."

On the bottom of the page, hardly noticed, was a story that would have been the banner headline on any normal day:

"FOUR DRUG KINGPINS MURDERED WITHIN ONE HOUR IN PHILADELPHIA."

The police are still investigating the murders. There are no suspects, and no clues as far as we know. We did hear that police were checking out a Chicago connection, but that's just rumor, and few Philly journalists are tracking down rumors these days.

During the first weeks after that fateful day, hovering between life and death, I knew little. But while medical teams patched me together, the local TV news business was getting hammered.

First off, the Feds. That lunatic FCC chief–the right-wing fanatic who is more concerned about bare nipples than real indecency, like those extremist, racist talkers on the radio–began an investigation the day after. I mean, the bodies were still warm in the morgue when Tommy Brown went to work on the industry. Brown was the architect of the giveaway to the big companies, the deregulation, but on the day after THE DAY, Tommy turned into a fanatical reformer. And the FCC investigation into what the president called a dark day in the history of journalism wasn't the only one. Tommy Brown threatened to break up the big station groups. Believe me, that will never happen.

I got apologies from Homeland Security when this was over. So that's good, but is it really enough for the pain they put me through while I was in the hospital? After all, I knew nothing.

All these months I've spent recuperating and watching my business go down the drain–along with all the mistakes I watched before 3/14–have taught me one thing: Don't hold back. When I testified before Congress, I laid the FCC out. After all, these guys set up the whole deal that allowed people like Bernie to bleed his stations. Profits are good, but bad information from people who care more about ratings than the public's safety? That's disgusting.

Of course Congress wanted heads. And three days into Congressional testimony, Bernie O'Malley, recovering from his physical and emotional collapse, was forced out. He took his gazillions and retired to Ireland. The White House asked the Justice Department to see if any charges should be pressed. But Buddy the dispatcher was in Venezuela, protected. Harvey was missing, believed to be in the Caribbean. In any case, Hopkins is not suspected of anything but alcoholism and stupidity. Danny Caldwell, suspected by the FBI as a part of a sinister plot, is still missing.

For some of our more distinguished members of Congress, the media haters, this was an opening. Senator Ted Backenbaugh of Missouri called for action to rescind the First Amendment. Can you believe that? Backenbaugh's attempt was laughed off the Senate floor, but the mood on Capitol Hill about the media is dark. And the Philadelphia debacle has hurt the credibility of local news across the country.

The networks are having a field day. The truth is that the River Edge story would never have made it to broadcast on a national network.

The state didn't miss a beat. Governor Shapiro, shocked that his state wasn't ready to respond more quickly to disaster, launched an investigation of his own government's failure to deal with the havoc of the exodus on March 14.

And in the news business, 3/14 now gets the same notoriety as 9/11. The business and its organizations, especially the Radio TV News Directors Association, have set up forums across the country to examine what happened. And Norcel Energy, owner of River Edge, hired a PR firm to teach Neil Gerber how to speak to the media and to develop a crisis communications plan for the company. A little late, don't you think? Under the circumstances, Gerber's "no comment" helped the hoax unfold.

The impact on local news staff was mostly terrible. Barb Pierce resigned and is now working in New Mexico. That's irony. The news director at Channel Seven was fired. Annie O'Brien is looking for a new career, one with no responsibility for handling information.

But there is some good news. Keith Byrne was named to the permanent co-anchor team at Channel Five and is given credit for stopping the coverage before it got any worse. Keith and Diana will be married next year. Diana has been honored by the industry for sticking to her ideals on the big day. And Warren Warren of News Radio is now the most celebrated broadcast executive in the nation, credited with bringing sanity to the hundreds of thousands of drivers trapped in their cars, depending on his station to keep them from going even crazier.

Veronica Victor is still the co-anchor. In August, she married Angel Esperanza, the Peacemaker. Boy, that was a shock. Who knew? Their marriage took place a month after Esperanza's former lover, Darianna Hoffman, was appointed Surgeon General of the United States. It's rumored that Esperanza's influence helped her nail the job.

As for how the hell this whole thing happened, none of the award-winning scribes or broadcasters who survived the debacle has managed to put two and two together. But my buddy Tony Avellino and Keith put some of the pieces in place. Esperanza was at the nerve center. We trusted him as a credible news source. But Keith is adamant. He will never reveal his sources.

But even if he's not going to get his judgment day on earth, the question remains: Why would Esperanza do it? There are some who say he was avenging Tony Perez's murder by trying to discredit Caldwell. That's still a mystery. Maybe Danny Caldwell could answer that, if he ever shows up.

Our plan is to wait and watch, but Keith has a problem. After all, his co-anchor is married to the Angel who's far from an angel.

And what am I doing? I finally retired. Should have retired years ago. I lecture and write books. I also monitor the achievements and failures of our industry. I'm happy and well and hold out hope for the business—a little hope.

What about the Cambria killings? Those guys had something to do with planning some sort of attack. But they were taken out first. It's a puzzle. Some of us think they were supposed to provide a distraction, but who the hell needs two punks when local news people, fighting to be first, create a panic on their own?

Incidentally, the officer who discovered those bodies, Garcia Perez, was recently promoted to deputy chief inspector of the Philadelphia Police Department. His main assignment: curbing the rate of homicide.

Across the nation, local news audiences continue to shrink. Local news is tempered by the tragedy that struck Philadelphia. But every day, news directors are still looking for ways to grab viewers. Some newscasts have turned into reality shows, with their own anchors giving birth on the air, airing their personal crises with shrinks, and sensationalizing the news with stunts in a way that draws viewers away to the cable networks and the Internet. That's okay with me, as long as local news directors, tackling hard news, make it an imperative to stick to the facts.

The good news is that, after Philadelphia, there are executives, anchors, reporters, and writers who will think twice before they rush to broadcast with information that could, if unleashed with the full power and fury of television, actually kill people.

I should know; I almost died. I often wonder what might have happened if I'd been in the newsroom instead of flat on my back on the road. But hindsight is always 20-20. It would be vacuous, vain, and just plain stupid to suggest that any of us could have stopped the momentum toward disaster. I'd like to think that I could have, but that assumption, believe me, is as bogus as the news reports that caused mass death by deadline in the Philadelphia suburbs on March 14.

12276411R00145

Date Due

SEP 11			
JUN 8			
JUN 30			
JUL 14			

19

ockshaw, M.
Double somersaults.

O (((

RICE: $14.00 (3559/go)

Double Somersaults

Double Somersaults

Marlene Cookshaw

OO

Brick Books

CANADIAN CATALOGUING IN PUBLICATION DATA

Cookshaw, Marlene, 1953–
Double somersaults

Poems.
ISBN 1-894078-06-3

I. Title.

PS8555.0573D68   1999   C811'.54   C99-932474-8
PR9199.3.C66D68   1999

We acknowledge the support of the Canada Council for the
Arts for our publishing programme. The support of the
Ontario Arts Council is also gratefully acknowledged.

The cover is by Alyssa Bettencourt – Panel, from Surrealist
Quilt from the exhibition 'Through the Eyes of a Child.'
Thanks to Studio Programs, and the Winnipeg Art Gallery.

Author photo credit: Julie Kenyon.

Typeset in Trump Mediaeval.
Printed and bound by The Porcupine's Quill Inc.
The stock is acid-free Zephyr Antique laid.

Brick Books
431 Boler Road, Box 20081
London, Ontario, N6K 4G6

brick.books@sympatico.ca

for Michael, most durable of tumblers

OO

Contents

Full of Itself   9
The Tree of Logic and Possibility   10
Roses   13
Over the Shoulder   14
Broken Islands   15
OrthoNovum   16
Between Their Bellies and the World   17
Daughters of War   18
I Keep Taking   22
St. Peter's, Thanksgiving   25
Handsworth, June, 1993   27
Jan Garbarek's Saxophone   28
Negative Space   29
In Any Case We Emerge Unformed   31
Shore Leave   32
Cheating Death   33
After Mantegna's *Lamentation Over the Dead Christ*   35
It Happened in May, While My Sisters   38
Open and Close   40
Playing Fair   42
Advent, With Friends   44
Solstice, Winter   48
Holes in the Snow   51
Charles Dickens Punch   55
House   56
Grandfather Harrows the Garden With Horses   57
I Make Noise With My Mouth   60
Praise   61
Grays Harbor County   62
Blue Mexican Glass   64
On the Ferry. On Hold.   66
The Dead and the New   67
Whoever's Responsible   69
Gli uccelli   71
South Island   73

What Is Promised 74
White Noise 76
Everything Necessary 78
What We Save for Last 81
Maybe the Body After All 84

Oh tiger, oh bone-breaker,
oh tree on fire! Get away from me. Come closer.

– Mary Oliver, 'West Wind'

Full of Itself

Who can be still for the Fire Dance?
Feet are up and moving. Though it
is not dance and is maybe the coffee

he will never say 'merely' again.
The rug a piece of sky or earth,
six by ten, the golden proportions.

Feet fly on the plain,
on the denser acanthus and pyramid.
He is happy with edges, they suit him.

Wool the spongy colour
of beach sand and flowering
heather, what sends him up

clean like a new shoot, budded
and full of the future in its own
astonishing package.

Worlds move. The music evolves
to Ritual Prayer and Recitative; this is
something else again, brings

him to his knees. Music
solemn and careful, full of itself,
not letting much go.

The Tree of Logic and Possibility

In grade eight she is selected
for special math classes. Driven

Saturday mornings for weeks
to the right side of the tracks.

In her astonishing velvet shirt she
discovers the tree of logic

and possibility, generates chance
and a new world, graduates

from ninth grade with the highest
marks in the city.

Math presents her
the honorary key to everything.

What we wear to new places we
never take off. In the newspaper photo,

hair schoolmarmish with unwanted curl,
there are no other faces. In that

floral atrocity her mother loves
because it is colourful and she loves

for its moleskin nap, she is
wild with the possibility

of no people, of a world
of numbers, causation, prediction,

stars. The music of it. Telemann:
vivace, con brio, allegro.

She cannot live there, so gradually she
brings there here. She crosses

mathematics with intent, builds a grid
she can inhabit without

intercourse or pain, over-
lays the people, exchanges, unruliness,

simultaneity, surprises,
till everything begins to die.

Math makes her think
of stars: cold and brilliant,

immense as her life was supposed to be
but isn't: instead

a mirror image, smaller, dusty, a lost
map. Neither answers. Who goes there?

Some trees poison their surround.
She is modest, honest, avoids

cameras and mirrors. And the body,
breathing little, that seed

of possibility starving for air,
kept only adequate, alive.

If you walk the road
toward her house, the yellow

centre line going uphill
points at the North Star.

Last winter underneath the brittle
Christmas tree, she unwrapped

a planisphere of the night sky.
This year takes it on the deck

and swivels one-eighty degrees
to midnight, December 31st,

holds the map against the stars
and tips her head.
                              Geese

in the next field screech with promise.
Cars crest the hill on the harbour road,

headlamps offer a wedge of the sky.

Roses

My father died four weeks to the day after
his mother died. He died reaching
for a hand he sensed resting on the blanket.
He died in hospital. His lips turned blue.

He fathered children who thought he was
the world, that the world was always
this way. Twenty years they thought this.
How could he remain unconvinced
in the presence of such certitude?

Who knows what my father wanted out
of life or what he wanted
in it. How he revelled
in his sister's coastal yard!
The lush greenery, the stream
dividing it from the neighbour's.

The nursery catalogues he read
erupted roses. His mouth opened
the words through long winters
while he lay on the couch,
hearing aid turned off, stopped
by the lavender-grey *Simone*.

Over the Shoulder

Guilt is a bag someone has carried
up the hill from the pub. A brown bag
the size of a good catch, or
darkish, and bigger than that:
duffel over the shoulder.

Guilt is a pool with ladders
rising in every direction.
We climb and fall back and climb again.
Who can make the connection between
what snaps underfoot and what drenches us?

We are not taught how to do nothing.
We're dragged from our busy infancy
and distracted for years till our
balloon of competence shreds.
There are secrets you know,

there is what happens when
what you haven't imagined occurs.
Pain or its absence. Wind
bares the back of a sparrow's head
underneath its buffer of down.

I believe in birds, the smallness of them,
their potential for flight, the way
they acknowledge this, even so

nodding and feeding in front of us.

Broken Islands

When you left I
climbed ladders, removed
the storm windows. The peas grew
six inches overnight.
I began to notice
building cranes, scented
geraniums, dust
on the top of the door. I began
to feel what someone might
in my place. This was
me alone, almost in
connection with the world.
The helicopter clearing
ground. One of us
shuddering.
         You paddled
the skin of that perfect blue.
The Island broken between us,
wafer on the tongue.
Out of the disconnection came
some line, the cord
on which tin cans are threaded.
What is the weather?
Mr. Watson, come here.
Hot enough at this end to drop
a starling from the blue.
You might believe the tropical
hum.
    Mr. Watson, I want you!
One of us shuddering.

'Mr. Watson, come here; I want you!' was the first articulate sentence
spoken over the phone by Alexander Graham Bell on March 10, 1876, when
he spilled sulphuric acid on his clothes. The receiver was a tuned reed.

OrthoNovum

The Sixties gave us a basket
to put all our eggs into. Lined

with radiant excelsior,
cut from a bleach bottle

with pipe cleaner ears and a tail
of flowering pink saran: Lay

all your eggs here. Anticipate.
Debbie Reynolds tied our frilly aprons

and showed us how to stock
the freezer for a family of four.

The Blue Flame Kitchen monthly
sent economical recipes

involving mashed potatoes and
tinned tomato soup. Meat = budget.

Food = love. Tommy Hunter. Bedroom
slippers, mules, with pink fur trim.

Some singer with a torchy voice
sets fire to the memory of

whatever I once wanted. A matching
peignoir. Straight hair.

What do you want, sweetheart?
To please you.

What I wanted after that was perfect
skin, a mask that let nothing out.

Between Their Bellies and the World

When girls who've learned to tilt
their heads to one side demur,
when these girls grow up,
who sees them? They've reached a pinnacle
of understatement. They've followed
the important rule of removing one
accessory before entering the world.

This has served them well; they
are shy creatures who get more
than enough attention for their smooth
skin and intelligent gaze.
They keep their knees together and
breathe, mouth closed. Then
at thirty they cut off their hair,

begin to confuse what they are
afraid of with what they don't
like. Shut out music and the city,
listen harder, watch till their eyes
ache. Refuse motherhood, tight clothes,
shoes that can take them
nowhere fast enough. See the reasons

for everything and want desperately
to be sometimes wrong. To be
essentially wrong.
They put the necessary padding
between their bellies and the world.

Daughters of War

Snow White drinks coffee with the happy
office workers on their morning break.
The red-haired waitress smiles and steams milk

for two women who talk
about the Vietnam war, how they were
four when it happened and no one
seemed to know even then what it was about.

The prince on his fortieth birthday
has taken a bus trip with no one he knows
to a canyon he's never seen.
What the next decade offers
is monumental, cavernous: he
has said several times,
'I don't know what is leading me.'

Snow White's hair is short enough to bristle,
the colour of iron. Though she's said
she recalls the soft gathering at her neck,
like a beloved animal that died:
it brings the same ache.

A half-life ago she was rosy
as the ponytailed busboy in his enormous boots
who arranges cups handle by handle
on the shelf. Now the daughters of war
talk software, overtime, data,
news.

I join her, late; the restaurant empties.

The prince, she says, spent his thirtieth birthday
eating fish and chips in front of a mirror
in England, rubbing one wool sock against

the other. His twentieth in Winnipeg,
hitchhiking after his first love,
drinking beer with her brothers.
Snow White cannot recall her own decades,
any of them. He doesn't know
what leads him. She wants advice.

*

On my twentieth birthday I leaned from
the car in my mother's drive
the winter after my father's death,
stood up from the car in my raspberry plaid dress,
hair curled for the last time,
to discover I had lost

a necklace. Under the car seat
or in the anemones, it did not shake
from any folds or pockets. But shines
twenty years later from my mother's mantel,
from the portrait I had taken that day
to give her just what she wanted,
the blooming girl behind glass,

pretty and pliable, with her curled hair
and the cross at her throat.

The photographer put some of her long hair
forward and some of it back, arranged her.
I let him, thinking, The last time. Now

she is dusted weekly, oversees the living room
no one lives in, the room where Christmas
unfolded like a Chinese magic box
into an endless universe of delight

and then suddenly folded back into
a place reached only in dreams.

*

'Go back to bed and think of Christmas,'
says my mother, lying mountainous
under pink blankets in the nightlit room,
her eyes struggling to open. Beyond her
is father, flat as the fields and snoring,
tuned to another world, glowing and immediate.

In the drawer beside him, wrapped in saran,
an image of me not yet taken,
mid-teens, a high school photo in which
I radiate possibility, that radiance a tunnel
he thinks we can crawl through to the new world,
the next world, the life everlasting.

Go to your place, my mother says,
where people expect you to be,
and act well. Think, says my father,
of what is magical, other,
what cannot last, what sustains you, what is
not this, not here, not now. No one
seemed to know even then what it was about.

In the end, of course, he went alone,
stopping just long enough on the edge
of the bed, eyes blazing and distant,
body rocking with heat, to turn his head and ask,
'Do you love Jesus?'
I can't imagine what I could have said to that,

or what I did say. Or what he saw
through that bright corridor his look made,
what image of me sent him
into the next world, left me

twenty years later in a restaurant
two thousand miles away swallowing
salt. Reaching for Snow White's hand
on the steaming mug, whispering, 'Go
back to bed and think of Christmas.'

All we can hope for is everything, I say.
All we are given's an old pair of shoes.

I Keep Taking

At certain points in the universe longing condenses
    – Roo Borson, 'The Limits of Knowledge ...'

I keep taking my life in hand, over
and over, and setting it down again
like a bargain I cannot afford.

Uptown, the women in rubber band skirts
tell me nothing has changed since
lions and Christians. When I ask
what they mean, they say
something about spectacle and desire.

What is this desire of mine
for new structure, this attempt
to reorganize pieces, to make them speak
sense?

I want to grow a greenhouse,
enough to feed us all through winter.
I want an In and Out basket.
I want the broccoli never to yellow
in the fridge, I want my favourite
black jeans to recover their seams.

I want two mornings a day.

I want homemade soup in the slow cooker,
bread in the oven, peaches
ripe at all seasons. I want
my thirteen-year-old dog to live another five years,
and five after that.

I want the canary, when he dies, to float
from the perch in his sleep, head under his wing,
like a dandelion blown before the colour's gone.

I want strawberries to send runners
to the empty spot.

I want stucco to metamorphose into brick
and this house to grow another storey.
I want my bed on the second floor. I want
nothing to match and everything to speak
its history. I want a salt wind
to parch the rivers in my head
and spring rain to startle the prairie wheat.

I want storms we know the end of.

I want swallows to nest beneath the eaves
and friends to visit for a season.
Private cars dismantled and hammered
into ploughshares, and fluorescent lighting
to cease like a bad dream.
I want the morning silence unsettled
by the neighbour singing laundry on her line,
by the rattle of starlings
beneath her loose shingle,
by the shriek of the early train.

I want men to speak softly and women
to walk with their heels on the ground.

I want to uninvent
perfectly interchangeable parts
– Eli Whitney, do you hear me?
I want the United States to become untied,

I want butter to stop sailing
across the ocean to a country full of cows.

Let us cease taking lives in our hands,
over and over, and setting them down
like a bargain we cannot afford.

Let's pull bindweed by hand, and raise
chickens to eat the earwigs. Take our own
bags to market, have
our shoes resoled and our animals neutered.

Let us not scoop dolphins from the sea
as if they were mould on a windowpane, not
cut loose our invisible nets, not cloud
the blue world with tampon applicators.

Let's begin to point a finger at ourselves,
organize the pieces, make them speak sense.

Let's allow what indicates the world
to enter us.

St. Peter's, Thanksgiving

> *... happiness,*
> *when it's done right,*
> *is a kind of holiness*
> > – Mary Oliver, 'Poppies'

Go to the far side
of the stack of bales.
The cat will abandon your ankles
at the barn of the yearling pigs.

Make certain the sun's well up
and your shoulders teased loose
by a night of manoeuvres
on the sprung floor of Danceland
an hour south.

The Olson Orchestra's *Yellow Bird*
has nothing on the voluptuous yawps
of the abbey pigs,
near market weight now,
who loll in godly satisfaction
on their sisters' flanks, or
root their bedding till straw
dusts their eyelashes

gold. Such bliss that the morning lies down
for the honourable sky.
The silo fans catch their breath
while poplar leaves shiver
the fall hedge. Mingle, they say. Ask

one of those old men to dance.
Or that lightfooted matron

in lurex shirt, defying the mirror ball
for magic. The last

of the crop is taken up.

One pig straddles her neighbour
en route to the trough.
A young woman with oatstraw hair
jumps her partner, is
jitterbugged into the air.

High-centred. Squealing. The pleasured
sift of the wind through young fall rye.
It's the birthday of the musical twins

and everyone sings. A foursome in seven-step
wheels like a glittering carriage
through splintered light.

Find the bale already shaped
to your body. Move in, snug
under the cantilevered stack,
bedded, overhung, taken in
by the bunched, the gathered,
the fall-silvered mass.

Rub your head in it.
Line the cuffs of your jeans.

Let the abbey bell ring ten times.

Handsworth, June, 1993
after a photo by Nick Hedges

I am looking at the black and white faces
of two workers in Birmingham, beautiful absolutes,
mouths wide and eyes nonexistent with laughter.

The love in their faces looks different directions.
One man wears the arm of the other like a favourite
sweater. Behind them a locker room wall:

the men have burst from an assembly line
into this passionate bud, eyes closed
in an outward blaze of faith. How

the eyes must be closed, the mouths open
for any of this to happen, the bodies
corridors of energy, empty and alive.

Bite air like an apple, exhale it like fire.
The men are a single knot of love at one
with two beings. They are black and white,

hatted and bareheaded, and look
to both borders of the photo, joined.
Nothing but passageway, straws to the light.

Jan Garbarek's Saxophone

Sea wash or tin rattle, tricks, he teases
with that melody I want more
than anything and he'll give only

a little at a time. All I remember
is being forbidden. A nine-year-old girl
fell from a tree on her head and died. Being

forbidden the monkey bars, all bars,
any play that parts her legs
or turns her on her head,

discloses bliss. Maybe my life
is falling around me now, how would I know?
When the rhythm stops I hear

roosters, songbirds, the twin lambs
bleating down the valley.
Rhythm returning

me to myself. Core,
ears, mined, ore, concentrate. Soprano
and drums, heart on five lines, five

fingers: piano. The ark of providence rises
on the pond. What is done becomes right. Even
the falling from tree. Even dying.

Peter Carey's *Bliss*, blue Mary
in the boat. Neighbours. Two
of every kind. How sound steps off

from the last note and then exists, sweet
pea, wisteria, vining thin air.

Negative Space
for Barbara

I'm making biscuits for my dog. That is not
what this is about, you understand, but
I'm rolling out dough
and cutting it in the shape of men
and hearts.
                It's late morning. The cicadas
began their unbearable hum
like eager bankers before nine; the sun
turns its gaze on the kitchen glass. The air
begins to liquefy, the dog
like Sambo's tigers to resemble melted butter.

My friend's dog in the city
knows fifty words, but not 'treat.'
'Treat' is a word my dog understands, or did:
deafness has scissored the links
between label and object.

When I go back to the city these days,
I notice trees. The cars are foreground only.
Beneath the birches, the sign on the moving van
on Tyee Road announces, We are 2 small men
with big hearts. Further up Selkirk
the faded bumper sticker reads
I   MY   .

The radio interviewer rattles off too fast
the title of Paul Ehrlich's book,
about the need to plant trees and reduce

our population, about the unacknowledged
living beings that keep this planet going.

When I rolled the dough I was able to lift from it
nine men but only one heart.
This is what I wanted to say. I   MY   .

The heart, the noble face
are what we read into it.

In Any Case We Emerge Unformed

When I turn for comfort to the window's wild
shrubbery, the Oregon grape, having exhausted
February's yellow bells, offers instead
a breast-sized cluster of blackened nodes.

This is your fist, it says. This is your heart.

Unendurable that we enter the world so
incomplete. All studies show that humans
should carry their young another two years,
or is it till the young are two years,

I forget. In any case we emerge unformed,

at odds our whole lives with the dispassionate
air. I cry part of every day now.
Yesterday a man I'd never met inserted
a needle into the flesh that harbours my heart.

I lay down for this. I unbuttoned my blouse.

Shore Leave

To live here is to live in a lantern,
so much clear fresh light

when the rest of the country's wrapped
in boots and down. This morning the rain

hammers on the eaves, and the whole valley
steams green and gold. I walk home

this afternoon down Amies Road,
the smell of cedar interrupting thought, and

every twenty feet a towhee or some brush wren
startles the trees. Everything seems

like a good idea. People, no people.
I wake the dog up for tea: toast,

goat cheese and garden tomatoes;
I make a study of Lee Valley Tools

and the Pennysaver ads. Now we hurry up the road
to walk the Otter Bay circuit before dark

which arrives suddenly between
a quarter and a half past five.

Cheating Death

No one up there knows much about it,
though people still speak of cheating death

as if it were a business deal.
Death has moved into our valley

too often this spring, the straw everywhere
pink with it, and there is no managing

but digging hard holes with a pick
and laying in the broken bodies.

I take to the house a feather
from each, one speckled, one green.

The drake collapsed a month ago
defending his small herd. His hen,

who cheated death that time, carries
her aching neck angled at earth.

On Thursday the smallest chicken vanished
into air. Last night the rooster and his hen,

who used to roam the valley till we shut them
in the coop at night for safety,

were pulled from their roost
and banged against the nestbox walls.

The morning empties. Even the wind dies.
The ducks uphill have heard the quiet,

refuse to leave the dark of their house. Death
undermines us. Now even

the smallest mumble sounds like terror,
a feather in the throat of death.

Death's only management is art. Dig
the gravelly hole, lay in the bodies,

pull the dirt back over, pile rocks on top.
Out of this will rise pain.

Mock orange scrapes the shingles,
the oven sides gain fire. At five to seven

drinks are poured, potatoes put to bake.
The chickless mother turns her eggs, lays

more. After the first pink rose is cut,
the signal bloom, the Elizabeth unfolds

another twelve, head-high. The sun
sorts through the evening light.

And the Rugosa like one of Lautrec's dancers
throws her cherry skirts in the air.

After Mantegna's *Lamentation Over the Dead Christ*

In my mother's room I pull the dress
from her ankles, drop
the nightgown over her head.
I kneel at her feet with slippers.
She lowers her hips to the edge
of the bed, and misjudges,

slides to the floor.
Surprised. Full-length. Amused.

Appalled, much of me flies,
as spirit does, as pigeons from the eaves.
Between bed and wall.
Resigned, there is this:

Her feet, which are helpless, prophetic.
Upright, they propelled her
like small glass sleighs over snow. Downed

they're unworkable. Her hands,
which flare from the wrists like wings
of a quail exhausted in chase,
trailing anticipated calm.

Almost midnight and I'm tired. I clamber
over the bed, step down at her head.

I am at the wrong end, cannot
accept the whole scene's pale surrender.
In my hands the neat coil of her hair unwinds.

The carpet reeks of Desert Flower.
The closet spills unmended clothes.
Porcelain dancers freeze mid-minuet.
Photograph frames shoulder boas of dust.

She says it takes two men to lift her,
as if noting her height or her dress size,
as if it's a fact that she counts on,
her puzzle piece that engages the world.

I bend behind her, double her dropped
head, match my ribcage to hers, press
my thigh to her back. Her belly and breasts
are soft Tuscan hills, yellowed silk,
caught in their own cloudy lace.

She says it takes two men to lift her, looks
at the planks of her legs and says,
No point in trying. No point
lower than this. Once I dreamed

myself in that laid-out pose
in the snow, the sky bright, faces
ringing my head like a horseshoe of roses
in trackless white. My hands tremble with rage.

It seems I have spent my whole life heaving
the body upright. My mother detached
from unruly flesh housing her,

only the eyes alive: we are to guess
the correct manoeuvres. What we do
never exactly what's wanted, never enough.

Let her mistake my shudder for compassion. It is

fury roars up from the green carpet, steels
my thighs. This is my life I'm trying
to haul up from the fallen

clothes, my own and hers too, up
from this placid pose
into the dangerous world.

*

I climb back over the bed
to the phone. She's worn me
like the robe I've laid over her
while we wait for the door to open.

My sister and her husband dress and drive
across town. They enter the house
like mechanics, move the bed to one side.
They lever my mother upright,
sit her down, say goodnight.

At the mirror she brushes her teeth,
winds hair into curls round her face,

the face that resembles so strangely now
her own at two, nuzzling
the photographer's black lamb
with fierce delight, with a clutch that says

Mine. I am in my old room in the dark,
rubbing the small of my back. There is
no point lower than this, I think,

no more care for the body possible.

It Happened in May, While My Sisters

navigated that corridor of treeless pasture.

I was with my husband. We were poking
our bills into morning-wet grass.

Something large enough to cast us both
in darkness shoved me to the ground.

My husband fled. There was no air
left in me, and I could not comprehend

the flash of the sun and the flash
of the sun cut off, again and at once.

Nor the senseless alarms of the chickens who
leapt sideways shrieking. The sun itself shrieked.

The shadow that rode me like a stone
from the great fir past the eucalyptus

bent a ray of the sun around me
in a thin gold blade that

pinned my breast to my shoulder.
What dropped, I know now, was a shadow

of the sun, elliptical because
it was morning. There are stories of this.

Lose your body in the grass,
stop your voice till shadows pass.

We see parings of this shadow sometimes,
very high up, and go to ground.

We lose our bodies in the grass,
we stop our voices till the shadows pass.

I shook off the shadow at the edge
of the honeysuckle, carried

the fragment of sun in my shoulder
under the spiked leaves of the Oregon grape.

The leaves opened my breath. The sun
went back to being above the trees.

I shoved deeper into the viny roots,
trying to shed what was left

of the brightness. Someone lifted me
into the light. I made myself shade.

Open and Close

The sea of milky air
at the bottom of the valley
is far colder than it looks
under one hot moon.
I walk through

the excavator's yardlights
along the road's yellow line,
a deer gone suddenly in the brush,
owl overhead, its bell-like call

tracking me down the moonlit open road
and up into the dark
shade of the cedars,
where Rhode Island Reds on Mundys' farm
roost in a silver Airstream.

Here comes Lydia barking at my
long strides, and the young farmer with her
who seems always puzzled
at how his life unrolls in front, just

out of reach. Fine night, he says,
breathless, and I say yes,
and the frogs agree, and we all
perform astonishing
feats of levitation in the wavy light

and then are set down neatly
in our separate worlds.
Lydia barks some more, and he's
embarrassed. I walk fast

back up the hill, breathing and
breathing, ribs full of night air,

stoked like an old stove.
But my legs can't seem to take me
far or fast enough and my shoulders

draw tight round the point
at the nape of the neck
where death has been known
to reel us in. Home,

I'm surprised to find I've locked
the door. I dig up the hidden
key, open and close,
sit quickly on the coco mat,
boots still tied.

While I unearthed that
bit of brass, a night bird
whined a small two-syllable sound,
thin as a skipping rope flung

in orbit. Hunting or hunted? Whee
whee. Hunting, without doubt.
The hunted are silent. We
stop breathing, we sink
at any rush of wings.

Playing Fair

Next, Michael and I walk the road to the Centre
between new-mown fields to buy whiskey for us

and greens for the ducks. Coffee and eclairs
at the picnic table beside the gingko – ancient,

long-lived – among other details make me weep.
I go into the grocery for lettuce but can't

get past the first line of a questionnaire:
Do you think you need a new Centre? Greenless,

we toss our cups and head for home,
stopping inside the cemetery gates

to drink whiskey from the bottle and watch
the chickadees and goldfinch. I cry again,

wailing a little at how one thing happens and then
another and what do I know and what good is anything

I do. So. From this place I breathe in, one
boreal lungful, then another, black-capped, knowing

this is the beginning of knowing I need
to yield to it, and of beginning. What

happens next is the ravens set in
with gluttonous horrific shrieks that Michael says

is just birds feeding their young but I know
is something somewhere being torn apart.

And since the Yes has already begun I say Yes
to the ravens, capitulate, raging,

despairing, relinquishing all at one time.
A truck roars by and preys on me too, and I can't

control the howls or stop my teeth
from chattering. After a bit we stand up

and walk between the first rows of graves,
dizzy in the sun, my teeth still rattling,

then back to our packs, where I tug off one shoe
and one pantleg and pee under a Douglas fir.

Then we pull burrs from our T-shirts,
examine their ingenious devices for attachment,

open and close the gates. Say Hello to the two
bicyclists who pedal up to us, thermos in hand.

They fill their cups. We head for home.

Advent, With Friends

In Lucy's study one morning, maybe Tuesday,
with a hot lemon drink and the unopened doors
of the Advent calendar. On the desk

a stack of student papers; above it,
tiny colour photographs of all the animals.

Crow and elephant. Elephant and crow. Giraffe
with her preposterous reach into leafy
solitude. My mouth closes

on another language that shapes exactly
messages of the blood. The air thins.

'They have been motivated to amass
stores beyond their need,' reads the last line
of the uppermost essay. The words

enlarge and waver. One person is not
the same as two. In so many minutes

more will happen: Those ungulate hoofs
ladder onto the veldt. Starved atmosphere
shatter the glass paths we've mapped

away from pain. Sitting on the floor last night
was perfect. Chairs are stupid. I used

to know that. Above us, all
the tiny coloured animals.

*

Terence chatters at dinner about
the journals of students and illnesses

of staff. Chaucer and the Wife of Bath.

I'm in the kitchen one Dimetapp into hallucination,
head no clearer, Jay sick at heart and mad,
mad: Why, he asks, is everyone so upset at a non-issue?

Patricia leaves the table to see if I'm all right.
Her daughter Clea in scarlet pyjamas, hair up,
has begun to whip cream for dessert. What I need is

sleep, sleep without the banging wind that tore
open the shutters last night. What is possible?
Looking at hands will not tell me this.

Getting thicker, says Patricia. Through the door the men
gesture wildly. If the tongue runs on long enough
something will out. The cream peak. The heart ache.

Mom, this isn't doing anything, says Clea.
It works, Honey, her mother replies. Without missing a
beat. It works all of a sudden.

*

Consider icons – of motherhood, muse, the word
made flesh. Also garbage bin rims
and the mouths of cylindrical holes in the sand
in which we've stored our irreconcilable pasts.

I am in a small car in the city, running late
for the ferry home. My sculptor friend drives.

He holds the view that icons are circular
portholes to the possible. Or
gestures in a black hoop, I suggest, barred

by a diagonal line from being what they

seem. Framed, says Barbara from the back seat.
Verboten. Al swerves.

He wants the flat inevitability
of their beauty. In his dreams, the black
seventeen percent of himself takes shape,
threatens Barbara. He grips the wheel.

It seems to me neither Mary with her pert breasts
spilling milk into the mouths of saints
nor the inarticulate shuddering muse
deserves the reproductions they've received.

The residential curbs are lined end to end
with cars at dusk. A driver delivers shrink-wrapped
miracles. Al navigates the junction. I figure

icons are moulds into which we pour
the unfamiliar. They may be the means
to discard our souls. I tell Barbara my dream:
holes in the sand large enough for a body upright,
as if a huge finger had plunged itself to the fist.

The Great Dibber, she says.

The icons are moulds. We
can throw them away. But where is
away?

*

On the longest night I dreamed I had a daughter.
About eight, and sturdy, with a mouth like silk.

My husband had fixed a band on her hair,
asking, Is this the right place?

She said it was. I turned off the TV,

slid my arm round her waist, and we tumbled
over the carpet, cheek to cheek.

I told her this was called double somersaults.
She told me her name was Arlene.

Solstice, Winter

With her hands on my back at a place
later identified as the Soul Gate,
this edifice, under a blue sky:

> brick wall, the fire hall from which
> my grandfather quelled years
> of upstart blazes in the prairie town.

> Much talked about at council, the building's
> massive symmetry no longer houses
> men, their families, and the matched pairs

> of horses who hauled silver linings
> to whatever needed wetting down. The last
> team perished, pulled backward

> in 1920 at the nuisance grounds
> by the wagon's weight, into the steaming
> purgatory of accumulated trash.

> But this is past. The great arch
> from which the eager horses broke
> is blocked with paler stone, rose-coloured,

which at her touch abruptly crumbles,
as if dynamite or a wrecker's ball
has blown the weak point skyward.

> *

I board a bus home, half-empty, rattling
to the ferry in late afternoon.

Evening drops its gaze over us
on the way, a starlit dark, so that

when the bus stops at the harbour we're poured,
almost seamless, into the night.

*

Furious, fierce, I pace
room to room upstairs
while he shivers over
his knees, head in hands.

When did the sun last stay
its course? I won't
go down, and can't be still, till

the poplared light of his dropped face
compels me to admit I don't

know what next will fall. Who

has done this thing? Someone pounded
on his back, refusing
his eyes' heat, battling just once
the unforgiving backward haul. Of this

what can be borne?

*

Four days until light's hold
begins to strengthen. Cold

fear outlasts the night.
A candle, barely lit, flares

up again to sear
a brief, kind pinhole in the dark.

Holes in the Snow

In Montreal storms alter the lives
of people we love. I think of shoppers
who no longer walk the streets buying
capicolla, hot baguettes, the freshest
Chinese greens. A man's heart
attacks him on the way to his front door;
another dies, monoxide in a drifted
car, blinded by what continues to fall.
A woman fishes in trash
for the butt of a cigarette
discarded yesterday. Pubgoers sneak
their dogs into cold stone corners,
give them ashtrays puddled with beer.
In Montreal living is cheap.
The flower shops fold into
themselves, and fists of daffodils
and agapanthus haunt the tiny caves.
A woman in Montreal smokes
over her words. In the top
of a house where windows have frozen shut
and snow festoons the exits,
she addresses 'Archangel.'
She wears black, she attempts
to scratch through the blackness.
I attempt to clean the woodstove glass
with fire, to burn through creosote,
the grimy vision. Are we outside
or inside? Here or Montreal?
                              In Montreal
the horses that work the old streets
are barricaded in barns, blanketed,
alfalfa piled within reach and
the man who grooms them wrapped
in the warmth of their breath,
unable to cross town.

A woman in Montreal paints
houses in Westmount, inside and
out, conservatories, sunrooms,
while snow piles up outside
the glass, and the begonias
grow long-stemmed and confused.
Montreal is a Disney city, glowing
at night with a blue fairy light.
Some of us are outside it: a place
we can't enter. Our steps would burn
holes in the snow; lilies
would turn their heads to us
and shrivel; the horses would snort
at our heat, terrified, refuse
to leave the burning barn.
                                        I begin this
conflagration with a finger on the map.
A woman in Montreal doesn't flinch.
Her second-storey room is full
of snowlight. She presses
her forehead into the palm of one hand
and thinks about the Atlantic, about
the language contrived
by rocks and the sea, the wearing
of words into pebbles of meaning,
how the death of a dog in the snow means
no words at all in either language.
                                        She burns
her way into permafrost, buries
the dog wrapped in her red sweatshirt.
In Montreal planes stop flying.
No one arrives or leaves. The spirit
burns or succumbs. The dog
returns in a dream, licking
its way from her toes to the inside

of her thigh. 'Who are you?' she
asks, pulling herself up into
the dark room, the words
pins and needles in her mouth.
In Montreal the snow creates another
element to swim in, the ghosts' own
medium; the dead communicate. They
bloom in our brains like astonishing
hyacinths, waxy, essential –
and vanish, leaving us
sick with their absence.
                              Inhalation
stirs the balsam poplar. I translate
its breath into something suggestive of
speech: branches in a terra cotta wine
cooler. In Montreal the endless snow.
When I exhale, leafbuds withdraw
into their apple-seed sheaths.
                              Hearts
encased, hatboxes of Barbie-doll
outfits for every occasion except
the onslaught of white, grain upon grain,
petals unending, ludicrous abundance.
The mobile possibility of each
crystal before it finally lands,
ash of the dead, egg timer upturned.
                              At last
in Montreal the trains begin to move.
'No, not yet:' this, desire that speaks.
The blue is dimmed by astonishing sparks,

the drifts near houses pocked with yellow.
The boys have written their names in pee.
The hydro reconnects in Montreal.
In Montreal the groom breaks ice
in all the water buckets and climbs

through the window into the light.

Charles Dickens Punch

When your lover walks to the shop for a movie,
brings back *Enemies: A Love Story*, the sky
grows dark, the snowy hills light up. Play

Carla Bley's *Reactionary Tango* at top volume, chop
inordinate amounts of chiles in the beans. While
you set plates, a dozen blowing crows

pluck a towhee from the air. Holly berries redden a red
deeper than imagined. The ducks sink,
flotilla of boats in the snow, feet rowed

under their wings. Simple. In this country
the onset of cold equals fear. Ebbing electric
support. Heat equals anger, force of the heart.

And there, in the city, the New Year. There,
cedar swags, ribbons, glass roses, enough
squash to set on the tiles, kneel before,

whack with the largest blunt knife. At midnight
the flamed paper boats drown in dishwater,
'bitterness' jettisoned, black at the edges. Even

the calendar flaunts its dull birds. Abundance there
beyond need: Mexican tin trees laden with candles, friends
in the front room who don't even notice your absence.

House

The soul is not flawed, nor is it
reachable. The body wants the body.
We are born into a heavier air

with only time till limbs become
ideas of themselves. *Analysis*, from the Greek,
meaning to loosen throughout. I've been

unhappy a long time. All
that would not speak settled
in me like fog. Spirits, claustrophobic,

en route to the second floor, collapse,
obstruct the stairwell. *Feng shui* declares
this is all that is wrong.

Grandfather Harrows the Garden With Horses

In the teahouse behind a screen
of bougainvillea I shuffle index cards,
divide them by months in the ground, divide
days of the week by reasons for anger,
annual rainfall by minutes till my husband
pedals home.

Potatoes grow well after corn.
A root crop, with the same requirements
as carrots, they need hoeing, hilling up,
planting early, drying in the ground.
But they're a solanum and must not follow
their sister tomatoes.

What will come up by how we go on?

From left to right the cards laid out:
desert storm, meteor shower, intoxication
by sufferance, over-inhalation of
possibility. I open a matchbook
from somebody's wedding, empty. The house
littered with what my husband has used up first.

Nothing *belongs* to me, nothing stays
put. Things circulate, rotate, coilbound
calendar pinups and the twelfth moon of Jupiter
and these uncooperative lives that
shuffle through time and space, consume
nutrients, draw up minerals, exude
allelopathic substances that poison future crops.

I wear black and sneeze, surrounded
by index cards pencilled with dates and the ashes
of cigarettes bought before I ever knew
that nights could be so dark.

The deck rail bounces with rain.
In half an hour my husband will ride in,
hungry and warm from the long hill. He will overlook
the bags of manure piled in the drive,
the landscape cloth rolled like an old carpet
on the living room floor, the unscrubbed sink.

In my inner world, dim and small,
full of promise, like an unopened box,
nothing has yet conceived of desire.
The pole chain swings between
plough horses, their crown pieces steadily
row the air.
Women in aprons lay crockery
on cloth-covered tables under the trees.
August, and the trees bear fruit
the exact orange of the Emperor tulips
that fired the onion bed in spring.
The fruit is the only colour;
this is after all
before the Great War.

The horses race like time inside
the fence, triangulate
the lettuce bed. The earth
has been waiting for this
wedding, this chance to spill
the hope chest and lay out
great-aunt's silver teaspoons.
The lovely horses! Men
stand in caps and braces,
hands on hips and pointing.
The plough has bitten hardpan
behind the snorting pair.

My husband comes back from town, from
a future I've almost forgotten,
brings a gift. A large, elaborate globe
of liqueur, eccentrically ornate,
like a coconut woven of pewter,
like an ammonite pried from the seabed
and polished with felt.
He drops it, a helmeted head,
in the ploughed earth
at the feet of the men
who acknowledge it sideways.

I watch from the teahouse behind a screen
of bougainvillea. The horses pass.
The children run after, bucketing stones.

Out of the open window of a house
invisible behind cedars
roll the wet low notes of a jazz piano.

Nothing has so far conceived of desire.

I Make Noise With My Mouth

Why do I need to be right?
I tear our scorched tablecloth
into eight squares
and dye them crimson.
I make noise with my mouth
and move air with my arms.
How do I know what I know?
My legs grow legs and
effortlessly walk the line
on which I hang the laundry.
Socks with thick soles
that take days to dry,
tapestried table napkins,
pinstripe shirts whose cuffs
are a miracle
of collusion and collapse:
I want to kiss
the wrist that's buttoned in them.
My legs grow legs; I walk
to the late morning ferry
with a ripe apricot pulsing
in my blue tin cup.
I move air with my arms,
summer's rolling promise.
When I take lunch
from my pack at the dock, the fruit
is a fuzzy purse of liquid:
nectar in a skin sack,
intact, what I know,
the whole flesh one
sweet bruise.

Praise

Beautiful stoppings, bubbles
we trail in the aeriform fluid to mark
where we've been. All of us
incidental, particular, necessary

as three aspen poplars
seen early winter
from the third floor window
in afternoon sun. Breath held

before giving in
to the world's eloquence.
The branchtips snare a resinous
light. Eye to eye to eye

to eye we meet, fellow beings,
luminous-trunked in a slow arc
skyward. Before this, trees
were all legs, and I knee-high

and in the way. How small then,
with what a large idea
of a life. Now lifted
to the beloved, now there is

this which is not me,
the world's face, crevassed,
beneficent, I lay
a hand against the skin of.

Grays Harbor County

I did not turn down Blue
Slough Road, I did not take

the Lempie turnoff. I drove
the highway from Montesano to Raymond

through an arc of willows
new to this world, Keith Jarrett in Köln

hammering their emergence,
no other car on the road.

People here try hard to be
good citizens. There is no doubt

they are god-fearing folk, in
troubled times, time being

one day and then another.
A man sits on the guardrail

in a suit jacket the colour of old blood,
hands on his knees, nodding

to the traffic – logging trucks now,
four-by-fours, boom cars,

the delivery van from Hutchison Floral,
the Grays Harbor highway patrol.

He sits a long time, bending
to dust his trouser cuffs,

lifting his jacket to examine
his belly, his hands. The piano

plays us a heartbeat percussion,
rhythm of breath. He looks

at the belly, the hands as if nothing
is his.

Blue Mexican Glass

Wind blows froth along the sand like soapsuds,
like plastic sacks from a bombed supermarket.
Seal pups, tea bags, sunbathe on the beach.

The sun again, not to be trusted, nothing is
to be trusted, where did the word come from?

And where that cold wind – California?
Japan? The maps are never big enough
to tell. That's why stars, and in us
the mirrors of stars, neurons
passing on whatever arrives, whatever
is formed. The news,
the new, the need. Oh.
                          This
is all there is, when will I learn that?
There is what comes, what I do
with it, what goes. What gives.
No matter. No matter at all, no
substance. Beneath my foot, the shattered

blue Mexican glass, picnic table worn to
chicken house planks, birdsong
at evening. This is *all*. This *is* all.

The bird sings the same long note and
hesitant trill, over and over, each
time new, expressive, untiring. I too
could listen forever. No tape deck
eats it, no engine drowns it out.

I walk back to my bed through the pointed
beach grass, striding over the faded strawiness
of it all, the warm sand. The broom gives off
perfume and then something milkily poisonous,
doubling me over with the memory

of my dog's death. I am inside it, the world
and the summer hazy around me, the trees
distant and the sun and grass dimmed by
pain, that dome of old glass lowered
over. Something to do with
the thin sweet call of the bird singing sleep
in the veins, how everything relaxes away.

Last thing at night I take out my left
contact lens, then I try to take out
the left lens again, then I try
again, the same lens, again, the left.
Knowing the world is in front of me still,
knowing there is something more to get to.

On the Ferry. On Hold.

For a drink, for Leonard Cohen
to sing 'Take this waltz,'
for a bath or a storm
or the bedding down
of the ducks. What
I would give.
            What gives is
one's beliefs or one's breath. Heart,
soul, sincerity, memory.
               We will
arrive in sunlight, walk
up the hill out of breath;
                 my cup
will clank in my bag. Often
this happens. One steels oneself.

The bus and the boat, unaffected,
they go as they go.

The Dead and the New

I have been driving six days; not place
but time alters the birdsong, the shore.

In Waco Texas the Branch Davidian compound
burns to the ground, revealing
what everyone has now predicted. Time

decides whether we walk on sand or stone:
the sea tongues rock for days or millennia.
What changes is the meaning of the word *range*.

Halfway to Charleston in the hot sun, full
of thoughts of what home is, of
rototilling the patient bean patch, I can't tell

whether the blue up ahead is water or
sky. I'm driving through a wasteland
of logged hills transformed

by English daisies and the hard blue overhead.
Benedicite. Forget-me-not. I have seed

for long-stemmed rhubarb chard and
Continuity's extravagant frill.

Home is this vista of logged hopes
and severed innocence; nurse log and

colonist: what opens the soil. Prairie
sky, washy blue, laundry on the line.
Where we pretend to live until the desire

to live returns. Cielo. Where
dogs go, into the queen's hand.

What changes is the weather: soft storm,
foghorn and fine spit, the salt
expanse, old as talc, still giving up

warmth. All the broom adolescent, the wild
peas open magenta. What animals know

is how to own time. We'll sleep upstairs,
paint the window trim red. Charred remnants
of Texas at our backs, the sun gone blind

behind the iron sky. Spring races us
northward, by tendril, rootlet, chemical star.

Whoever's Responsible

When you got up this morning how did you
avoid thinking about death?
    – Spalding Gray

1

That morning we made love, we made it out of
the dreams of mink and eggs and anxiety.
A plane roared overhead and roses opened
to such a raw corona. We closed
the animals in and they died.
Not the storm but their lives blew in
from the mountains. We turned attention to weeds
and mowed down the four small oaks that survived winter.
Wind came up cold. When earth covered the bodies,
they loosened at last, they let the world in.
The walnut leaves were as big as my hand.

2

This morning we make love, we make it
out of nothing. A plane roars overhead
and the hazelnut waves its branches.
I pull on my yellow rubber boots,
a monarch lights on the toe. The blossoms
of hornbeam are wedding lace, coral,
heady and rippling with history.
Water drops, water, into more of itself.
Ocean spray and honeysuckle drip over the wire.
I open the door of the duckhouse and
four black bodies demand daylight and an icy tub.

3

Tomorrow I'll sit on the balmy deck,
eating warm fruit cobbler with cream
dabbled by dragonflies. I'll cut my nails
in a little pile at my feet. I'll learn to smile
in a room by myself, tap my shoes like Charlie
Chaplin's dinner forks, the oceanic roll. I'll give over
absolutely to Leonard Cohen, Clint Eastwood, Sergio
Leone, whoever's responsible for that
little Western whistle that takes care of
nothing. The hammock will whup its blue and white
stripes in the wind.

Gli uccelli

On your back on the foam, feet up
on the driver's seat. In the rearview

your eyes, the pillow, blue
of the headrest. Chamber music,

Italian. St. Martin-in-the-Fields
carries you, lymph, out of the body

to fists of ocean spray, the fine
mist pacific. Over the Hood Canal

both ends of a rainbow: the meaning
of bridge, of bow, that oiled gesture.

And through its iris of colours
an outcrop of land, then another,

headland, point, the earth taking shape
beneath gasoline hues: see this, see what is

here. Consider the lilies. Right eye twitching
a long vision of road. Engine and tires

quiet in your head, bourbon the heart's
hum: delicate misuse of resin and bow.

Dove. Hen. Nightingale. Cuckoo. Ghosts
of the real, three centuries before,

birds you too have lived with,
in the blood, its disinterested music,

piped notes, in-the-fields, small birds
that pierce the night air and your heart

with magnanimous grace. Birds that run
the sea grass and broom at your scuffed

approach. Twitch. Right eye or left?
Voice from the throat for nothing, no

one, not you, not even the bubble
of its life, just sound

of its being, being. The word bladderwrack
crashes against rock, against the drifted

shipwrecked barriers you don't know how
to scale. The left unlettered, the right

in contact with the world. There
is the question of food or no food,

breath and voice or the curbing of both.
Of whether you'll wake

in time to choose the ferry inland
through islands or the one due north.

The question, after docking, of two homes.
Sleep the long night or the day's threat,

vision shifting, fibrillating, wings
and never-never. Close your eyes

and think a happy thought.
What matters? Close your eyes.

South Island

> *I want*
> *just the flash of its*
> *spirit.*
>   – Constantin Brancusi on *Fish*,
>   one of his animal sculptures

After sunrise over Gowland Point
I lie on the carpet listening
to Steve Reich's *Tehillim*, whose fragments
lured me onto rocks when the seal

swam near. Now sun

lights up the fishline which,
last spring, suspended the hummers' feeder
outside the east window
                     so the fishline glimmers
not like some forgotten hook but with

its own sinewy fire. It comes to me I'm afraid
to want what I want. Brancusi. *The Seal*, also called
Miracle. Yesterday I learned

'confidence' means 'with faith'

and the word has swum with me since, rising
up out of everyone's speech. It leaps again –
flight, what bliss! – after a perfect
poached egg on toast, after my friend Barbara calls,

setting 'denial' end to end with
'mystification,' wanting

a recipe for trifle.

What Is Promised

Arc of yellow-green where the grass
first shouts spring, flashes
its underwear, whatever. Lately

I've been sensing something,
vibration of the atmosphere,
back in Oregon with the engine's shimmy,

things cross your mind behind
the wheel of a car.
The arms of an overhead fan lay slices

of light on a plate. A long row
of animals threads the lawn at dusk. Flowers
unfold or fold up at the edge of vision.

I expect it's about light and movement.
About time. It's about time.
So these images are

ghosts from before or later, one world
laid over another, plenty
of fish in the sea, the depth

infinite, too dense
for the hooking of any one
image, fleeting. But always we

do just that, we hook
a lover from all the partners there,
raise a child or two, despite

the millions. We are
driven to it, we tour
one layer or another of the veil. This

transgression of indolence.
The fly crawls up the window glass,
crawls up the landscape

of road, field, bush, sky,
up the reflection of hand
lifting teacup, up the desire for

this afternoon, this tea, what follows.
My mother says her mother said
bubbles in tea are promises of fortune,

drink them quickly before they
burst. Yellow-green
the colour of sunlight rising through grass,

the way heat steams from the garden
on summer afternoons. What is promised
on one scrim. What happens on another.

Where are we in this series of visions?
What do two people mean
when they walk like the blades of scissors

into evening, facing the end of the day?
What do they mean seen
from the next farm, over the deck rail,

from a singular distance? I am afraid
of the days before you leave, the years
after you come back.

White Noise

How is it I am so unfailingly pulled
to scowling men, undershirted
in doorways, lean-jawed and liminal,
unsummoned, unshaven, unable

to believe that time could trickle
into any hands but theirs? I don't believe
in any hands but theirs. Dark souls who
turn me on and then off like white noise,

collect mail from the sill
before meeting my eyes, who won't
meet my eyes. Morning. The long
afternoon. Before whom I want

to apologize, for rainfall, the dog's
loose-lipped snores, the tea's aroma
of smoky bark. For speaking, for drinking
and dreaming, for covering them over

with sheets, for pulling the sheets
from their hips and tonguing
them into daylight. For the low-level buzz
that is my solar plexus calling to theirs.

Do they know any of this, blinkered,
thin, dangerous, wound in their own
beds till mid-afternoon? I can't
tell you how often I've lain

down, the door open. When will I learn
to fall into sleep and then
sleep. Deeply. Without each breath hinged
to the corridor, clock. What

does this tell you about me? Too little,
too much? Down the long hall
of the heart, soon now, someone
will come in sock feet to kiss me goodnight.

Everything Necessary

I

First the noise: flap, tick,
small thump of its body against
the glass. The cold woodstove
tuned to astonishment. Swallow
in a steel box. This means
what?! This means what?!

The bird weighs nothing, resists not at all,
is vivid, brilliant, thrills
in my hand. Take it outside, open
the towel. Thrum, thrum, bright eye.

Bursts from the red cloth,
through the limbs of six arbutus before
I draw a breath. I raise
the towel to my mouth. Nothing more
need happen, I could repeat this

a lifetime, fulfilled. The red cloth.
Astonished vision of the trapped soul.
And the hum in my hands,
St. Veronica: time happening at once,
out of any order I thought I knew.

*

A car travelling fast past the window
sits you straight up in bed. This
means what?! This means what?! You look
for the clock's green face. It isn't there.
You're in completely the wrong house,
not knowing anything at all. Frog song
slows into summer. The doors close

at the island pub. You've done
your breathing exercise last thing at night
and gone to sleep trembling. This means
what?! This means what?!

*

Inside the house are letters or no letters,
the phone's violent wrench or the long quiet.
Out of the quiet the cello beckons. Twin
of the solar plexus, it moves you sideways.
Out of your rib is drawn a plant whose spring leaves

tremble of their own accord.
You walk out into the wet field,
wade in buttercups and orchard grass
under the balsam poplars till you are buried

in scent and the lime-new leaves. Sun
arrives from a far place, falling
like glass or new moons or the faces of Asia.

2

Collecting. Home. Our queen
has gathered half the workers to her
and set off. Bodies swollen with honey,

we've gorged, taken nothing but our hum,
which we give and give into the valley's heat.
The tall grass steams. Where to,

where to? We hang like a dark tornado
from the branch of the plum.
We are the arm of the plum tree, breath

of the long grass, birdsong and flight,
the valley's still shape. We are water,
clay-bottomed and full of hope.

Give us new comb to pack, sunny
days to fill with work. We'll do everything
so much better than before.

We are golden, comets, the stuff
of pure light. The young we'll feed
are chaos in gold leaf. What hums!

The land shapes itself from our desire
while we hang in a funnel of life,
breathing, mouths open to the sun.

We've abandoned the old hive, shell
of propolis, larvae gone sour.
Fear lives a while longer:

we can see it from here.
We're not lost though, watch us
circle the new hive. We'll figure

how far to May trees, the opulent
rosemary, that last tulip bent double
with sunlight and fire. We know

everything: how to breathe,
how to live in our bodies, how to
set ourselves free, how to hum.

What We Save for Last

Dessert. What we've been taught
is not good for us, what we've been
taught to want. The equation of that.

We hold to us for the longest time
late rooster calls, sagged barns,
mashed potatoes and peas,

moats of gravy – saving
gravy as long as possible after
potato walls have collapsed.

We let go what no one asks of us,
we say whatever we've imagined,

vast intricate bridges, the longest
high-level bridge in the world.

I'll give you that.

We pass out biscuits of information,
bunches of dandelions, fine stones,
we hoard very little, only

our names and what anyone might want
from us: who are we really?

What we save for last proves
our difference, what is left
on our plates is for us, alone.

Some think everything is eaten, that
lovers want to eat the world
and those they love, or that
they need to, that we are

agents of mystery, that this
is bigger than both of us.

We live in the span between
one time and the next, the longest
high-level bridge in the world.

What we save for last rots
in its lack of generosity.

What we save weighs us down.
What is kept keeps us, in place,
out of other places, without room
in our baskets for anything new.

My mother's cupboards stocked
beyond balance with tins and boxes,
so full she's unable to find
or remember what she'll never need again,

forcing vases, mermaids on rocks,
urns with inscriptions: Make new
friends, keep the old,
one is silver, the other gold.

Gold is what we keep longest,
in our teeth, round our necks,
weighing one hand over the other

into the grave. What we save
for last is what we once thought
we saw of ourselves: small jug

to pour ourselves into, containment,
still possibility. We forget
something closes, we forget about

webs, and birds who steal shining things,
and the cumulative weight of

the dustmice under our beds.
What we save for last
outlasts us, without us, without

ever having been us
except in the taking.

Nothing saves us but what we
give away, what gives us away.
What neglects the origin and end

of the gift. What crosses and recrosses
the longest high-level bridge in the world:

what touches us and what leaves.

Maybe the Body After All

Fiat, Latin for *Let it be done.*
Maybe the old car simply wants to die.

This afternoon we buried the frail canary
in a black jewel box under the Douglas fir

in a generous hole from which the Kiftsgate rose
will launch its hundred-foot briar. I hate most

how ordinary we are. You'd think
by now we would know what to do with grief.

Begin with the word that haunts you:
victim. Pretty child. Remember your mother's

voluminous skirts, that brown-and-white two-piece
whose pleats, blade-thin and permanent, formed

a corrugated vista of daisies in parched grass.
Later, the same rain, same sun. The rose

working a fantastic faith in its own
tangle. And to what end? Waking

no different than sleeping, same moving toward
or away, same unuttered pain in the gut.

The one clear dream's a stage set: house
lit up and hollow. Fiat abandoned, doors open,

in the valley.   Not quite home.

Acknowledgments

I'm grateful to the Canada Council for the Arts and the B.C. Arts Council for their support during the writing of these poems.

Many have appeared previously in the following publications: *American Voice, Arc, Event, Fiddlehead, Grain,* and *Prism International;* in *Bottomland,* a chapbook from Reference West (Victoria); and in the anthologies *Meltwater, More Garden Varieties 2,* and *Vintage '97-'98.* Thank you to the editors.

Thanks also, heartfelt, to the strangers-become-friends who made my stays at the Banff Writing Studio and the Sage Hill Poetry Colloquium both joyful and productive.

To ten-year-old Alyssa Bettencourt, who dreamed her twin in astonishing colour and allowed me to use the result on the cover of this book, many thanks. I'm grateful to Gail Ryckman, whose work helped this come about.

To Marnie Parsons for her unfailing warmth and faith, and to Don McKay, whose skill and generosity as an editor match his kindness, my deepest gratitude. Hugs to you both.

Marlene Cookshaw was born and raised in southern Alberta. She studied at the University of Lethbridge before moving to the west coast of B.C. in 1979. She has been a member of *The Malahat Review*'s editorial board since 1985, and is currently Acting Editor. She lives in an old farmhouse on Pender Island with fiction writer Michael Kenyon and a Hungarian Vizsla named Géza; she keeps a large garden and a dozen ducks. Her poetry, fiction and reviews have been published in such magazines as: *The American Voice, Arc, Books in Canada, Capilano Review, Fiddlehead, Mississippi Review, Prairie Fire, Quarry, Raddle Moon* and *Waves*. Her work has also been featured on CBC Radio.

'Jan Garbarek's Saxophone' won first prize from the League of Canadian Poets in 1997; 'Open and Close' won first place in *Arc*'s Poem of the Year contest the same year.